Emily Hill is a dating columnist at *Sunday Times' Style*. She has written for the *Guardian*, *Spectator*, *Evening Standard* and *Mail on Sunday*. She lives in London. This is her first book.

BAD ROMANCE

EMILY HILL

Unbound

This edition first published in 2018

Unbound
6th Floor Mutual House, 70 Conduit Street, London W1S 2GF

www.unbound.com

Text Design by PDQ

A CIP record for this book is available from the British Library

ISBN 978-1-78352-496-9 (trade hbk)
ISBN 978-1-78352-497-6 (ebook)
ISBN 978-1-78352-495-2 (limited edition)

Printed in Great Britain by Clays

1 3 5 7 9 8 6 4 2

MIX
Paper from
responsible sources
FSC® C018179

For Angela Blacow, beloved but dead.
And Alex, who kept me alive.

'... she only smiles, I laugh'

Jane Austen, *Pride and Prejudice*

Dear Reader,

The book you are holding came about in a rather different way to most others. It was funded directly by readers through a new website: Unbound. Unbound is the creation of three writers. We started the company because we believed there had to be a better deal for both writers and readers. On the Unbound website, authors share the ideas for the books they want to write directly with readers. If enough of you support the book by pledging for it in advance, we produce a beautifully bound special subscribers' edition and distribute a regular edition and ebook wherever books are sold, in shops and online.

This new way of publishing is actually a very old idea (Samuel Johnson funded his dictionary this way). We're just using the Internet to build each writer a network of patrons. At the back of this book you'll find the names of all the people who made it happen.

Publishing in this way means readers are no longer just passive consumers of the books they buy, and authors are free to write the books they really want. They get a much fairer return too – half the profits their books generate, rather than a tiny percentage of the cover price.

If you're not yet a subscriber, we hope that you'll want to join our publishing revolution and have your name listed in one of our books in the future. To get you started, here is a £5 discount on your first pledge. Just visit unbound.com, make your pledge and type **romance5** in the promo code box when you check out.

Thank you for your support,

Dan, Justin and John
Founders, Unbound

Contents

JULIA'S BABY

Julia should not have come to the wedding. That much was clear as soon as she arrived. Late, she was, and massive in belly. Her hat festooned with tropical fruit, her dress – hideously colourful. She made the hinges shriek on the great church door and winced as it slammed shut with a shudder. Puffing out her cheeks, she waddled slowly towards the nearest pew. She had a fist jammed into the small of her back, as if she were expecting to give birth at any moment.

Everyone turned round to stare. The vicar got confused, forgot his lines, began to stammer. The bride stood at the altar, in an ill-advised orgy of organza and tulle, said something no one heard. The groom started coughing and the best man also. A hissing came from the bridesmaids, taffeta skirts bristling, as they squirmed to get a better view. Someone, somewhere committed a laugh.

(You cannot remove heavily pregnant people from weddings, as a general rule.)

Flushed, Julia did not appear to notice. She settled in at the back, stared up at the angels in the eaves. Felt her hat, caressed her bump, sang the hymns over-loudly.

The wedding passed off as weddings usually do. Julia did not interrupt. If there were any just cause or impediment, Julia declined to mention it. The bride threw up her ornate veil, the groom seized and kissed her. The organ struck up in triumph. The wedding party swept down the aisle, plump in love, flawless with smiles. Everybody cried. Just as you'd expect.

Outside, the sun shone and died, shone and died, as clouds raced across the sky. Julia disappeared. Confetti was thrown, dried petals flew off, the gravel path littered with silvery shreds. Two turtle doves were let out of a box. One dazed itself, flying out disorientated, straight into the church door. The other refused to perform at all, sat cooing where it was comfortable. The photographer set about his formations. The maid of honour, humiliated in mauve, frowned between shots. The tiniest bridesmaid misplaced her violets and started to cry.

Then the rain came down, in sprightly gusts, so the bride and her mighty dress were borne back inside the church, dabbed down with handkerchiefs and rearranged for the car. And it was while the wedding party was stood, in the vestibule, that a thin plume of smoke was spied, rising from a distant tombstone. Julia crouched there, lighting one fag off the end of another. She must have thought no one was looking.

The scandal reached the reception before Julia did. It was agreed that she had done very well to keep her figure, her slim ankles, shapely legs, and slender arms. But if that was how she managed it…

Julia did not seem to mind that she was getting wet. She pulled her ghastly hat down further on her head. Finishing her cigarette, burying the ash, she picked at the blackened moss that filled up the cracks in the gravestone. She tore up a handful of grass to scrub down the letters. The shower ceased and the sun emerged, with a little more conviction.

There wasn't a space for Julia at the wedding breakfast, but she sat down before a plate, crumpled the name tag, and dared anyone to move her. Many of the guests, who knew the whole sorry saga, were hoping to draw her out. But Julia just smiled, her eyes glassy, giving answers of remarkably few syllables. After some prodding, she at last came to admit that it was a boy, and she was going to call it George. Another woman, in a dubious hat, asked if Julia had a picture.

'Of the foetus?' asked Julia in the lull as the room laid down its dessert forks for the speeches.

The best man's speech was not a success. Seeing Julia before him, he had to ditch half his routine and all of his jokes. He settled for a rather pitiful story about the tightness of the groom's running shorts.

When the groom had thrown Julia over, almost eight and a half months previously, everyone had expected her to go to pieces. For Julia was the sort that would. And Julia duly fell apart, over the weeks and months. When first she found out, she would not believe it. Carried on, as if everything were normal, refused to give the groom up. So the bride had to step in, to clarify matters. Then, there were a series of confrontations. Firecrackers through the groom's letterbox. Vandalism of the bride's car. Julia had stapled a letter, full of bitter accusations, to every lamppost on the street.

The bride had wanted to call the police. The groom said it would blow over. And so it did. All hushed up, so that now no one was sure what Julia did, or did not do. The only thing anyone knew for sure was that Julia had disappeared to her mother's house. Nothing more was heard. The groom forgot to feel bad, made a proposal. The bride tried on wedding dresses, set her heart on the church with two spires. Neither of them had wanted a long engagement. The groom had been through one of those.

As the big day approached, the bride felt it only right to issue an invitation to Julia and her mother, Julia's mother being her godmother and Julia her oldest friend. But neither Julia, nor Julia's mother, had made any sort of reply and the bride credited all concerned with doing the decent thing.

The bride was not to know of Julia's subsequent history.

Of Julia. Sobbing Julia. Hysterical Julia. With one leg hoisted over the Highgate death drop. Julia. Persuaded down. Much to her own embarrassment. Julia three days later. Caught in a scarlet bathtub. Minus a pint of blood. Julia. Patched up in hospital. Julia. Sobbing Julia. Unable to sleep. Taking all the tablets at once. Found just in time. Another admission. Stomach pumped. (No heart to be mended.)

And there lay Julia. Julia's sobbing mother. Julia's sobbing sister. Hysterical, the lot of them.

But tonight, Julia seemed pretty much serene.

As the guests became increasingly drunk, everyone began to discuss, quite openly, the father of Julia's baby. The whole marquee was doing the maths. If Julia was due any day now, and the groom had left Julia less than nine months ago, then it was perfectly probable, creditable even... for Julia was a loyal sort, everyone knew that. She was not the sort to cheat and lie, not as attractive as the bride, not as engaging as the bride. But all the same.

The bride and groom took to the parquet. Their first dance marred by the death looks of the bride. The groom, poor man, near death without the looks.

Julia was faring quite well. She had chosen a seat with a magnificent view on the edge of the dance floor. A great space cleared around her but she did not seem to mind. Julia's hand flitted to pacify the kickings from within, as she swayed, ever so gently, from side to side. Smiling vaguely to herself, thinking her thoughts.

She had been spied, from under the door of a toilet cubicle, nipping from a hip flask she had hidden in her handbag. She had then shared the contents with the flower girls who had discovered her. They were all of twelve, and now turning various strange shades, a match for their unflattering dresses.

Sometime later, when the music stopped for the cake to be cut, everyone held their breath and tried not to stare in Julia's direction. It would not have been polite. At a certain point, Julia must have forgotten she was not supposed to be seen drinking, and had finished off the table wine. Now Julia had her face down in a flower arrangement, groaning at volume, her last cigarette burning a hole in the opulent tablecloth.

The bride's expression could not be read. Certainly there was contempt and incredulity in her eyes, but her smile confused it. Bravely, she plunged a knife into the swan-shaped cake, with her new husband's hands about her waist. But, as the camera began to flash, her features broke out in fury.

She strode over to Julia, cake knife in one hand, a fistful of her dream dress in the other, ready for the showdown.

Julia roused herself. Shaking her head, she brought herself up to her full height and clamped both hands on her great belly, fingers spread. Julia stood proudly in the middle of the room: so much taller than the bride – always had been, always would be – and possessed of riches that the bride, in her tight white corset, had not.

Julia opened her mouth. And Julia said, pointing at the groom:

'IT'S HIS BABY.'

Only three words. And she said them very loudly, just like that.

The marquee erupted. The bride began to shriek. The groom collapsed. The father of the bride had the best man by the lapels. The flower girls were sick on their shoes, everyone screamed, the place turned into deafening riot. So no one had their eyes on Julia, as she slipped out.

Heavy and waddling, she made her way, crab-like, towards the exit.

Outside, the night was cool and fresh and, as she neared the car that waited for her, Julia's tread became surer, her stature more erect. Julia wrenched open the back door, tossed her hat onto the seat, and clambered in.

As the car moved off, Julia watched as the marquee disappeared from view.

And the car rushed forward, down the empty track. Julia took one last glance behind her. When the last of the lights were eclipsed by trees, she hitched up her dress, withdrew a little knife from the recesses of her purse, and started to sever the uncomfortable prosthetic bulge strapped tightly to her middle.

GODDESS SEQUENCE

It was while sobbing, desperately, most desperately, into a mustard-coloured cable-knit sweater, on the last train home, that the goddess came into being. She had left marks, was tired of making marks, on that sweater, into which her face was pressed. Her mascara had leaked off, smeared off, bled off, her face.

But feeling this sudden force burst within her… she jolted upright, clutched at the metal pole, tore herself away. Only to catch sight of her face in the window, as the train rattled and slowed to a stop. Her face, her terrible face, and her head throbbing.

So it was not a case of leaping, fully armoured, from another god's head. Nor of being birthed, like Venus, on the crest of a wave. She simply stood up, on the last underground train, and by some mystical act…

Goddess she was. She could feel the thunderbolts forming in her fingers.

Off through the night air, blindly tripping the pavements home. She took off her shoes, threw them away, and went barefoot through the empty streets. She felt so light, so perplexedly pleased, to find she was a girl no longer. Goddesses, she knew, were not troubled by men. They were not cheated on, shouted at, nor trampled upon. Goddesses did not cry. They did as they liked and liked what they did, subject to no indignities. They were caressed by gods and luxuriated on clouds. If a man troubled a goddess, he would be put an end to, with a thunderbolt. Or driven mad.

The goddess's face was no longer wet. She was walking faster, with divine enthusiasm. She flew around the final corner, gliding through puddles, which felt pleasing to her toes. She scraped the key up the side of her door and, after some wrangling, turned the lock. She stumbled into that awful place which used to be home, and was now just some reeking hole she would have to abide in before returning to the heavens.

She practised a thunderbolt on the mewing cat. It went running off through the cat flap, into the garden. She sat in the darkness of the kitchen, in deep contemplation, dazed by the silence. The transformation had made her hungry. The goddess opened the fridge. Nothing in it save some grapes – small, and somewhat withered – and liquid, liquid the colour of ambrosia, which is the only sustenance a goddess needs. She drank this. It made her feel more alive. She started to dance alone, and span into the sink, saucepans clattering to the floor. A faint noise down the corridor, as a mortal cried out in his sleep. It made the goddess feel suddenly tired, unable to keep her eyes open.

She floated up to bed, and lay on top of the covers, on top of the colours, thinking more, and harder. New goddess thoughts that had not struck her before…

At some point, she fell asleep.

Next morning, as the sun peeped at her shyly through the broken windowpane, she woke far earlier than usual. The golden rays caressed her awake, illuminating her godly lashes, provoking low goddess moans. She felt a little strange – but having gone through such a profound transformation the night before, what could one expect?

Yes, she felt very peculiar: best to have a bath. So the goddess descended the stairs. And on the landing was confronted by her reflection in the mirror. She had to admit – feeling the mess of her hair and pressing her own blotches – she did not look much like a goddess. What was the point of being a goddess if one was not radiant? She saw how the black streaks would come off easily enough. So she entombed herself in the downstairs bathroom, which she was not supposed to use, ever, at that time. But goddesses do not obey rules, they break them and laugh.

She took a bath, a long, leisurely bath as all sorts of mortals hammered at the door. The goddess sighed and kept her eyes closed, as she felt a beautiful warmth spread through her bones. After an hour or so one of the mortals tried to get in at the window. She stood up, naked and gleaming, to slam the casement on the mortal's fingers. Lucky, he was, not to be blinded, or turned into a stag. She got back in the steaming tub, topped it up with more hot water, and filled it with more salts. She lay down again, allowed her legs to float up, until the skin on her stomach crumpled completely.

Emerging with new, dewy, dripping, goddess skin, she cleared a face shape in the glass and looked at herself frankly. She smiled at her pinkish flesh, moist and puffy, but not quite glowing, yet. She left the bathroom, taking a steam cloud with her. And as she slammed the door, the mould on the ceiling above started to buckle, and the plaster came down with a crash. Up in her room she sprayed herself with all the dregs of her perfume, the scent she had been saving for a special day, and put on her best dress, even though it was Tuesday.

Yes, it was Tuesday. And she wasn't going to work. She would never go to work again. For goddesses do not bother with things like that. But she felt the need to leave the house, since there was a lot of shouting going on in the bathroom below, a battle for cold showers. So the goddess sprang lightly down the stairs, opened the door and rushed off into half-deserted streets.

The birds sang their little hearts out, trying to cheer her. The sun beat down quite furiously for the time of year, making sure she was warm. The clouds had packed up and retired for the day, to fluff themselves up, ready for her return to the heavens, should she want to take a nap in the sky. The goddess felt so light and happy, traipsing through the dirty streets.

The goddess stopped at the end of the road and climbed aboard a mode of mortal transportation. She went up to the top deck, to sit and watch, as the buildings bowed down before her and the trees trembled and waved. She stared at all the little mortals below her, carrying on oblivious to her presence. Arguing about things, and worrying about things, and hoping for things that could never, ever happen; oh, the goddess felt pity for them all.

The goddess squinted and made the traffic lights go her way. She was gliding, flying through the streets. And then, seeing she was near her destination, she flew down the stairs and off, back into the street again, catching sight of herself in the window as she went. There she was and her face, her ravishing face, luminous and smiling.

Her pockets kept making noises, with earthly devices, as all the wicked mortals who'd done their damnedest to destroy her yesterday called. She decided to have done with them, threw her coat, and its contents, in a bin that appeared. She went on. From now on, mortals would do as she, a goddess, decreed. Else there would be thunderbolts.

She felt a little too elated, rushed headlong down the street trying to regain her composure. On the corner, she caught sight of herself in a window once more, and was appalled by her own hair. It was sticking up on end where she had run her hands through it, and she must have electrocuted it by accident, for it was not correct. The goddess twisted a great strand of it around one finger and held it up to the window.

It must be fixed.

The crowds began to part before her as she glided, once again, down the street. She plunged in one direction, then another, until she found a bright salon, with chequered floor and rows of dryers. She blinked at the expensive signage. This, most certainly, this would do. Magisterially she summoned a mortal, who took her to a chair, and sat her down, and spread a sheet across her like a gown.

Her hair was washed, very carefully, just as it ought to be. And her skull was felt, very tenderly, before all her hair was cut off. Off it came, all the old, mortal hair, to reveal the new goddess hair beneath. And her godhead was revealed to all, as the salon girls gasped, and the hairdresser lay down, prostrate before her. The pristine, shining hair of a goddess new.

Emerging from the salon, the goddess gazed down at herself, and saw that the clothes she wore were not the clothes of a goddess. She summoned another vehicle and it took her to a large and gleaming shop, where she tried on many beautiful things, and watched herself, carefully, in the mirrors. What a beauty she was. But at the counter her card was returned to her. There was talk of cutting it in two. The goddess understood that she did not need these clothes, these ghastly – she now saw – ghastly clothes. Other goddesses would mock these clothes. All she needed was a silk sheet to wrap herself in, for that, she knew, is what goddesses wear – in statues and paintings.

So she went to sit in a garden square and felt a fresh prickling sensation in her fingers. She looked, and wondered how thunderbolts could form in such ugly, hard-bitten, varnish-chipped nails. She must fix them, too, she saw that now. It was really quite important. So she opened up her purse and found the crumpled note, which she had long saved, for total emergency, and she went to a little place that she saw, with a thousand tiny vials of brightly coloured paint arranged in the window. She entered, to the trill of a bell, and sat down, allowing a tiny woman to feel her fingers and toes, sawing away, like a violin virtuoso, making them iridescent and smooth.

The goddess closed her eyes. She felt very tired. For she knew that soon she would have to return to her earthly dwelling, to get dressed for the evening ahead, and even as a goddess, she dreaded to return to that awful shared dump, full of groans.

On her return, she went to fetch that single white sheet, kept so smooth and perfumed and pressed, in the recesses of the laundry cupboard. She went to take it, endured the annoyance of the mortal in whose room it was kept. There was awful noise and much grappling and then rending of that beautiful sheet. The goddess's fingers itched to end the dispute, with a great crackle of electricity. But she refrained. And, though the sheet was torn in two, she bore it off, triumphant.

The goddess had a drink. And put some music on. And wound the sheet tight around her, pinning it fast with hair-pins and tape. Soon, very soon, she would be ready to go. As the sun went down, she made up her eyes. Her lashes, her godly lashes, she made black as night. Her lips, her godly lips, she made red as the dying sun. Her face, her godly face, made radiant and irresistible.

She finished off the last of her drink.

She emerged, it was dark now, to shaking streets, and shivering lights. Tiny green men dancing for her and neon shopfronts wanting to seduce her. She veered towards the hovering sign, turned and went down the stairs, through the barrier, and down the escalator. She stood and waited for the whoosh, and the air, and the whimper, as the carriages rattled to a halt and the doors burst open to welcome her.

She entered and swayed, feeling the clatter of the rails beneath her feet, clinging on to the pole, as she sought to remain upright with all the strange convulsions and sudden slacks in pace. She smiled her divine smile at all those mortals who played around her, faces blurring, faces whirling, and all that awful noise, again.

The train halted – just as she held out her hand for it to halt – and she emerged, giggling at the thought of herself among all these mortals in the press of the crowd. She allowed herself to be carried along. She stood and waited to be transported up, bustled in, bustled out, expelled, exhaled into the city.

The crowd, the great crowd, spewed into the street, as the air cooled down to bathe her face. More noise, more mortals, and neon, skipping neon. Rows and rows of people, all jostling to greet her, all making the pavement difficult, rushing rickshaws and bikes and cars. But she navigated her way to where she knew she must go. Where it was all dark, and the music was loud and deep, where the noise made the blood rush to her ears, pulsating through her limbs, until she felt it suffuse her, head to toe. Down again, and down again, down she went…

Into this new place, this new state, which seemed so familiar. From her old life, the old sad life, that had ceased the night before. That pre-goddess time, when of course nothing would happen as it would now…

The goddess flew off to get another drink, asking for more of the same. And she rocked, with one hand on the tabletop, and one eye on the blinking lights, breathing in the smoke, the perfumed ice, the sounds and beatific vision. The tiny lights all around her, tiny little lights, dancing little lights, pink and green and yellow, tiny little, tiny little mini gods, and they danced together, and they danced all gods as one together.

And then she saw, or only half saw, somehow she sensed... the source of all the trouble. Standing, so heartbreaking, by the bar, in the same old sweater that had been her undoing the night before. And then she unravelled. So immediately, she unravelled. Just as she did, each and every time.

And as she fell to the floor, the sheet slipping away, the goddess returned to her earthly state, as she knew she would, as she knew she should, for she knew she would never be a goddess truly... It had all been so stupid, such a fervid, fantastic, foolish thought...

The man in the corner looked up. He stood there, on his second pint of the evening, wearing that mustard-coloured, cable-knit jumper, from which he had not so much as soaped her mascara from the night before.

He surveyed the ex-goddess, as she fell to the floor, and directed his attention back to his beer, turning to the barman, with that so-charming grin, as the bouncers prised her off the floor. He raised his eyes, skyward, as if to say, 'The girl is quite mad... and she has nothing to do with me.'

And later that evening, as he hurried home, through a thunderstorm that no one had predicted, his mustard-coloured, cable-knit sweater utterly sodden with rain, the source of all the trouble was struck by lightning, and died, fried, on a wet pavement. Freak weather: a bolt from the blue.

HOUSING CRISIS

So I moved to the city, got myself a job no problem. They're always hiring and firing at American Success. Give me a headset and numbers and there's not much I can't do. I sit next to people who constantly complain that we're being worked to the bone. Well, I sit there, twelve hours a day, already a skeleton. I have ambition. I have pluck. I have stamina. Yet still I can't find a place to live.

The rooms disappear before they're even vacant. You read a listing in the morning, call up, immediately, to fix a viewing. The room will be free in six weeks, they say, come and have a look at it. So you say, very courteously, I'll come straight by after work. You force through what sales you can, manage to leave five minutes early, an exceptional thing. You speed across town, even the traffic goes your way. You arrive, triumphant, to find they picked another person who visited that afternoon. And if you express your annoyance, just watch their faces harden, as if you've only confirmed that they made the right choice.

But that's not so bad. There's something to be said for the sudden blow. Worse are the places where they interview all-comers and sit there like a committee, firing all these damned questions at you. 'What do you do? Where do you come from? How do you spend your weekends?' Occasionally, they make you sit through a meal with them, to see if you're a good fit. May as well stick pins in me. Shine a light in my eyes. I learned right away not to tell the truth. I work so hard, we never have a thing in common. Plus they don't want a flatmate, they're searching for their next best friend. And I have as many friends as I can stand, at the minute, if you really want to know.

My lies got better, more elaborate. I grinned so hard I gave myself permanent wrinkles. Still I had no luck. I was getting chucked off one sofa after another. People profess to love you, until you ask to stay. I was told to lower my standards. As if that were the issue. So I went for the places in newsagent windows, faded yellow adverts that propose abiding on the murder mile, where you get to your room via a ladder, bed down in asbestos. You clap yourself shut like an ironing board and live horizontal, the ceiling is so low. And you're not allowed down again between eleven and six, since you mustn't disturb the person sleeping below.

Well, I fell on my feet with that one – lovely place, great views, silver insects crawling all over the bathroom floor, keeping you amused while you did your business. The gas gave you a headache if you forgot to open the window, but even in winter it's good to get your air. The next-door neighbours made it difficult to sleep – visitors at all hours, floors shaking, walls trembling, day and night, with industrial bass. Then, in the quietness, low, exotic moans. Worst were the occasional bouts of dawn yelling. After two months, one of their visitors fell out of the window and all of them left straightaway.

The police turned up, went about questioning all the

neighbours. And I told them. Gas is highly flammable. Makes sense to smoke hanging out of the window. They squinted at me, frowned and knocked the next door down.

Oh, I curse myself for leaving that lovely place. But those were the days when I was too easily upset.

At the next place, my stuff kept going missing. The drugs squad took a battering ram to the communal door. My flatmate, very friendly, who said she was a waitress, but was quite clearly nothing of the sort, kept thieving the electric money. She'd be out, having five-pound notes stuffed in her underwear, and I'd be sat, trying to read my magazines by the light of the moon. The washing machine broke down under the burden of her lingerie, with its petrifying hooks and teeth, and we'd row over the foaming flood. The fridge overheated due to her jars and unguents. And she started bringing men back home, in blindfolds and handcuffs, who made these noises. It was hard, very hard, trying to sleep, three feet from all that.

I should have bought earplugs, drunk more gin.

But instead, I phoned round everyone I knew, asking if they knew of a place. And a friend of a friend of a friend knew of a room going in Stepney. All they wanted was a cat lover. I got on it straightaway. I stuffed all my possessions in the back of a taxi and, to distract myself from the expense, spent the journey making up stories about my stepmother's Siamese kitten. In fact, cats are the only thing I hate on earth more than my stepmother. Try as I might, I cannot see the point of them. Their fur gives me a permanent head cold. My eyes stream, my nose explodes and they take it as a positive invitation to rub up against my legs.

But my stories worked a treat, I got the room. And it served me right, for telling such lies. The cats tormented me. There were two of them, both obese. All day and all night they laid siege to my door, and whenever I was out, set up camp on my bed. They left neat oval piles of black fur on both pillows. I couldn't breathe. I never invited friends round, since those I had always wriggled their noses and asked about the smell. The cats were taking it in turns to shit all over the carpet. And they were useless specimens when it came to defending their territory. At night, the wild cats from the alley would break in to attempt a rough seduction and, having failed, spray the whole place down, screeching like a party of the damned.

With all that noise, and the terrible stench, I was becoming somewhat vexed. Plus the cats had left fleas in the mattress and my flatmate passed on his nits. Then the boiler broke so we couldn't take a shower. The landlord wouldn't fix it. First thing in the morning, we'd all fight over the kettle. And I tended to lose.

People started to move away from me at work.

So I took action, since it was summer, and the mornings were bright. I got up an hour early and went for a swim every day before work. I walked a mile, across the motorway, under the flyover, to reach the municipal pools.

But even that didn't do me much good. The pool was empty, and bitter with chlorine, which killed all the bugs, the musk of cats and my fragile hair. But then, one day, unbeknownst to me, a wasp crawled into my cap while I was getting changed. So when I put my cap on, I got stung, and went into anaphylactic shock. Another swimmer called an ambulance. I missed two days of work, recovering in the hospital. And that's just not advisable, in the current climate.

Well, I panicked. Felt I couldn't hack it any longer. I was so soft back then.

I should have calmed down. Thought about things rationally. Drunk more bloody gin.

The next place, well…

The moment I saw it, I thought: this is a better tenor of life. A nook on the outer reaches of the Northern line. A room, very large, going cheap, fashionably stripped-down floorboards, futon bed, alpine-scene wallpaper and a vast window that looked onto a walled garden, shady and green. The ground floor of a handsome mansion block – oh, it looked so evocative in the rain.

Later, the person I viewed it with told me it looked like the scene of an Edwardian murder. But I stood there staring at it and thought: now this is the place for me. The landlord took a liking to me. I could tell right away. Once you've got a place, it's easier to get a place, if you see what I mean. He said I could move in immediately, since he hadn't liked anyone else who'd come round to have a look.

Well, I got cocky, started haggling him down, said the windows would have to have curtains put up on them, the view was perfect, but I needed my privacy. And I couldn't be doing with the sinister china ornaments in the lounge. And the bathroom tiles… He stroked his neat little moustache, clicked his heels, said he would put up blinds and have the gargoyles removed next day. The bathroom tiles, however, were non-negotiable. Nothing could be done about them. And it wasn't a fascist insignia, it was Buddhist, entirely the other way around. Furthermore, he could save me £50 a month in bills if I agreed then and there not to turn on the heating, under any circumstance whatsoever. There was a fire in the living room, he said, which heated the house. I could always sleep in a hat and wool tights if it got nippy, that's what he'd do. Besides, he said, most of the time I'd be at work.

And I thought – at last, someone who appreciates thrift and hard work. We shook hands. He told me some repulsive stories about a famous person that he claimed to have heard from a friend of a friend. Even asked if I would like to join him in a roast pigeon, which he'd found dead in the garden and stewed in wine. Usually he'd stuff it and add it to his bird collection but since this was a special occasion...

Well, I moved in that day, I was in such a hurry to get away from the other place. I hadn't slept in days and was terribly tired.

I lost a load of my stuff on the trip across town. On the bus, some bastard nicked my cactus plant, my tape deck and the corkscrew. But that's buses for you. I lost my favourite pillow on the train. The first snowflakes were falling, a cold snap, odd weather for October. I arrived just in time to catch my new landlord dragging the futon out of the room, saying he'd rent it back to me for £50 a week.

It was then I recalled that he was reminiscent of someone. The moustache was just exactly... his tiny build and staccato speech... dressed in brown, head to foot. He spent all his time... in the living room, blasting out Wagner, painting wretched watercolours. Kept harping on about a squad of local rabbis, armed with samurai swords under their prayer shawls, on patrol in Stamford Hill. I said that sounded very reassuring, just my sort of neighbourhood, and he frowned, stuck his hand in the air, did an about-face. Went on and on about the local maidens and his urgent need for greater living space.

He was always surprising me, at night, in the hallway, when I was hurrying to and from the bathroom. He'd pin me to the wall and talk my head off, even when I was half asleep. One thing he was very upset about was what had happened with the flatmate before me. She had accused him, most insultingly, of sexual harassment. He was indignant about it, most hurt. All he'd done was go into her bedroom to retrieve a pair of his scissors, which she had borrowed and failed to return. He needed them, and she was asleep, so he didn't want to wake her. He knew exactly where she'd put them, in her underwear drawer. And she'd given him such earache, sitting bolt upright in bed, and screaming, screaming, screaming, as he rifled through.

Well I was so fed up, after the move, and, not wanting to make another error, made the best of it. I was sleeping on the bare floorboards, coming down with a chill. I had a water bottle strapped to my feet and another around my middle; I'd wake up, sweating madly, in the night, and then rigid with cold, at 6 a.m. And what were they thinking of me at work? I'd been turning up, utterly off my game after another night on the floor, teeth chattering, coughing up half a lung, spraying green phlegm with projectile sneezes. My numbers were down. I was living off flu pills and Vicks inhalers, reeking of Deep Heat and Germolene.

I felt I had, at least, to tackle him about the lack of curtains. I was tired of the freezing air rushing straight through the windows. And I kept hearing rustling at night. When I turned round, all I ever saw was myself, reflected in the great black windowpane. All very well, you might say, but after a shower, I like to air dry. Not wanting to annoy him, I left him a note, a little scared, I'll admit, to confront him directly. And I was right, because he didn't take it at all well. Started shrieking. What did I prefer? Curtains on the window or hot water between 6.30 and 7? We couldn't waste money on both. We weren't *dilettantes*.

Well, I didn't understand or know what to say. But I'd clearly made a mistake. That morning, when I woke in the early hours, I found he'd snuck into my room and was rifling through my drawers. I lay there, perfectly still, with one eye open, watching as he read my correspondence with a tiny torch. And much good it may have done him, reading my unpaid bills.

But I wasn't having that.

As soon as I heard him go into the bathroom, and the water gush from the taps, I leapt up, threw the quilt off my floor, and burst into his room to teach him a lesson. Unfortunately, I was confronted there by a gigantic watercolour of me, in the nude. My moles were captured, just so. The tattoo only two people know about. My nipples, violet with cold. No, I wasn't having that. I kicked the canvas down the hallway and left him a note, pinned to my behind, demanding the immediate hanging of curtains. Plus a new regime, which would entail the return of the futon bed, hot water on tap and all of this gratis, in compensation for embarrassments suffered.

Well, he chucked me out by the end of the day. Refused to return my deposit, held my knicker drawer to ransom.

You see, those were the days I was too easily upset. I should have apologised, bought a bottle of vermouth.

The next place, you see, was so much worse…

HOW TO BE SINGLE AT PARTIES

I'll tell you how to be single at parties.

I met a girl who told me on Saturday night.

You know the parties I mean: the ones where the hostess greets you with a squeal of 'you must meet so-and-so' and dumps you in the corner with a man intent on telling you his entire life story. How, last year, he quit his job, left his girlfriend and went to India to find a better narrative. Only he contracted hepatitis, in the second week. He'd been in such a rush; he'd forgotten to get vaccinated, so he finds himself in hospital, staring death in the face. And suddenly – he says – he saw it all clearly. The girlfriend he'd just dumped had been *the one*, he missed her quite desperately. So he calls her up, at great expense, livid skin, kaput liver, riddled with the tubes that attach him to life, and asks her if she'll be his wife. Death itself reminded him of her. And all she says is 'NO' before hanging up (*the unfeeling, inconstant hag*).

So he's come back to no job, no home and no woman. Having seen nothing of the world. Crippled with medical expenses and still the wrong colour. He's sleeping on his sister's floor. But, by the way, he says, not to worry, he's not infectious.

And so you say, 'Oh, I know, you can't catch hepatitis through talking.'

And he says, 'No, I mean *for later*.'

And if you escape, with a savage shudder, and reel on into the evening, you'll only run into that woman who asks you one question after another, each more charming than the last.

She'll say: 'You do go through them, don't you?'

And then, 'Actually, he's quite a catch.'

Followed by, 'Of course, you're always *working*.'

Concluding with: 'If you don't mind my saying so – you look like *death*.'

Your whole face is moving, but no sound is coming out of your mouth. And while you're so distracted she'll introduce you to her friend, with the megawatt smile, who keeps tapping her ring finger on the rim of her glass – the Morse code of the newlywed. She's so captivated by the sound her wedding band makes – that delicious little tinkle of gold on glass. And it is she who trills,

'Have you thought of internet dating? That's what I did and you can see how that turned out.'

And you say, 'Really? You advertise yourself on the internet? How clever. I'm still putting adverts up in public phone booths. That must be where I'm going wrong.'

But not until six hours later, when you sit bolt upright in bed, beating your pillow about its head, paralytic with insomniac rage.

Sisters! We must stop going to these parties occupied by the enemy. Our time would be better spent in the bath. I say to you! We are veterans of the sex war. We need not be patronised. We have seduced men on the beaches. We have fought them at the taxi ranks. We have kissed them in the fields and in the streets. Party after party. Night after night. Drinking, drinking, drinking. Till the sky turns black. The floor fills. Stilettos stamping up and down, up and down. And then, in the corner, dancing alone.

Oh, the agony of bikini season, the crippling price of lingerie. A host of bad-luck dresses, hanging on the rail. And all those endless weddings we go to alone, teeth clenched, eyes raw, hearts of glass. The bridal chorus: a victory parade. And just to round things off, she throws the bloody bouquet at us: a retiring vigilante tossing her final grenade.

I never try to catch it. Why play their game? But last time, I was the only one still standing. I kept my hands resolutely by my side. But the bride's aim was sure. It hit me right on the nose. And then her mother prised open my tightly clenched fists. Insisted I take it home.

Yes, I'd say that was the nadir…

Well, I'll tell you how to deal with these situations. I met a girl who told me on Saturday night.

I saw her enter in a provocative dress, impossible to ignore. She swept through the crowd straight towards the hostess. Loudly declaimed something, but I couldn't quite hear. She held her hand out – smiling – when thrown into the path of a pudgy divorcee. And as he started talking, she shrugged her shoulders, put her hands on her hips and, gesticulating wildly, launched into some speech so fantastic, he scuttled away. Then she was shepherded towards the hepatitis, but countenanced no talk of diseases. She rolled her eyes, opened her purse, took out a piece of paper, and began reading from it, quite earnestly, for ten minutes, before moving on.

After that she cut Mrs Questions dead, with a single insouciant nod, and a photograph that she flashed like a police badge. And sailed, majestically, straight towards me.

We'd met once or twice before.

'Hello, hello, what are you doing here?' asked Maria, for that was her name. 'Couldn't get out of it either, I imagine. There's no doubt about it, I'd get more pleasure biting my nails off and spitting them on the floor than talking to any of these swine. But the hostess is so nice. There's no getting out of it.'

'I know what you mean,' I said. 'But you haven't had any trouble.' For she'd had none of the usual remarks. She had conquered obstacles in a matter of minutes which had been destroying me for more than an hour.

'Ah, but that is because I have a man. In society, my dear, you're still deficient without one. So I keep mine in my handbag. You should do the same. He must be relatively obscure, devastatingly handsome, and you must have plenty of information about him, to share for hours and hours, should you be accosted by people sure to bore you rigid. I would suggest a writer. Or an explorer. Or a painter would do. And then you just talk loudly and straight over them.

'I can tell you're interested. So allow me to introduce you. This is my boyfriend, the poet Vladimir Mayakovsky. Look at his picture. What a sex god. Here he is holding his dog. Here he is scowling. And here he is sitting on a chair, looking fierce. This one was taken in prison. He's had a colourful career.'

I dutifully looked through the faded black and white images of a man with an impressive jaw.

'See here – he has a very large head because his brain is so huge, he wears the most outrageous clothes, and he likes to play billiards. He bursts into tears during poker on account of his nerves. Nevertheless, he always wins. I often wonder if his addiction to playing games will be the end of us. Of course, he never accompanies me anywhere because he is a poet and a hypochondriac. He worries, too much, about germs. He prefers to stay at home, playing mah-jongg all night, or he goes out, pounding the streets alone, to compose his poems, tapping out the rhythm with his steel-capped boots. And you should read his poems, they are the most brilliant thing you'll ever hear.'

She took a drink.

'He is also a genius.'

'But Maria,' I said, feeling, somehow, that I might be breaking cruel news. 'Anyone can tell… these photos are very old… and look at his clothes… he's clearly been dead for a century.'

'It's true, he shot himself dead in 1930 – but no one bothers about that,' explained Maria. 'The important thing is to have someone you can bore on about for hours to strangers and bastards. They do not usually ask for visual proof but if you find it useful, you just flash it at them. And it doesn't matter because no one ever comes to this sort of party to listen to *you* anyway.'

I didn't know what to say, so I told her I loved her shoes.

'Oh, cut it out.' Maria screwed up her nose. 'You just watch me. Anytime anyone tries to hand me a baby, I begin.'

'You begin what?'

'I begin reading poetry.'

As it happened, a woman jiggling a baby on her hip used this pause in conversation to introduce her gigantic infant. We'd known the woman, once. Before. Her name was Sheila.

Maria held her hand up. The woman stopped.

'Maria—' Maria yelled. Everyone turned.

'You won't have me?
You won't have me!
Ha!

Then once again,
darkly and dully,
my heart I shall take,
with tears besprinkled,
and carry it
like a dog
carries
to its kennel
a paw which a train ran over.'

There was a pause.

Maria said, 'My man wrote that about me yesterday. Isn't it powerful?'

The room was completely silent. I was thinking I ought, perhaps, to clap, when all the babies in the room started howling as one. This did not hinder Maria. She explained that her boyfriend – who wanted babies sooner rather than later – had written these particular lines after she complained of a headache in bed. 'His appetite is insatiable – if you know what I mean,' Maria said. Sheila's eyebrows rose, as she swayed about, trying to calm her screaming baby.

Maria said, 'May I? I do so need to get some practice,' and took the howling baby by its underarms. She stared at it for two minutes, as if she were thinking about eating it, and handed it back. 'It smells very nice,' she said. As the baby gurgled, Sheila started to talk, concentrating on me, rather than Maria, of whom she evidently disapproved. Of course, I was lucky, Sheila said. I really wouldn't believe the stress involved in having children... the agony of childbirth. The constant screaming. The lack of sleep. How he shot out nearly two years ago now, and she still can't get him onto a bottle. He guzzles away at both breasts, can't get enough, sucks and sucks and sucks, such a lusty little chap. Just like his father...

'And would you believe,' she said. 'The second time around, they called me a geriatric mother. And me, just thirty-two.'

Maria surveyed the baby with renewed disgust, and then thrust her face far too close to Sheila's. 'Why on earth,' Maria demanded, pointing at me, 'do you think she needs to know any of that? You've inserted images in my mind I may never scrape out again.'

I went red all over and stammered an apology, but Maria had thrust her arm through mine and dragged me into a corner of the room.

'You can tell, just by looking, the people who are going to ruin you with their conversation,' she said. 'Stay away from women with babies. Stay away from men with beards. Now, enjoy more of my man's verse:

'As the years go by,
        you wear out
                the machine of the soul…
There's less and less love,
                and less and less daring,
and time
        is a battering ram
                        against my head.'

And she commenced, at the top of her voice, rising to a deafening crescendo, very much like a wail:

'Then there's amortization,
        the deadliest of all;
amortization
        of the heart and soul.'

The room was quite still. Everyone was staring at Maria, who said, 'Don't you think that's poignant?'

And, then, since all the babies had started wailing again, she added: 'Fuck this for a game of soldiers,' and knocked back her drink.

'Now just you see,' she said. 'No one else will trouble us for the rest of the evening. We can stand here, in our corner, with all the crisps, and have a lovely little chat, all by ourselves.'

And it was quite true. The party meandered on around us, as we chatted amiably, with half an eye on the clock, waiting until the time at which we could, politely, make our excuses.

'Of course, ideally what we'd do right now is behave so badly we'll never get invited again,' Maria said, casting her eye about the room. 'But... well... not much chance of debauchery here, I shouldn't think.'

She was silent, as if thinking carefully. I was lost as to what to say.

'I suppose,' she said, with a sigh, at last. 'The only trouble with my methodology is – I really do love Mayakovsky. I never go on dates anymore. I mean what is the point, anyway? How many dismal evenings must one woman endure? I prefer to sit at home and read what he wrote. I'm never going to meet a real man who stimulates me like that. At night, sometimes, I line up all my pillows in a body shape hoping he'll visit my dreams. Oh, it's awful to wake up alone.

'Of course, everyone expects you to be miserable if you're single,' she said. 'They want you to be – it makes them feel better, since they lost their freedom.' And with that Maria burst into tears, knocked a vase over and spilled red wine all over the carpet. So I went to find the hostess and told her we had to leave, right away.

'Thank you for a lovely party,' I said. 'But, I'm so sorry, we've caused a bit of a mess. And I think I ought to drive

Maria home...'

Maria threw her arms about the hostess and kissed her affectionately, on both cheeks, thanking her for a 'stupendous' evening, as we sped towards the door.

As soon as we got outside, and into my car, Maria stopped pretending to cry and started to laugh instead. Laughed so hard she got hiccups. 'Oh dear, it serves me right,' she said, struggling to draw breath. 'You know the Russians say you hiccup when you remember the dead.'

I bombed across the bridge while Maria wheezed a series of directions, in between painful breaths, insisting on a right, then a left, then a left, then a right, until we finally arrived outside what I mistook to be her flat and turned out to be a bar, for she was insisting I owed her several drinks.

And when we got inside, she slapped a waiter on the back, and said, 'I'll have a French martini, and she'll have Sex on the Floor, please.' And laughed her awful laugh again. And then she winked at me, rather beautifully, as she explained, 'If you can't avoid those sorts of parties, you have to get out of them as soon as you arrive. For that you must develop a foolproof exit strategy...'

*

Later that evening, I started dating Che Guevara, to the delight of all concerned.

Maria thinks politics might appal people even quicker than poetry.

RIP HER TO SHREDS

Maggie took two fluorescent drinks, served in hollowed out pineapples by a girl in a hula outfit, and sucked on all eight protruding straws at once. She could see, from where she stood, behind a large waxed plant at the end of the bar, that no one else had taken the dress code literally.

Maggie cursed herself, in language too foul to repeat. It was the sort of mistake she was making a lot, just lately, and she did not know why.

'Oh dear, you've taken things a little far, haven't you?' said a woman in a little black cocktail dress, a zebra mask over her eyes.

Maggie turned and sighed. 'How was I to know, when told to dress as my favourite beast, for a party at the zoo, that no one else would dress up properly? I suppose I'll just have to drink my way through the embarrassment.'

'I shouldn't if I were you,' said the zebra, lowering her voice, conspiratorially. 'You know what you're like when you're drunk. You'd mount anything. You tart.'

'I beg your pardon,' said Maggie, all of a sudden struggling to breathe. But the zebra woman sprang off and disappeared into the crowd.

So her reputation had preceded her, Maggie thought: nothing wrong with that, not necessarily, for it had taken many years to build. But she did wonder briefly what she had done to upset the zebra before abandoning the thought as unnecessarily reckless. She finished her drink and started to search for someone she knew.

It was a rare event, escaping the office at such a reasonable hour. It was important to enjoy herself. Lately, her life was no fun at all. For four evenings in five she sat at her desk as the night slid away from her, because she had reached such a position that they expected her to do so for hours on end, waiting on decisions that might never come.

After eleven hours of work there was next to nothing to do but the editor, who set out to wreck her daily, never wanted to go home. So the whole department was forced to sit there proving itself indispensable. Agreeing that lunch is for wimps. And dinner is for wimps. Weekends are for wimps. Sleep – also for wimps. Admitting to an interest in anything outside the building at all – a wimpish thing to do.

Maggie sat there, filing her nails, applying and reapplying her lipstick, and thought that she could understand this attitude if she were working on a cure for cancer. But she wasn't. She just sat there, with all the rest of them, spending hours, countless hours, trawling the internet, waiting to be torn apart. Not that any other job would be better, Maggie knew. Jobs are all the same.

She had been so excited, leaving on time, telling everyone about this crucial networking event. But now she was in two minds as to whether she ought to stay. On the one hand, she looked and felt ridiculous. On the other hand, she had gone without a man so long, there was such a sharp and pressing hunger in her heart, that, she feared, if left unsatisfied, she might well burst. Maggie finished her pineapple drink and returned it to the girl in the hula outfit, who replaced it with a new drink, in the form of a plant pot bursting with equatorial flowers.

Maggie tried to engage the waitress in conversation, but the girl just frowned at her and looked perplexed. She stood in silence at the end of the bar, her embarrassment concealed by lolling palm trees and rich green overhanging ferns, trying to summon up courage. The air was hot and tropical and the more Maggie drank, the more she came to notice her beautiful surroundings.

For it was a fine summer evening, the sun still bright in the sky, its fierce blaze reflected in the streams and pools and rivulets that spread out across the zoo like a maze of gold. Maggie abandoned her drink, moved away from the bar and went to examine the pond. She peered at the luminous insects skating across, and put her face too close to the water, to look at the coloured fish darting underneath the surface. She inhaled a fly and started spluttering, returned to her drink, trying to swallow it, held out her glass for more drink, and stumbled back, away from the bugs and into a glasshouse, which proved to be stiflingly hot, and full of orchids.

Outside, she could hear the popping of champagne corks and gusts of laughter, so she wandered back out, into the crowd, trying to find a good-looking man. Finding none, she attempted conversation with several people who happened to be standing on their own, but they just glanced up and down at her dress, with startled expressions, as if she were talking a foreign language.

Maggie tried, very hard, not to take these failures to heart. She knew this evening was just going in the same direction as everything else. It was all symptomatic of her luck. Just the latest instance of this year's luck. And last year's luck. And, yes, Maggie thought, the luck she'd had the year before that. 'When one falls into such a dismal luck rut as I've had,' Maggie said to herself, 'it's very hard to get oneself out of it…'

So she sat down by the bar, and tried, once more, to admire the trees and the fish and the flowers. And when that didn't work, she dug one perfect leopard-print talon hard into her wrist. It was awful to think how, just an hour ago, she had been so pleased, so very pleased and proud. Delighted – yes, delighted even – to have got herself into this infamous dress.

In her youth, her recent youth, this dress had had that effect on men a great dress will have. It dragged them to her, inexorably, as the moon creates the tides. But the men at this party weren't even looking. They were too busy talking to women in outfits you could wear to any old party, with tasteful and dull animal accessories. These men sweated profusely into their standard-issue suits, until their shirts were wet through and their faces melted like waxworks left near a fire. They seemed unaware of the heady atmosphere here at the zoo, with all its potential for wild romance.

Maggie pressed her face into her leopard-print thighs and stared hard at her leopard-print shoes. She put both hands on her little leopard-skin hat, with the tiny leopard-print ears she'd sewn on that morning. How gleeful she had been in her bedroom, stuffing her body into leopard-print hosiery. The dress itself had slid down, just so. And then she'd wriggled and grappled with the zip and a coat hanger.

Wrestling with herself in the two-way mirror, she realised how hard it would be to extract herself without assistance. And she had imagined meeting some sort of manly bear – or a lion or a leopard – who would race off with her, into the night, to tear the whole outfit off with his teeth. But none of these men looked the least bit carnivorous. None of them were baring fangs at her.

But, while it failed on the men, Maggie's dress was having its usual effect on the women. Other women rarely appreciated her sartorial adventures, and tended to sneer at her in a manner most deflating. Maggie smiled at a trio who came near, and they drifted past without acknowledging her, trailing an odour of mothballs and Chanel. One of them started to talk knowledgeably – and at top volume – about how zebra print was the only chic thing this season.

'It makes leopard print,' the woman shouted, without looking behind her, 'look vulgar. As leopard print, of course, *is…*' Then, a lady in a monochrome dress, with a discreet little badger mask, sat down next to her, so Maggie stood up.

'Christ,' said the woman, as if suddenly alerted to Maggie's presence. 'What are you wearing?'

Maggie felt something pop, looked down at her dress, and found that her stomach had triumphed in the war with her underwear. She stared down, miserably, as the great protuberance overcame her leopard-print tights.

'You don't remember me, do you?' asked the badger.

Maggie could not say that she did.

'That'll be because you're an awful slut,' spat the badger, before flouncing off, towards the exit.

For a terrible moment, Maggie thought she might cry. But, if that happened, she knew it would be the end. That her tears would finally confirm what she must never admit, that her life had gone wrong, and irredeemably so, many, many years before. So she sniffed and pulled herself together. First, she would take a tour of the animals. She would get her money's worth. That would show she was not defeated. She would look at the animals that interested her, and then go home, have an early night.

She had only been to a zoo once before, when she was small, and she hadn't liked it. She had been mad keen on big cats – tigers and leopards and jaguars and lions – animals that roared. But when her parents took her to the zoo, on her seventh birthday, the animals had all looked so depressed, like inmates in a jail. The lion, so lackadaisical in his fake savannah. The tiger, so lethargic, bedraggled on a heap of rock. The jaguar had died, apparently, the day before. And the leopard lay purring in the sun, like a pampered, overgrown housecat. So Maggie set off, walking erratically, trying to follow the signs to the dangerous-animal enclosure, until her head began to ache with the booze and the fumes rising off the tropical plants, and she ended up at the very end of the zoo, clinging to a set of railings, staring at a pair of – what the sign said – were Visayan warty pigs, grunting aggressively.

Maggie attempted to retrace her steps, hoping to stumble across a more thrilling beast, only to get lost following a labyrinthine water feature, which the sign said was full of otters. Maggie stared hard, trying to spot an otter, before deciding she wasn't really interested, and after a great deal of wandering this way and that, Maggie found herself in a vast ice-blue igloo, in which the temperature had plunged below freezing. Hugging herself, Maggie tried to walk out again only to find herself staring at a despondent penguin.

A waiter appeared, from nowhere, to offer her a drink served in a plastic rhinoceros, and it was while trying to take leave of the kidnapped Emperor of the South Pole, while also attempting to get at the alcohol in the rhinoceros, that Maggie happened upon a tall, sharp-shouldered woman, who was draped over a bench. A woman very obviously drunk, and already staring at Maggie in a hostile fashion.

'I do like your dress,' Maggie said, hoping to ward off any hostility with a compliment while frankly admiring the lady's dress of tight, sea-green silk, which made her look – Maggie thoroughly approved – like an indecent mermaid.

'Thank you,' said the woman. 'I'm supposed to be a grass snake.'

'You look exactly like one. I'm a leopardess.'

'Yes, that's what I thought you were,' the woman said, squinting at Maggie as if the sun were in her eyes, which it wasn't. The woman then fell off the bench and Maggie got her back onto it, and helped her to sit up straight.

'You know, I thought this party would be fun,' the woman confided. 'But it isn't fun at all. "Come as your favourite beast," he said. "For a party at the zoo," he said. Well I don't count wrapping some mangy old ferret round your neck as sticking to the theme, do you?'

'No,' said Maggie. 'I do not…'

'Or digging up some snakeskin thing that someone died in, that should have been buried with the corpse. Or carrying around the remains of some crocodile killed just to perper— perper—' the woman sneezed, 'perpetrate a crime against fashion. You know, usually I don't come to these sorts of things. They're so full of bitches…'

The woman blinked at her, as if expecting some sort of response. Maggie tried to think of something to say, but her head ached, worse and worse.

'But Lord Pabham happens to be a personal friend of mine,' the woman continued. 'The sort with benefits if you know what I mean… so I assumed he'd be here, only he's not, and of course, I know this place very well so… it's really not my fault that I made this… mistake.'

'Something should be done,' said Maggie, with conviction. 'Maybe, if we took a good look, there might be some place to dance, later, or maybe there will be some sort of after-party?'

'Oh, later,' said the woman. 'Always later… and why would you think I wish to dance? It's impossible to move in this damned thing. No. No. I didn't come here to dance. And I'm not waiting. No, I'm not putting up with it. A bloody insult, that's what I call it... and so now, yes, you've got it right... I will get this party started. Or die in the attempt.'

Maggie felt a surge of hope, which promptly dissipated, as she watched the woman stagger in the wrong direction, away from the party, making tiny steps, very quickly, so that her tight, sea-green sheath shivered and shone as she went. Maggie was just thinking that if she ran, she might catch her, and steer the woman back in the right direction, when she saw the woman haul herself up the side of a tall gate and slither over the top with remarkable agility. The woman had either ignored, or not noticed, a sign which said: 'Do Not Enter – Control Centre – Dangerous Animals'. And Maggie was not going to follow her there, so she sat down on the bench that the woman had vacated and closed her eyes for a second.

The cocktails overcame her. The moist air made her feel sick. She rested her head against the back of the bench and found that, if she copied exactly the same pose that the woman had adopted, she felt almost comfortable. Indeed, Maggie may have drifted off into a prolonged and restorative nap, had she not, sometime later, been seized awake by blood-curdling screams and a crowd of terrified women running past the bench on which she sat, pursued by roaring bears.

Maggie stayed, petrified to the spot, as the bears passed and, when they were gone, turned around, only to be accosted by the penguin, made furious by the intolerable heat, flapping his wings very violently at her. Maggie did her damnedest not to scream. She kicked off her shoes – in which it would be impossible to run – and hurried, as unobtrusively as she could manage, back through the party. She saw monkeys wrench the fur hats off the elegantly dressed ladies trailing the odour of mothballs and Chanel; the hats were launched into the air as the monkeys swung violently from lamppost to lamppost. A llama was sniffing a waiter, with evident approval, as the waiter tried to disappear under a tablecloth. A lion was roaring arrogantly at three men in black tie, who were scrabbling on top of one another, trying to keep the beast away with a picnic umbrella.

An elderly couple were being groomed by apes. Lizards, snakes and spiders were crawling across the ground, scaling up trembling legs, causing squeals and hysterical yelps. A hippopotamus was charging the bar, knocking down the pineapple and pot-plant drinks like so many skittles. The girls in hula outfits were hugging each other and wailing.

The catastrophe only seemed likely to escalate, and Maggie's head cleared with the adrenaline. Time slowed, and she crouched down flat, to begin crawling, on her elbows, as quickly as she could, towards the exit. Silent and nimble, kicking away snakes and spiders, she could just see the great white stone lions that marked the arch through which she could escape when she felt a powerful tug at her foot.

The Leopard, who soon had his paws all over Maggie, was very taken by her, this voluptuous, great leopardess, who had spent all this time wiggling her behind at him seductively to show off her delectable spots. Never in his life had the Leopard seen such graceful colourings, nor such a fine, healthy specimen of the opposite sex. Her coat alone was irresistible, not to mention her form, and her strange, powerful scent. He had never found anything like it.

Several leopardesses had been paraded before him by the zookeepers over the years, hoping he'd be tempted... the zookeepers had worried that their Leopard was not quite as other males. But the Leopard was a thoughtful, and deeply passionate, animal. As it was, the Leopard had his standards. In the desert, in his days of freedom, he'd anticipated having his pick; he would not settle for some pre-arranged sham romance, he wanted the real thing. He knew he could settle for nothing less than a *coup de foudre*. And this had now struck him down.

Maggie looked behind her and screamed. She should, of course, have been pleased that her dress was finally delivering her the powerful male for which she had so fervently prayed throughout the evening. But single women, these days, are so hard to please. They are fanatics. Who want it all and are determined to get it. And if they don't, they won't settle. So Maggie continued to scream and wail, in a manner wholly contradictory, not to mention hypocritical.

The Leopard, of course, interpreted this noise as a positive invitation to pounce. Maggie's timid little mews were so alluring to him. And he was halfway through his seduction when a deafening burst of laughter was heard above. The woman in the zebra mask was crouched on top of the large, ornamental lion, shrieking uncontrollably.

'Oh dear, oh dear, Maggie, what did I tell you? Bestiality, now! BESTIALITY! I knew it! Just you wait until I tell…'

And Maggie, feeling quite desperate, and utterly unable to help herself, started to cry. Since it was the end, anyway, she pushed the Leopard away forcefully and scrambled to her feet. She turned, dashed forward, and hit her head so violently on the stone statue, she passed out. So she did not see the Leopard attack. Nor what was left of the zebra afterwards.

But as she came around, in the back of an ambulance, to the ministrations of a very handsome paramedic, Maggie found, somehow, that her faith was restored. For she was dimly aware in the great gloom of her head: that other dresses came and went, but leopard print had never failed her.

LA FOULE

Yesterday I was mugged. Just off the Commercial Road. I should have seen it coming. She came straight at me. Shouted 'gimme yer stuff'. Hit me twice. Once in the back, once in the eye. That's the absolute last time I smile at a child.

All my fault. Took a short cut, didn't I? Drunk in the dark, wasn't I? But oh, my eye.

Still, I like to think I had the last laugh. Off she ran with a bag full of complete crap. Dead lighters. Snot rags. Athlete's foot powder. A £500 phone bill Gravy ran up speaking to a call girl in Caracas. A mobile so big you could brain a duck with it. And I hope she speaks to the people who call me. It'd serve them both right.

May their feet rot. Yes – like anyone with a shred of sense, I keep the bulk of my cash in my left shoe.

Well, I was just checking my sock and thinking about getting a bus when I cursed myself – I saw him coming. He asked me if I had the time. And like a fool I looked at my wrist. Why, I don't know – I never wear a watch. And in an instant he was on me. He took my shoes and he took my sock. I didn't struggle. He was armed to the teeth. And I'd only just thought what a strange colour they were, like he'd been gargling red wine and flossing with strings of beetroot, when he started screaming at me to stop looking at him funny. He sprayed deodorant in my other eye.

And lamped me one for good measure.

When I woke up there was a crowd all around me. Somehow I'd lost my tie and my keys. Someone was hauling me towards the hospital for medical attention, and someone else was dragging me towards the police station, to report the thefts. I made a scene. Thrashed about. Insisted I be taken to A&E.

They hauled me off, and I still couldn't see, so I resisted. Eventually they took me by my arms and legs and pushed me into the back of an ambulance. After a short ride, sirens on, which made it difficult to understand all the questions they were asking, they took me out, and instead of rushing me in, straightaway, for medical attention, they sat me down on a chair. I asked for a doctor. They said they'd try to find one. But whether they did or not, it's not for me to say.

Straightaway, I felt a finger jab me between the ribs and a voice shouting, 'What the hell's wrong with you?'

I said I couldn't see.

'Lucky you,' the voice said. 'There are some real ugly fuckers here. But I know you from somewhere, don't I? You look familiar.'

'I can't see you. So I can't tell.'

'It's Barry,' said Barry.

Well, I racked my brain, and it was Barry-less, so I said, 'How are you, mate?'

And he said: 'Very well, very well thank you.'

'What are you in for?'

'I don't want to talk about it,' he said. 'What about you?'

'I was mugged. I blame myself. Happened twice in five minutes.'

Now, the first lesson is: never act friendly to a stranger in London. They get excited. Think that it's OK to have a little chat. Which it isn't. Give them an inch, they'll steal your tape measure. Barry didn't stop talking for the next hour.

'That's bad, very bad. When I started out I was always getting mugged. I remember when a group of seven-year-olds set upon me and took my last fiver. I was wandering round Bow, couldn't find the boat where I was supposed to be staying, asked them for directions. I never made that mistake again. I'm from the country, myself. The kids here are feral. Well, I felt very stupid. But, I tell you what, I made some changes and it's never happened since.'

Then Barry told me his entire life story. It was brutish but mercifully short. The details struck me as highly improbable. What I needed to do was get up and demand to see a nurse. But he was clutching my arm and there wasn't any stopping him. Eventually I reminded him I'd been assaulted and asked for his help.

'It's very simple. What I did was this. First, I stopped washing my hair and I let it grow as long as it liked. Then, before I left the house, I would run my hands through it, making it stand on end. And whenever I had a nip of something, I'd dab a bit on my wrists, so I smelt more interesting. On the street I would talk to myself about whatever happened to be on my mind, taking care to shout every tenth word or so. I half run, half walk – scout's pace, you know – so no one thinks I'm drunk. This is important. I run four minutes in a dead straight line, and then I stagger about erratically for six. No one comes near me. As a solution, it's genius. If I do say so myself.

'The thing I find is that no one ever lets you alone in

the city. Every road you go down is crammed with cars. Every pavement is full of bicycles. Buses are a scrum. You never get a seat. The Underground is just some foul game of Twister. I've seen them sweating down there, contorting over other people's body parts like they're trying to reach the spot. I shudder just thinking about it. So I came up with the solution.

'On buses, well, I'll admit it, I sing. Not pop songs, the kids do that. All the hymns. Doesn't matter if you can't remember the words. 'God Be in My Head'. 'Morning Has Broken'. Stick to the classics. You can clear a whole deck with 'Kumbaya' alone. Doesn't matter if you can't hold a tune. In fact, it helps.

'The Underground – I know what you're thinking, there's no clearing a crowd down there. Those carriages are so brimful at rush hour. What's to be done? I'll tell you. It's obvious. You come to terms with the fact that it's a long journey – you're spending forty-five minutes on one line, far too near the earth's core. You take a suitcase. Nothing in it. You go into a carriage. You leave it in the middle of the aisle. People get on and off at the next stop. No one pays attention. Then you stand up and look about you, and you say, "Whose bag is that?" with frightened eyes. Then you walk, ever so quickly, down the carriage, telling people to move.

'Don't say, "it might be a bomb" or anything like that. You'll just shut the line down. A beginner's error. No, you move gingerly down the carriage, as if you're afraid it is a bomb but don't want to look stupid if it's not. Well pretty soon the people next to you will start moving. And before long the whole carriage has dispersed. And then you can sit down again, put your feet up, read a newspaper.

'I know what you're thinking – changing lines. Surely that's sending you right back to square one? Well, it's perfectly simple, when you're in the tunnels. You can't sing – they might mistake you for a busker. That wouldn't work at all. No, you dance along the yellow lines. Pretty soon there will be announcements on the tannoy. "Can the man on the westbound blah blah please step away from the platform edge." Well, move away, just to please them, and then do a little jig, the Hokey Cokey, one foot on the line, one foot off the line, in out, in out, shake it all about. You'll soon find a space clearing. No one wants to end up on the rails because they stood next to a mentalist.'

Barry's voice was getting louder and louder, pitching higher and higher.

'It's so simple, when you think about it. The natives don't like to make a fuss. They're loath to make eye contact. They'd rather die than have to deal with a tourist. They just move away from your baggage as quickly as they can. Stuff themselves into an even fuller carriage – just to get away. Thinking, I'm away from the blast, *and* I'll still get to work on time. They don't tend to get off altogether. But if they do, and they're really worried, they don't cause a panic. They might look silly. And get to work late. Once or twice, I've heard someone talk about telling a guard. But good luck finding one, that's what I say. If it's a false alarm you won't get in trouble. Foreigners are always leaving their bags at one end and taking a seat at the other end. It's quite natural for them. They've never set foot in a capital like ours before. They're ignorant. Ignorant – of the carnage we exist in!'

I still couldn't see but I could hear noise increasing around me. I had the distinct impression that people were trying to distance themselves from Barry, who, as he kept hitting me, I assumed was making a series of ever more extravagant hand gestures.

'Honestly, follow my lead, you'll never get mugged ever again. Look wild, look dangerous, behave erratically. No one will touch you. You could live in the meanest street, in central badlands... no, no one'll touch you.

'And as for the high street. Well – nothing could be simpler. You go up to a homeless chap. You give him a tenner. Take a bunch of his magazines. And then you just walk wherever you like, shouting *"Big Issue, Big Issue"*, thrusting them at random people in the crowd, whistling occasionally. You can count on them all being miserly bastards. And so you will find a clear path opening before you. Mark my words. The effect is biblical. Like Moses separating the Red Sea. Or whatever.'

'Well,' I said, relieved he'd finally stopped talking. 'I can see this all sounds very clever. But how come you're here if you've got it all figured out?'

Barry went quiet. I could hear more rustling. And footsteps. Then my name was called. Finally, I thought, they're getting me to the nurse. But that didn't happen, since I was sitting in a police station. They informed me that I had assaulted a police constable in the execution of his duty. And I informed them I couldn't see a thing since some bastard had sprayed deodorant in one eye and punched me in the other. And after a second hour spent blind, they cautioned me and sent me off to hospital.

Barry, I hear, was not so lucky. He was sent down for six months for communicating a bomb threat.

His advice, however, has been quite useful. I've not been mugged since. And tourists never ask me for directions.

THE DINNER PARTY

I had never thrown a dinner party before. I'm not much of a cook. But Jack insisted. He thought it might help him at work. He wanted to invite his manager, Geoffrey, and some other guests. So we asked the new next-door neighbours, his cousin Judy, mad Barry and that couple I can't stand.

Judy was busy. Mad Barry could not be reached, by telephone or any other method. The couple I can't stand can't stand me either. The next-door neighbours cancelled in the afternoon. Claimed their kid had croup. If that kid has croup I'm certifiably deaf.

I had trusted the manager to cry off too. I kept my hopes up right until the doorbell rang. But there he stood, with his girlfriend, on the doorstep; with a bouquet of blue chrysanthemums they must have thought kitsch.

The girlfriend has so much hair her head looks like a tree in leaf. There were kisses all over the place, very professional. They knew exactly how to behave. I don't know who made kissing complete strangers a thing you had to do. But I was prepared. I didn't slap anyone, as instinct dictates, when moist lips are launched at my face.

I showed them straight into the living room, which I'd brightened up with a printed tablecloth and flowers. But when I asked them to sit down, it was like I was seeing the room for the first time. Overnight, the plants I'd bought to cheer the fireplace up, potted begonias, hydrangeas and a dark pink orchid climbing a frame, presented a rich diorama of death and deformity.

I started pointing at the photographs on the mantelpiece and talking utter rubbish, distracting their attention, as I pushed the nearest pot underneath my chair, pretty skilfully, with one foot. Talking, talking, talking, I poured them large glasses of wine, all the while pushing the other plants towards my corner of the table. I don't know why I get so embarrassed. But I was sweating too much to calm down.

The girlfriend has a very loud voice. It launched into a series of blatant lies: how nice the house is, how up-and-coming the area is, how she loves what we've done with the place. We haven't done a thing to the house since the previous owner died, allegedly in the rocking chair she happens to be sat in. Our estate agent told us that, he must have had his reasons. We bought it up very cheap, furniture and all. There's a brothel above the hairdresser's opposite and the house shakes whenever a lorry passes, which is six times an hour. I smiled back at the woman's abundant head and said, 'That's very nice of you to say. I do love how you have your hair.'

I'd been so diverted, wondering how much hairspray must have been in it to make it go so horizontal and yet so vertical at the same time, I'd quite forgotten her name. She smiled, so I said:

'Where do you get it done?'

I went to check on the dinner and racked my empty brain. The pots were boiling over. The chicken had shrivelled up. I turned everything off and went to find Jack. What I wanted to do was stick my neck under the tap and my feet in an ice bucket. It was too hot for a roast. But Jack insisted. He said you can't invite people to dinner and not give them meat. And then he said my barbecues give him ulcers.

As I climbed the stairs, I looked through the crack in the living-room door. The girlfriend was sat on Geoffrey's lap, giggling, quite blatantly, at our wallpaper.

Upstairs the kids are running around half dressed. So I ask Jack, 'Why aren't they in the bath?' He looks at me as if I've asked why Tokyo isn't in France. We have a set-to in whispers, which he ruins by slamming the wardrobe door shut and stamping off to the bathroom, making both the girls cry. He stubs his toe, curses imaginatively. The kids start chanting the swear words and jumping up and down.

We're about to start arguing when Geoffrey pops his head between the banisters asking if everything is all right. 'Oh yes,' I say, blowing my fringe up out of my eyes, and accidentally winking at him. 'We're just putting the kids to bed. I'll get you another drink.'

He says he doesn't want another drink. Which as far as I'm concerned is bad manners. I go into the kitchen and prepare the hummus. I wanted to buy those fancy crudités and breadsticks you can get in M&S but Jack said the girlfriend has a wheat allergy. Clearly, she is a woman who likes to make life difficult. Or perhaps eating bread crusts really does make your hair curl and she recently overdosed. I deliver the hummus with an array of celery sticks and mini cucumbers I sliced with my own fair hand and try to make conversation.

We talk about their holiday plans. And then we stop talking because I used a name which is clearly not the girlfriend's name, and she is too polite to correct me. I was about to deploy fresh inspiration when we hear the unmistakable sound of heavy rain, indoors. It appears the bath has overflowed and water is pouring through the ceiling. I look at Geoffrey and his girlfriend. Jack is effing and blinding upstairs. The water continues to cascade through the ceiling, the floorboards sodden and the plaster dripping above.

I am overcome with a desperate urge to smoke. 'You OK, babe?' I shout upstairs, as Jack continues effing and blinding. Geoffrey and his girlfriend look at me and it dawns on me that I didn't want them to come round, Jack bloody asked them to come round. So I don't know why I am the one downstairs, feeling ridiculous. I foist more wine on them and start asking questions.

How long have they been together? Where did they meet? I mention wedding bells and the pitter-patter of tiny feet. It comes to me – in a flash – hallelujah – that her name is Chloe – just as her eyes pop and she looks at Geoffrey, who smiles and squeezes her hand. Chloe starts chattering, on and on, God knows what she says, I wasn't listening. I want Jack to come downstairs and take over. So I wait for her to draw breath and excuse myself.

He's fallen asleep. The twins are rolling about on the floor, squabbling over the wind-up mouse. I shake him, prod him, talk at him. He doesn't move. So I lick him in the ear, which he hates. Finally, I get the kids to bounce on him. He wakes up. I can hear them downstairs, laughing at our shambolic decor again. Jack goes down. I read the twins a story. I read one, then another, then another. Then they want another. I say, OK this is the last. They smell like Labradors and talcum powder. He obviously hasn't washed them. Jan nods off on my arm, Fran soon follows, so I tuck them in, put the nightlight and the baby monitor on, and go downstairs.

I fix my hair in the mirror and start getting the plates out. Jack has turned the oven back on so the chicken is a black lump. I open the fridge and start fixing a salad. Then

I hack the chicken to bits and dump it in the middle of the dining table.

'Babe,' I say. 'If you go and get the rest we'll eat.'

My grin is so large my cheeks are obstructing my vision. They have been sitting there for an hour and a half with swimming pool-sized glasses of wine and they're not the slightest bit drunk. We start talking about Geoffrey and Jack and their work, although mainly about Geoffrey's job, how much travelling he does, the state of company profits, expansion plans, the dire economy, how he intends to vote in the local elections.

In revenge, for having to listen to such boring information, I start talking about how much we blew on IVF and Jack's irritable semen. Jack looks at me like he wants to stick the chicken fork through my throat. I ruffle his hair with great affection.

I pour everyone another drink. And I realise they aren't getting drunk because they aren't drinking any of the wine I'm pouring them. Those absurd oversized glasses Jack's mother gave us for Christmas are bottomless pits of perfectly good booze. Although, by this point, I've managed three. The dinner is disgusting but, in testament to their formidable politeness, Geoffrey and Chloe are eating it and pretending that it tastes nice. I, for one, can't force myself. Jack has already finished his. But then he'd eat a plate of used tissues if it was put in front of him.

My cheeks are red, I feel so drunk, I go into the kitchen and have a bit of toast.

When I return, it is clear Jack has taken quite a liking to Chloe. They're deep in conversation, which leaves me with Geoffrey. I can't think of a thing to say to him. And he can't think of a thing to say to me. So I say I need to pop out to the corner shop because I forgot to get ice cream. And I buy fags. I light two at once. And expel the bad thoughts that have seeped into my ribcage.

I get back. I make up the dessert. It's actually quite good but I can't eat it. My stomach hasn't deflated since the twins were born. Jack is avoiding my glances. Somehow Chloe has noticed that Jack isn't feeling much fondness for me, and reckons we need to talk, woman to woman. She swaps chairs with Geoffrey and starts talking, urgently, about how she'd like her wedding.

Silk, tulle, chiffon, lace? Sewn by Belgian nuns. White, cream, eggshell? Quite fancies a headdress. Champagne, ice sculptures, a ukulele quartet. Lilies, roses, vintage foliage. Flower girls in lemon, bridesmaids in apricot, sunflower bouquets. Oysters, as a starter *and* an aphrodisiac, profiteroles or a macaroon tower? No hymns, they're not religious, Meatloaf played on strings, as she walks up the aisle. A photo booth with comedy props. Origami swans. Turning up to the church in a tractor. Since they met on the family farm. Photographs to be taken in a field of wheat. And so on and so on and so on. I read somewhere that marriages last in inverse proportion to the amount of money you spend on them. The cheaper the ceremony, the longer you're married. If this is true, I give them six weeks, while Jack and I will still be bickering in a care home.

I drain my glass and am just about to ask her if she would like more pudding when she takes my hand in both her own – so soft and beautifully manicured – stares deeply into my eyes, and says, 'You don't seem very happy.'

And that is when the chronology of the evening became a bit confused.

I must have felt a desperate urge to smoke. For I took out my emergency lighter. And it was while I was casting about, no doubt carelessly, in my apron, for the emergency cigarettes, sparking up the lighter while I looked, as is my habit, that her hair went up in flames.

It was lucky, in a way... the plant pots were just there, under my chair. I immediately made use of the dry soil, smothered the conflagration before her face was damaged. And setting aside the terrible stench, and all the hair that ended up on the floor, I think it improved her look. Overall.

That was a fortnight ago. Jack didn't get his promotion. We have only recently started talking again. The first thing we agreed on was not to have anymore dinner parties.

SHOPLIFTERS

The Major's house is on the hairpin bend, with the only bit of pavement. The cars round here make kamikaze lunges, so there's no sneaking past him. Many times I've had to throw myself flat on the grassy verge to avoid being run over when walking on the other side of the road. And since I got huge, it seemed safer to waste whole hours and days listening to his latest conspiracy theories.

Sure, odd things have happened. Last month, a helicopter fell out of the sky, landed on the nature reserve and killed a party of birdwatchers. Only the Major says they weren't watching *birds*. Then the fire station burned down, with the fire engine inside. The Major found that very amusing. Says he's long predicted it. Arson has run in the sub-officer's family for three generations. He said the Greasy Pole was a blatant fix. And correctly identified the winner, a month before the competition started. He opened a book on it, cleared me out, along with half the street.

The Major recounts, in frightening detail, his midnight spine spasms. He rehearses, with sound effects, the travails of his bowels. Meals on Wheels is trying to poison him. The bin men exist to thwart him. Rose at number 3 is sleeping with her son-in-law. Binkie at number 10 had her cat run over – the drunk next door did it. (And everyone knows it.) Number 46 is missing post. Suspects number 64. The Major says it's the postman's fault. Says he's got an IQ no better than a chimpanzee. 'Equal opportunities,' the Major says, his eyebrows reaching to heaven. And all the while, morsels of spit land on my cheeks. Saliva in the air like rain in the wind.

I don't know why they call him 'the Major'. He's said nothing about a military career. Sure he's big on deportment, tough on law and order, and the second time I met him he showed me his Luger. He'll rant on for twenty minutes about the price of fry-ups down the pub before shouting, 'But the Major knows the price of eggs. Yes. Oh yes. The Major knows it.'

It's hard to know what to believe. First time I met him he went on about the weather. We were in for a run of sun that would break all records, he said. It rained non-stop for a month, and he stood outside, every day, ranting and raging about the duplicity of weathermen. Standing there, laying in wait for me, in his bright red anorak, pretending to clip the hedge. As water dripped down his shears, his artificial leg sank further into the sodden ground.

The villagers have long avoided him. They think he's bad luck. A few years ago, he used to ride a rusty old bicycle, causing rash overtaking, road-rage incidents and car crashes, since he pedalled it in experimental fashion, exactly where he liked, and that was usually in the middle of the road. Since the accident, and the loss of his foot, he drives a mobility vehicle in much the same way. Traffic jams build up behind him. His mad tufts of hair sail in the wind.

If I make it down to the shop without the Major holding me up, there he is, prowling about the aisles. And while they order me to leave for spending forty-five minutes looking at the magazines, and sniffing all the perfume samples – and I need to do that, to relieve my constant nausea – the Major is treated with the greatest respect. The girl at the checkout practically bows every time he comes along. Totally oblivious to the bulges, shaped like Scotch bottles, most evident in his trousers.

The Major has *technique* when it comes to shoplifting. He goes up to the checkout, bold as you like, and slaps down a packet of cocktail umbrellas on the counter. Then he hums and ahs as to the cost of them, as he pats the booty he's stolen. The Major just can't help himself. So the shop assistant traipses off to double-check the price of cocktail umbrellas.

And the Major just stands there, whistling tunelessly, pounding his good foot on the bottom of the counter, as if flexing it on an imaginary piano pedal. The shop girl returns. Confirms that they really do cost 99p. And then the Major will mumble into his moustache, which generally has toothpaste in it, 'Good grief, that is not what they cost in my day.' And he shrugs sadly, as if he couldn't possibly afford them. Pushes off home.

Once, when I left the village store, a French stick stuffed up one coat sleeve and a cucumber up the other, the Major rode his mobility vehicle right beside me and offered me a swig of his swag. I shouldn't have done, what with the baby, but somehow I felt I needed it; the shoplifting gives me such a rush of adrenaline, afterwards I feel somewhat disorientated. We climbed the hill, as he cheerfully told me that the doctor was trying to kill him.

'Perhaps I have not told you how I lost my leg?' the Major said, with a sigh. 'It is a long and interesting tale… one day I was riding my bicycle, with Hound, my dog. He was a proud animal. A noble animal. A true Alsatian. He slept at my feet. And went with me everywhere. One day, we were coming down the hill, Hound racing at my side, when a child from the local gypsy encampment ran straight into my front wheel.

'The child bounced out of the way, it was I who fell badly, on the old shrapnel wound in my leg. And Hound, ever loyal, seeing my injury, began barking at the little rogue. Then the doctor, who was on his own bicycle, took it upon himself to drive between Hound and the child. And Hound, taking this as an act of aggression, which, I think we can agree, it certainly was, then bit the doctor, in order to disable him.

'Next thing I know, everyone begins to whisper that Hound is a danger to the public. That he must be put down. This in spite of the fact that the stupid man practically shoved his hand in Hound's mouth and then incited him further by running away. Asking to be bitten he was, practically begging, that fat rump of his bobbing about before my hungry Hound's eyes. A provocation.

'And so they took Hound away. There was the usual stitch up. That dog had heart. Never flinched in the face of death. It was the vet that whimpered. So the doctor has taken my dog. And, later on, he took my leg. And now,' the Major cried, his voice wandering up an octave, 'he plans to take my life.'

The Major, who was driving without any hands, hit the side of the pavement and skewed hard to one side before righting himself and offering me another slug of whisky.

'Don't believe it, eh? You're too young, of course, to know a thing about the evil that lurks in human hearts. But just you look about you. He's already done away with most of the biddies up and down this road. And I'll tell you why for nothing. Not for money. Not for power. Not for the thrill of it. That I could understand. No, he's doing it because he doesn't want patients distracting him from his amateur dramatics.'

The Major paused, as if expecting me to say something. He stared hard, with both eyebrows knitted.

'They're closing in on me,' the Major said. 'Yesterday I rang up, my other leg was giving me trouble. They said there were no appointments available. So I said, put me through to Dr Death. Those very words. Doctor. Death. And do you know what they did?'

I did not.

'They put me straight through. Well, it's obvious why. First, they know what we call him. Second, he's not got any appointments because no one will see him.'

He looked at me, again, as if I really ought to say something, so I told him he should ask for another doctor.

'But the others are *women*,' he said, with a terrible grimace. 'He's singing... duets... with the butcher's daughter. You can hear him. Trilling away in the surgery. But no one listens to me. I don't know why.'

The next time I saw him he didn't look very well.

'Another spy, eh? Keeping watch on me,' he said, rattling his garden shears, and coughing over me. 'Every time I come out here, to tend my hedge, there you are, creeping past, trying to draw me out. You all want me dead.'

I tried to explain to the Major that, as far as I could remember, he's the one that accosts me. And it would be difficult to carry out a murder in my condition. In the end, we went down the shop together, and tag-teamed liberating the Scotch and cheese.

It might have been the unaccustomed excitement that sent me into early labour. I should not, of course, have been shoplifting. But no one tells you how dull it is – moving out to the country, heavily pregnant. No one tells you what the hormones do to your brain. I yearned for one last thrill before my life came to an end.

The Major had informed me that, judging by the shape of my bump, and he had extensive knowledge of this, being the eldest of seven, and having made two himself, I was going to have a boy. I told him we hadn't wanted to find out. 'Quite right,' he said. 'There are so few surprises in life.' Which is a statement I profoundly disagree with. So I had a girl. And it was a difficult birth. I might have died, she might have died. But neither of us did, so we were kept in hospital for a long time. And when I got home, the doctors having cut my nether regions into ribbons, I didn't leave the house for six weeks.

When I finally managed to get myself together, to face the world with the squealing bundle, the Major was nowhere to be seen. I assumed he was sulking because I hadn't taken the baby to see him. He said he liked babies, very much, and they, in turn, liked his moustache. We started to walk past, quite regularly, and he didn't appear once.

When we got down to the supermarket, he wasn't lurking there either. His absence was so disconcerting, I found myself walking past every afternoon. But the Major was nowhere to be seen. The curtains in his house were drawn. The lights were off, even in the evening. His garden shears lay abandoned and rusting on the gravel. His hedge was quite unruly.

Finally, I asked at the shop if anything had happened to the Major.

'Oh,' said the brawny girl with the ludicrous eye shadow, who always used to serve him with elaborate rigmarole. 'He's dead. And I can't but think that I killed him.'

I said I was sure she hadn't.

'Thank you, but…' Moist blue powder and black mascara began an inexorable slide down her cheeks. 'The manager said I had to watch him because he was stealing so much of our stock. I couldn't believe it. Such a nice old gentleman. Even the smallest things were too expensive for him. But you know what old people are. Anyway, I was told to follow him round the store. And I did. He didn't take a thing. Then he started shouting at me, saying that I was trying to kill him. And then the next thing we know he's dead. I can't help but think... he was so insulted... it might have brought on... a heart attack...'

She looked so distressed I thought I ought to say something. But, just then, I felt a sudden twinge, and felt like letting out a sob myself. So I said: 'Old people die. It's what they do.'

'I know,' sobbed the girl, wiping her nose on her bib. 'That's just what Doctor Death said. He said the Major had been very ill and, for a long time, refused his treatment. He gave me two tickets to the pantomime and told me not to worry about it. Apparently, it's all in rhymes. You should come and see it. Everyone says it's ever so good, you know.'

Well, when Christmas came I thought I ought to go and see this infamous production. I booked a babysitter, thinking we deserved an evening out. And to my surprise, as I endured two of the worst hours of my life, I found myself thinking that the Major really might have unearthed a real conspiracy at last. To see that doctor, jazz handing across the stage, high kicking with a girl in tan tights, doing unspeakable solo tap dances and singing in unspeakable rhymes, you couldn't help but suspect his smile barely masked the steely demeanour of a killer.

And as the doctor grinned through the curtain call, bowed, waved, clapped – and ran back to bow once more – I found myself longing for the Major to crash into the hall, with Hound at his side, poised to chew the doctor into bits if anyone dared call for an encore.

But he didn't. So the next time I went to the shop I stole a bottle of Scotch.

And left it on his grave.

BLOODY MARY

My sister has the worst taste in men. So when she told me she was getting tattooed with the name of her latest boyfriend, I advised her, pretty strongly, against it.

'A tattoo is for life,' I said. 'Not just for breakfast.' And since she happened, at that moment, to be buttering her man's toast with a loving attention, she took offence. She pushed me out of the back door and refused to speak to me for six months.

You might think that an overreaction. But Mary never does anything by halves.

I know my sister very well, so I wasn't worried. I knew she'd get back in touch the second she ran out of babysitters. Her little one, Byron, is seven years old. My sister says he's special. The doctor says he has ADHD. Jehovah's Witnesses run on sight. When he's not kicking Rottweilers or ploughing his tricycle into the disabled or spitting things in little girls' hair, he leaps around the house, screaming and shouting, sticking his clammy fingers into electric sockets, dangling from the upstairs banisters, throwing himself down the stairs.

They have only just moved into the new house and it wasn't in a great state to start with. Paper peeling from the walls. Lights hanging out of fixtures. But my sister doesn't have the money to fix it just now; everything she had went on the mortgage.

Mary is a nurse by profession and she is sceptical, when it comes to medication. On principle, she doesn't think her boy should be drugged and she doesn't want to curb his 'creativity'. He is, she says, 'what they used to call "full of beans"'. But she can't stand up to him and that's how things go wrong. He wants cherryade and has a tantrum about it. So she buys it for him and the E-numbers turn him into Godzilla.

Last week, he cut his babysitter's ponytail off and confessed to the murder of his imaginary friend.

So I picked up the phone, right away, and I said, of course, I'll drop everything to look after my nephew. In truth, I had nothing on that evening. Plus, I love the kid, I can't help it. I drove over, I told Mary to have fun, very solemnly and straight-faced, so as not to upset her.

She'd had the tattoo, in the crook of her arm; it was still a little raw, so she had a bandage over it. I didn't ask if I could have a look at it, in case she got annoyed. Mary said it hurt like hell. More than the stars on her neck – which I do not believe – the naked lady on her wrist, and the massive rose that's growing apace with her thighs.

I thought she'd be off the minute I arrived, but she must have missed me. She spent an entire hour telling me about the love she shares with her man, in detail quite disgusting, as she applied false eyelashes and fleshed out her bra with chicken fillets.

There's no denying that my sister is a beautiful woman. She tottered off, in her towering heels, her long, long legs poking out of her tiny skirt. Her black hair, which reaches down to her waist, has been teased out with hairspray and swept up into a huge chignon. Her perfume lingered in the air. She says it is vital to spray it wherever one wants to be kissed. And behind one's knees just in case. She always smells, I must admit, like all good things come at once.

Byron started screaming the second she went. She doesn't often go out in the evening and, when she does, he doesn't like it. I tried reasoning with him, I made threats and bribes, but he was absolutely hysterical, in such a state I didn't know what to do with him. So I went up to the bathroom, took a pill from the prescription the doctor gave him, smashed a quarter up with a rolling pin and sprinkled it in the kid's Angel Delight. I bet him he couldn't eat the whole thing in a minute. And since he managed it in thirty seconds, he took his prize, and resumed his destruction of the house as if his brain was firing on tartrazine and speed. I picked him up, still kicking, and bet him double or quits he couldn't sit still for five minutes. He cleaned me out.

I was watching carefully, wondering what the hell to do, when he conked out on the AstroTurf. And then I started to worry. So I went to pick him up and put the TV on and he seemed OK, just unusually calm, which was a little scary, but very nice, and then I carried him up to bed, and put him in his pyjamas. And, frankly, it had all the makings of a lovely evening. I was thinking after the bedtime stories, I'd do the crossword, and settle down for the nine o'clock thriller. Maybe, after that, I might make myself useful, sort out the electrics, find some paint, try to tidy up the walls. But then there was a great thud downstairs. Because a dead-drunk Mary had walked with full force into the patio doors.

I ran down to find that she had slid to the ground, with her hair tangled up in the garden gnome. So I went over and picked her up, carried her indoors. But she was crying so much I couldn't understand what she was saying. I propped her up on the sofa and wiped the tear snot from her chin, still unable to make out a word. I unknotted her hair, patted down her face with a damp flannel and then she said she felt sick, so I fetched her the washing-up bowl and a glass of water. I asked her how she managed to get into such a state in less than three hours and she told me she's just not used to the night life, now she's a mother. And that's when her man turned up, hammering at the door. Like magic, she sobered up. Forgot how sick she's supposed to be, ushered him in, and started throwing anything that came to hand in the general direction of his head. The remote control, her phone, her shoes. All of it missed him. And they started bickering at top volume, so I ran back upstairs to try to find some earmuffs to put on the kid. Preserve his state of slumber – because if he were to wake up there would be no pacifying him. And then we'd all be sorry. But I was only halfway through riffling around in the drawers trying to find something to insulate his ears when the tone changed downstairs, as Mary and her man started making up. And that's the sort of noise I cannot stand, because Mary being Mary she'd have had her knickers off already.

I kissed Byron goodnight. Cranked up the baby monitor. Took all the beer out of the fridge, sneaked out the back door and drove home.

The next morning, Mary was in a rare good mood. She rang me up to apologise for all the kerfuffle of the night before. She explained that when she'd met her man at the pub he had dropped a bombshell. He had been promoted at work, she said, and, unfortunately, that meant he'd have to move abroad. There wasn't anything to be done, and so on and so forth, but she'd been so upset at the time. Now, though, she was coming round to it. In fact, she was going to throw her man a leaving party the following Saturday and would I like to come?

Ordinarily, I'm not a party person, but since it was a special occasion – and we were getting along so well – I said, of course, I'd pop along and would be delighted (to make sure he went as promised).

I took care, when Saturday came, to arrive very late, exactly as everyone was going home. But I misjudged it and could tell, the second I opened the garden gate, that all the kids in the neighbourhood were still in the backyard, screaming at just the pitch to give you a migraine, from inside the bouncy castle she'd hired.

My sister's man was slightly sunburned all over. He looked like a giant pink balloon animal. The screaming came in waves, as he limbered up, kicked empty beer cans out of his path and bellyflopped onto the side of the bouncy castle, squashing the children inside. He took ever longer run-ups, jumped to ever increasing heights, plunged with increasing expertise, to make the interior of the bouncy castle ever more terrifying for the children inside.

And I was just starting to think that I ought to find a sharp implement to let the castle down before he made sandwich filler out of the tiniest tot and we who witnessed it were all sent to jail, when the castle started deflating all by itself. My sister's man double-checked all the lager cans were finished. He looked at his new watch, which is twice the size of his beefy hand, and goes to kiss my sister, who was sober for once, and intent on giving him a send-off to remember.

Mary had bought fireworks by the crateful. It was already getting dark, as far as it ever gets dark in the city. The sky is a perpetual purplish, you can never see the stars. But it was black enough for fireworks as far as they were concerned. So he started setting them off, with the damn-fool fearlessness of the far-too-drunk. He set them up on the back fence, standing far too close, with the children pulling at his shirt in excitement, as red sparks fizzed and sprayed all around him, and smoke engulfed them all. I was restraining Byron, by sitting on him, there was no other way, and I started to call to Mary, suggesting that she ought to take her man to the airport soon, since you're supposed to allow three hours for international departures.

But, just at that moment, her man tripped over, and in an inexorable domino effect, one crate toppled onto another, collapsing into the conflagration which Mary had left to its own devices after she'd charred all the beef burgers, and all of a sudden rockets were going off in every direction. All of us screamed, as the gunpowder detonated in our midst; the yard was a war zone of terror and carnage, as we cowered and crawled and cringed and squealed. Flattening ourselves on top of the children, with hands over our eyes and our ears.

The only one who scarpered, running free, was the flabby coward meant to be taking his leave. I espied him, making his getaway as fast as he could, dragging a suitcase behind him, crying out that he'd get a taxi, he couldn't miss his plane, leaving Mary at the mercy of the fire brigade…

My sister's relationships exist in dog years. She can go from being single, to engaged, to married, to divorced, within roughly a week and a half.

But, for some reason, that summer, she didn't seem interested in finding a new man. She batted away new prospects, rather lazily, as she would a droning fly. It might have been the weather. It was excessively hot and humid. Too hot to eat and too hot to sleep and too hot to do the myriad other things she's good at. Or perhaps she was in love. It didn't matter, it was so nice.

We spent the whole of August sunbathing in the backyard, lathered all over in suntan lotion, feet in the paddling pool she made out of the bouncy castle the hire company refused to take away. Our skin roasted darker and darker, and even Byron slowed down a little, now he had his mother's undivided attention. I had to give her credit for her patience, and unaccustomed equanimity.

Once, I asked where her man had gone, since it hadn't previously seemed to matter, and spent an hour listening to her tale of woe. He had gone to the Congo, she said. He was going to the mineral mines to get rich, she said. It was dangerous work and he wouldn't be reachable by phone or email. There was no internet in the jungle. But he would be back in a year and then he would propose with the biggest diamond I ever saw and they would get married, somewhere in Africa most likely. She in a white bikini – that way she wouldn't be able to compare it with the first one, and the giant froufrou confection she now regrets. Each wedding would be special, in its own way.

So I was surprised to see the round, pink hulk a week later, as he cut me up on the roundabout in a rusty black taxicab. His great mistake was slowing down to give me both fingers, so I had a perfect view of his pudgy face. I took off my sunglasses, tooted my horn, and waved at him with the window down. Judging by the speed at which he reached the bypass, I'd say he wasn't best pleased to see me.

I thought about telling my sister but she seemed so happy, lazing in the garden, waiting for her lover to return. Everything was going so nicely. And I managed to convince myself that I might have made a mistake. It could, so easily, have been another balloon animal.

I let it pass.

But later that week, she called me up, crying in that way she has, with gut-wrenching incoherence. I drove straight over, and mopped up the tears as best I could, with still absolutely no idea what she's saying. I took Byron to our mother's and, when I returned, Mary had calmed down. She told me her man never went abroad at all. He had no intention of giving her a diamond as big as an everlasting gobstopper. He was living in a village five miles away, shacked up with his wife. She cried and cried and cried. And then, over and over, repeated that one dreadful word: 'Why?'

To which all I can ever say, when it comes to men, is: 'Who the hell knows?'

But she wasn't satisfied with that answer. She tried calling his phone. Number not recognised. She went online, began checking through all the sites he had used on her computer. And the thug had neglected to sign out of all his accounts, so she had ample chance to torture herself with photographs of him and his wife and kids. He'd only ever been a taxi driver, he'd never speculated in minerals abroad. And that's when my sister starts scratching the crook of her arm, with her sharp, manicured fingernails. Tears flooded over her inked skin. His name staring up at her. A rank insult, to her pride, and faith, and love.

'Well,' I said – for some reason I thought I'd try to make her see the funny side – 'don't let yourself get down. I'm sure you're not the first woman he's tricked, and I'm sure you won't be the last. It's good, now you've seen through him so quickly. And as for the tattoo... it's only skin, not your heart. And, look on the bright side; it's not an unusual name. I'm sure we can find you a better man with the same one.'

Well, she didn't take it as I'd meant it, and started screaming at me for taking the mick. She pushed me out of the back door. And, no matter what I said, or how hard I knocked, she wouldn't let me back in again.

Later that night she drank far too much vodka, took too many painkillers, and set to work on her arm with a scalpel and tweezers. Carefully, very carefully, she sliced off the skin, and peeled it back. She placed the bloodied, tattoo skin on a plate in the freezer. Then she dressed her wound, very carefully.

Next morning, she woke up very early, with a filthy head, and an idea. Mary took out her tattoo, let it thaw a little and packaged it up, with plenty of ice, so it was perfectly legible. And then she appended it to a letter addressed to her former lover's wife, with full rehearsal, of details quite disgusting, of all types of things they had been getting up to in recent times. And wrapped this all up very carefully in a big box addressed to her, marked 'Private and Confidential'.

She went to the post office, queued up, feeling – she said – quite impossibly sick – and posted this parting gift to his unsuspecting wife.

Now, you might call that an overreaction. You might think it hurt Mary more than it will him. That it's no sort of victory at all.

But, as she sits there, at the computer, hitting F5, waiting for the online tracker to say the little grenade she sent has blown up in her true love's face...

I think I might agree with you.

SPIRITS

In the final eighteen months of her life, my mother lived on rye crackers and boozed like a Soviet tramp. That is not meant disrespectfully. They drank vodka by the pint glass there. Everybody knows that. She wasn't a tall lady. She wasn't big boned either. She put it away all the same. I say nothing of tables. She would drink you into the ground.

I was a desperate disappointment to her in many ways. Try as I might I cannot hold my liquor.

As a child, she'd trick me into sipping her foul drinks. She'd switch our glasses round and play the innocent. Never once take her eyes off the racing and yet she got me every time. I'd start spluttering. Then she'd laugh and laugh until the bubbles popped off her tongue. The sofa clinking with all the bottles she'd secreted behind the cushions.

Then came bouts of hiccups during which she'd drop her tooth plate and I would scream. Later on she got to doing it deliberately, when we had guests she didn't like. She'd drop it when she knew only I'd be watching. And it looked as if her whole mouth were falling apart. I would scream and scream and no one would know what the matter was. The guests would clear out, just as she'd hoped, and then she'd get me to fix her another gin and tonic.

When I went home the last time I'll admit it was a shock.

For years her lipstick had been wandering off her lips and into the province of clown make-up. I say that with no disrespect to clowns. They paint giant red lips up to their noses for professional purposes. She wasn't even trying. Her face was smashed all over with smears and scarlet. I'd go at her with a wet wipe. But she was a lady really, and kept re-applying.

I'd been working hard. Damned hard. It's hard to get ahead, you know. Damned hard to get ahead. You can't be calling home, always, and checking on your mother. She expected me to earn a living. Or at least, I think she did. Perhaps she never thought about it. But the fact is you have to get on in life. You can't forever be at home, looking after your mother. And at any rate, she wasn't alone. Father was still there, mowing the lawn, pulling up the weeds, raking out neat stretches of earth.

We all make choices. And she abided by hers. It wasn't that she lacked charm, it's just she never used it. She could have made friends, could have gone out. But she preferred to go about things in her own way, alone. She liked to sit for days and fail to complete the crossword. She liked to smoke and read murders. And she loved to drive.

It was a year ago she got the driving ban. That was when the downward hurtle began.

She was a small, elegant lady, my mother, and she always looked her best when she went out for a drive. She put her driving gloves on, and checked her make-up in the rear view mirror. She made sure not a hair was out of place. Her feet barely reached the pedals in her little car, which she drove very fast, cross-country. She went through wildlife like death's own scythe. Foxes, pheasants and rabbits all reached their natural conclusion beneath her wheels. Their flat, tufty bodies were up and down whatever route she rode. She got a deer once, wounded him fatally in the side, and lost a wing mirror doing it. She tried and failed to get it in the back seat, thinking she'd butcher it for dinner. And that was fortunate, really. She was never any good at cooking.

In spite of myself, I admired the way she drove. She had the spirit of a racing driver. She put her foot down into corners; she was master of the handbrake turn.

But as time wore on she did forget how to operate the sticks coming out of her steering wheel. She would flash her indicators in the rain and set off her windscreen wipers at roundabouts. She retained a firm grip on the use of her horn, but that didn't help. She became a terrorist of the pedestrian crossing, causing untold heart palpitations in the OAPs as she drove through the town.

She had a few warnings, a few tickings off. Then she ran down the neighbour's cat. Everyone was very sweet, when the breathalyser test proved damning. They all said alcoholism is a terrible disease. I'm not sure the drink was much of an excuse. She hated that animal. And I watched her drive straight at it.

She'd always had a foul temper, of course, but usually it was directed at Jehovah's Witnesses, and the garden gnomes. She must have spent many an afternoon lamenting the destruction of that cat. Driving had been her one true pleasure. Sitting at home, day after day, unable to drive, unwilling to walk, seething and raging and bored, she spent all her time in a fug of her own smoke, simmering in gin and burning the dinner. She sacked the cleaner, couldn't get another one. The walls went yellow. The house stank of burned potatoes. All of a sudden, the lawn ornaments were launched at Father.

I'd been indignant, but not particularly surprised, when he found solace, a number of years ago now, in a gypsy woman down the road. I forget her name. She sold her own pots, painted all over in folk design, with red and orange flowers. Or used to, before my mother went and smashed them all, and started a bonfire with all the paints and brushes.

The woman was not a patch on my mother, of course. And no match for her either. All that autumn she stood outside, Father said, burning things, flames singeing the trees. He wanted me to come home and talk to her. But whenever I did she started crying. I didn't know what to say to her. And I didn't stick around for long. There wasn't any point trying to remonstrate with her. I didn't want any lawn ornaments hurled at me. I bruise easily. All in all, I fail to see what I could have done.

They had a terrific row the night she died.

He had poured the last of her gin over the petunias. After tearing off the leaves and screaming, she got in his car and drove down to the shop. Refused service, she turned back, got in the car, revved up, screeched right the way around the roundabout, and then another notion must have struck her because she veered back all of a sudden, took the bend hard and drove straight through the plate-glass windows.

It's all there on the CCTV. Her head went right through the windscreen. She never would wear a seatbelt. And her little body, so thin, was all done in. Her arm seemed to be pointing, the way she came out, at a display of discounted Lambrusco.

She died in hospital, several days later, without ever waking up. It made the local news and everything. I cut the picture out of the paper. For weeks people tied flower posies to the dismembered drainpipe. 'Hypocrites!' she would have called them.

Father sold up the house not long after. He's moved to

Spain with that woman. Every birthday I get a new pot.

I feel bad now, of course I do. I dream a lot of dreams about her and miss her all the time. In the church, they said she had only gone into the next room. So I got to thinking she might come back. Haunt me, for a while.

So far, she has not turned up. But, I feel, if she's going to appear anywhere, it'll most likely be the liquor aisle at Tesco.

Recently, I've been spending a disproportionate amount of time there. Just on the off-chance she turns up.

PITCHFORK

At sixth form I was first impaled – on the pitchfork of love.

The whole thing took me completely unawares. The other girls were better prepared. They would have developed a working knowledge of the situation. But I had spent my formative years at home, practising calligraphy and patisserie. You have to be in school to think fond thoughts of acnified members of the football team. I'd not spent wet lunch breaks tarting up my signature with a different surname each week, the dot of the 'i' a love heart, with curly flourishes beneath.

No, I was taken by that filthy feeling unprepared. And it was a filthy feeling. They don't tell you that. You never see it written anywhere. First love is filthy.

His very name (which I'm not about to reveal here – for I can't very well use his real name, and no other name could match the effect) causes a very specific prickle to cakewalk up my forearms. I close my eyes and see him entering the laboratory, always late, for fifth-period physics.

As the term turned from winter to spring, a green light fell across his head. An experiment with plant life had crammed the windowsill full of tendrils which spoiled the late sunlight that cast an oblong across his desk.

He was dark, with pale skin. Not tall, but sinewy – like a boxer – with closely cropped hair and eyes of such a deep blue that you might mistake them, if your eyes were out of sync, for two black points, hole-punched out of his head.

At first it was just the feeling. And I quelled it. Then he started pitching up in my dreams. Quite often he was just there, in the background, doing nothing in particular. Occasionally he would appear in fancy dress. Another time he came through a window and placed the small paper circles that were his eyes very carefully on my bedroom floor.

The most recurrent dream just featured a tractor, which would drive very slowly up my pillow. I knew he was involved somehow. Sometimes, I wouldn't sleep the whole night for fear of it.

Once, in real life, he spoke to me.

He had dropped a worksheet, which flew up in the air and then down under my stool. I got off, bent down to retrieve it and handed it back to him. At the time I was not used to bending, and could feel that I had begun perspiring around my nose. He put his arm around my shoulder, leaned in to my ear, and then whispered, very low, 'Your face looks like it's been reflected in a spoon.'

Another time, on a field trip, he stole half of my sandwiches. He left the crusts on a bench. My mother had packed me six, so I pretended not to notice.

His moods yo-yoed. One minute he was morose. The next he was unable to keep still, legs jiggling up and down like a five-year-old full of orangeade. The majority of the time he was downright insolent. He talked constantly, and loudly. After several months of close observation I could see why. He couldn't close his mouth properly. If we were forced to sit silent his mouth would gape open, wide enough to throw grapes in. I felt I was communing with him in these moments. I would stare with extra intent at him on these occasions.

There must have been something wrong with his jaw.

Reader, I loved him. There's no denying it, no rationalising it and no point dwelling on it. And it was just a tragic coincidence that at this point in my physical development, years of refusing to walk anywhere and getting through my mother's three healthy meals a day (plus all the crisps snaffled up my jumper at the newsagent) had made me a rotund specimen. Broad hipped, washerwoman-armed and prematurely saggy.

It was also, at this point, that my mother refused to buy me any clothes from high street shops, insisting that she could make any of the fashions better herself from patterns and wool. So I would turn up to school in a skirt which looked like a deflated tent and elephantine knitted jumpers. And she did not approve of cosmetics. God had made me beautiful – so while all the other girls had Max Factor to make a clean sheet of their perfect ovals, my round circle was a red dot-to-dot, occasionally numbered with pus.

I knew that nothing would happen between us. I knew, just as you would know, if you had been there. I was perfectly content with this. I was happy just staring at him. Cock your head and just look at him. He's a piece of work – dark hair, squat chest, strutting, preening young peacock that he is – he's as tasty as a teenager is ever going to get.

That is, until she arrived.

It took her nine months, but she came in the end. I don't know where she came from or how she was invited to our end-of-term party. I'm not a detective. But at our end-of-term party she was, smoking a cigar without inhaling. Her mouth would open, she would slot it in quite slowly, look about her, wipe around the end with her tongue and then pull it out, immediately, pumping the ash onto a corsage which was balanced on the chair arm.

Her hair was crackled up in waves and held there with a waft of hairspray strong enough to kill garden pests. She made repeated trips to the bathroom, with a little string bag full of cosmetic weapons. I had my eye on her. I'd had my eye on all the girls. But she had been drawing near his table.

Her slight and brittle little frame, covered in striped silk which rippled as she went, like the wind in a sail, was moving towards him. I had been watching him, unobtrusively, for three hours. Oh, he wasn't interested. No, he wasn't. He kept shrugging off the arm she kept draping across him. But she kept at it. She was persistent. She was determined.

This is the sort of can-do attitude out of which true and lasting romance is made.

I watched them for hours. Her eyes became two drunken dark slits that blinked when she moved in: beautiful big brown eyes, squishing themselves under a weight of suggestion, as she put her head down, and looked up, and slid her thin little fingers up his knee. Two sets of lashes batting down, over wide, watery pupils. The hollow half moons underneath blackened up with sweat and mascara. Those perfectly dead nails, crammed full of tobacco leaves and ash.

From the second I saw her she made me feel ill. I knew it, just as you would know, if you had been there.

It was as inevitable as pheasants getting shot in October.

I perched there on the edge of the dance floor, on which no one had asked me to dance but which was anyhow too swilled about with lager for anyone to do much but stand and slide ... I looked past the circle of tassel-trimmed chairs – on which drunken teenagers sank into one another like margarine on hot potatoes… I knew it was not going to turn out well.

I was near enough to spit at them, in my excruciating dress of sea-green polka dots. A girl squirming beneath the captain of the rugby team kicked me in one side with her stripper's stiletto – the bruise lasted six days.

But I couldn't move. I couldn't take my eyes off – the horror.

Naturally, when the lights came on, and the music died, there was nothing to do but go home. To sit in the bath, until it went cold, slamming head on tub, staring at the ceiling, and groaning like the dying. To spend the summer holiday in bed – eating myself from Friar Tuck to one of those people who have to be cut out of their homes. I came down with flu, after a seventh successive bath taken, while it rained, with the windows open. I became quite delirious.

In the heat of my fever it became quite simple and I saw clearly what must be done. All I needed was some metal thread to stitch up the hole in my skull that she had created – with all her flirting, with all her walking, slinging her hips about as if she was drawing a pattern with them. And a great deal of glue, to hold it all back together and prevent him from getting back in. I would lie in my bed, half lucid, telling my mother this, very solemnly tracing how I could be stitched, in the air. There I was raving, raving.

'Shall the world, then, be overrun by oysters?'

My mother stayed with me. My mother mopped my brow. She called out the doctor. He prescribed some pills.

After several weeks, I came back to myself. Pumped full of protein shakes, brainwashed by night-time relaxation tapes, I decided to stop. Just to stop. Nothing more. The sheets went unchanged. And nothing happened.

Then I had a little relapse.

When I tried to throw myself out of the first-floor window my mother telephoned the emergency services. An overreaction. It was the matter of a metre from window ledge to lawn below. I'm not sure I would have managed to sprain my ankle in the attempt. But the paramedics arrived as I lay there, upper body flailing out, bottom wedged, legs wiggling up and down, as I raved incoherently about the fishes. I was given some sort of injection.

My father put his head in the room and suggested that my mother would have been better off calling the fire brigade. She screamed at him to fetch a ladder and began to cry.

My prescriptions were upped. They gave me all sorts, pills to make me happy and pills to stop me fretting. After that, just to thwart my mother, who really was becoming intolerable, I would save all my pills up, secretly, and then pop a load of them at once, on Fridays. It gave me a most tremendous rush of screwed vision and nausea, which made the weekend go off with a bang.

After that, I began to have all sorts of fun.

One day, I woke up and he was sat there, watching me, cross-legged on the floor. He said he'd got tired of wriggle hips and thought I was cool. We drank cider in the telephone box, sat up on the green hill and watched the wind caress the corn below. We'd smoke his joints and sit in the garden until the air tickled and all the greenery had been re-made out of velvet. Cut out with a Stanley knife and smoothed off with a file.

I giggled until my cheeks hurt. And he began to multiply. I saw his image everywhere. Took it with me wherever I went. When I looked down, his imprint was all across me, like an old tattoo. His head I saw on haystacks and pot plants and tree stumps. He was there, on my mother's apron. He was there, coalescing from the smoke of my father's cigars. At dawn, the birds sang his name, sang his name. At night, you could trace his outline in the stars.

He stole my mother's credit card and got us pills of all sizes and booze of all brands; we were up for days. I danced so hard I dislocated my shoulder, he snapped it back in again. I was wedged up against the headboard. He pushed with his whole body, it snapped back into place. Nobody noticed us. Sure my mother was there, hammering at the door, but it was time to be doing things for myself. The things you can fix if you only put your mind to it.

I was taking back control, and the rumours that reached me didn't cause a flinch.

One night, towards the end of August, I went down to the quayside. Paddling off the slipway he pushed me, playfully at first, but I went right over, swallowed dirty water until I choked. Mud went in my eyes and stuck in my nails, oil was thickly pasted across my whole head. It took two long hot showers to get it all out of my hair. I'd said a few things. I made my feelings pretty obvious. As I dry retched and squeezed all the water out on the slipway. I swore, spat at him, and went home.

That was it. I thought I didn't care.

The sun was dying and the summer was almost at an end. I thought I could calm down a bit and get back to work. Make plans for the future. I started to draw up a reading list for him, so he could get more on my wavelength. We talked about letting other people know that we were going out. But part of me was dreading it, I suppose. The return to routine. I feigned illness on the first day back. And Tuesday crept up.

Now that I don't have to go to school anymore, now that I enjoy peace and quiet, a life of waiting for nothing at all to happen, attending groups, fattened up by the tablets they make me take, writing my music. Now that I have space and time to think and dwell on how my life turned out, I can see that whole little episode was nothing to get upset about. That the twenty-first century is full of second chances. The stakes aren't very high for anything anymore. Not when it comes to love. Think of all the romantic heroes of literature. There wouldn't be a story, today. Anna Karenina would have divorced dull old Karenin. Sued for custody. Rejoined society. Cathy and Heathcliff – a clear-cut case of antibiotics and social services. Romeo and Juliet – witness protection.

But right then, I felt abused.

First period, he cut me dead in the corridor. As if he didn't even recognise me. As if we'd never spent any time together at all. Lunchtime, she was back. I saw her pick him up in the car park.

I smoked several cigarettes in quick succession and ground one of them out, accidentally, on my foot.

I was not in a humour.

It was clear now that he was doing this to upset me. Our tussle at the quayside had been smoothed over, we'd made up – or so I thought. We had carried on as normal. I had mastered my jealous feelings, six weeks before. And I had won him myself.

I became very calm. Absolutely calm. But my ribcage was tight with rage. I decided to write her a note, an update on what had happened over the summer, and tell her to get away from him. I couldn't very well say it to her face. He didn't want a lot of fuss. When the car returned after lunch I watched him walk away before approaching her, I was waiting for her, having another cigarette in the back alley. I passed the note to her and strode off, waiting for events to take their course. She'd clear off to wherever she came from. Probably she'd call him up to say goodbye. No doubt she'd have a little cry. That couldn't be helped.

In the afternoon lab session, there was an incident.

Someone – I suspect it was she – came in wielding a pair of orange-handled, all-purpose scissors, and stabbed the rusty point, with force, right through my beloved's hand.

An outbreak of hysteria. A malicious pattern of revenge of which I had not guessed her capable.

Somehow, they managed to implicate me in the whole nasty debacle. Somehow, and to this day I don't know how, it all seemed to be my fault.

The last thing I remember, before I was hauled off, was seeing his face, reflected in the glass of the classroom door. He was smiling – such a terrific grin. Full teeth, wide eyes, as if he were about to burst out laughing.

He came over to me, put his hands on the bench. I saw what was happening, though, and averted my eyes, just as the tops of the scissors began their downward smash. I was never able to bear the sight of blood.

I saw the scissors raised – alive in the air – my brain repeated it, over and over, in slow motion afterwards. The scissors raised – and plunging down, to stab the browned point right through the hand.

And that hand reached out its fingers, in shock, before a bright stream of blood began rolling down the worktop, dribbling to the floor.

I can remember no more, until I met my mother, come to collect me, from the nurse's office. They had me sit there, on my own.

Yes, somehow he managed to pin it all on me. And things didn't go so well for me afterwards. Ten years on, I miss him still.

First love is always the worst, I hear. It should have put me off men completely.

RED IS BEST

I woke up this morning and the world was all red. The streets, the sky, the birds.

Every day, I hope it will be different. I stay up as long as I can, holding out for the apricot dawn. I'm scared to fall asleep. For when I sleep I dream in red. The sky changed first. A peculiar orange light, like the sun setting under storm clouds. And then the sun seemed to grow larger and sit longer, fat and bloody all the time. A sun fit for war, the pink papers said. And that was when they started burning the other colours in the yard.

The bonfires blazed for days, and the embers piled up. The ash like heaps of rubies, removed before it turned dead and black.

I can't go out in daylight now, I only look correct at night, under scarlet bulbs. I didn't buy the right things when they were still for sale. My curtains were a gift. A love token of sorts. I have little to do but stand behind them and look at everyone in the street. Buttoned up in red coats, hats and gloves, with their sunburned faces and regulation hats. From above they look like old-fashioned pillar boxes.

After the riots you couldn't get the right equipment. They looted all the tanning salons and hairdressers, stripped the stores, spray painted the mannequins. The men organised themselves into working parties and painted cars and doors and windows. I watched the tins pile up in the basement where I hid my illegal rubbish. Cochineal and Dragon's Blood, Autumn Leaves and Redcurrant Glory.

Every head changed. Teenagers went for the full fire-engine effect. The workers corralled all the henna. Ladies who lunch have tangerine bobs. Elderly ladies sit under the dryers, still half-price on Wednesdays, all a shade of deep maroon, their dogs like tiny foxes tied to the lampposts outside.

After the Prime Minister was elected, with his shock of vivid, pre-Raphaelite curls, the promotions became automatic. Bald men cultivated large moustaches and beards, which they could dye like un-red women. They exfoliated their heads vigorously, took to painting their nails. The government announced a huge stimulus package to get the country in order. The roads were re-tarmacked, grass pulled up and replaced with red clay. They pulled up all the weeds and replaced them with roses, carefully painting the stems. The trees were cut down and replaced with copper statues hung with leaves made of silk. Of course, not all colour has yet been obliterated. But we are making great strides.

The young girls all have new names. Coral or Poppy or Cerise. The boys are all called Rufus or Carbine or Cadmium. Vermilions are the worst behaved.

I must do something, if I am to go on. But I would need to find contacts, on the red market, yet even if I managed that, I haven't the funds.

And, besides, I do not want to be Red. I want to keep my paperbacks and a decent light to read by.

I don't want to burn my skin or inject my eyes. My eyes are

green. A statistical rarity. Chameleon eyes, they change with the light. I have taken a picture. I am keeping myself busy. Making a time capsule which I will hide. I'm not sure where. But I remember when I was young, when all the walls were plain, finding old wallpaper down the back of the radiator. And I used to wonder about all those people who had been in my house before. Living among all those patterns of blue and gold.

My door is correct, my cape is correct and no one ever stops to chat in the hall. So why do I feel their red eyes stare at me, when they catch me climbing the stairs?

They will be aware of my history. My history gives me credit. I had a man, before the redness started, with hair as real as the harvest moon. The only Red in the building, and he certainly made himself known.

It's so long ago we started, I forget how it came about. We met at a party. And then we met in bars. And he was with someone and I was with someone and somehow we drifted together, in the unknown. He would come up and stay in my room, where we would drink and talk, and one day he stayed, and lay about all year. Enjoying my cream sheets, reading all my books.

He said he didn't want to go out anymore. It was a waste of money. So I would go out to work and, when I got home, he would tell me about what he'd been thinking about during the day. He had great plans for the reconstruction of society and did not want to work anymore. The jobs he'd had never lived up to his talents. He liked that I did not mind supporting him, he said. That I understood his inherent greatness. He would expound on his theories for months on end. But after a time I started finishing his sentences. That made him bad tempered and sulky. He didn't talk so much anymore. I only have myself to blame.

One day, it could not have been long after the sky went orange, he was approached in the street. On account of his magnificent hair. He was offered a position, a salary too large to turn down. After a few weeks he became a valued employee. By the end of a fortnight he was out drinking with his colleagues every night. They had ideas as to the rectitude of things. I went along a few times but they didn't appreciate my suggestions.

When he came home he began to complain. I should be so lucky, to have red hair, why did I not dye it? He couldn't take me anywhere, with me looking as I did. Why did I not replace the carpet? Why did I not buy new sheets? It was very hard to keep him happy. Naturally, he was highly strung – all true redheads are.

In a rage he put up new curtains, painted the door, bought me a cape that made me look like Red Riding Hood. And he stayed on, for whatever reason, coming home or not, just as he pleased. Smelling of new perfumes. He won promotion after promotion. His days were long, his sleep became fretful. More responsibilities were heaped upon him, there were so few real redheads in existence.

He found it all very stressful. He screamed at me every night as his curls began to moult. He cried, one morning, when he came out of the shower in his little red towel. He held a little mound of hairs that he had dug out of the plug hole. Dark, thin wisps in his red-raw palm. There was already a patch of hairless skin, spreading out from his crown. The beard he grew was not as bright as his hair. Bald, he might not have passed for a real Red at all.

I did my best to make him laugh about it, but he had sensed the way things were going. He was right and I was wrong. He was obsessed with keeping his follicles sprouting. He spent all his money on tonics. I would massage them carefully, into his scalp, as we watched the Red dramas on the television. He started to read the latest findings on how to provoke optimum redness. He only ate red food.

This was long before the official guidelines were published, before the chefs caught on and the food conglomerates mass-produced the right colorants. We would eat nothing but raw meat, cherries, tomatoes, raspberries. I could see him, gingerish eyebrows knitting, fed up of it all. Swallowing mouthfuls, with his red fork and his red spoon, saying not a word.

When he left I threw it all away – the red saucepan, the red chopping board, all the red utensils he bought me that final Christmas. That was my first mistake – the caretaker found it all downstairs. A notice was pinned on the board, regarding suspicious anti-Red behaviour. I didn't admit to it. I hid behind the door and pretended I wasn't in when they knocked as part of the routine enquiry. I'd already fixed the spy hole by gluing crêpe paper over it. If they ever watch me, they cannot suspect.

I never see him now but I hear that he is doing well, that he switched careers and under less stressful conditions has retained a few of the hairs on his head. He hasn't lost his special status. He is an academic, I believe, specialising in Red matters. There are still too few children whose hair does not have to be dyed and we are lingering behind the rest of Europe in this respect. I heard he found himself a real strawberry blonde and got married, not long after he left me. No doubt they'll be trying, furiously, for Red babies. It's their duty now.

I am surprised he hasn't informed on me already. I know, now, he never loved me at all. But no doubt he doesn't want to taint himself so publicly. It wouldn't be wise to admit to having lived, for such a time, with a woman with barely a freckle on her body.

When he left he didn't take much. I've still got his razor blades and his gun. He had begun to arm himself in preparation for the Redness. He knew it was coming. I only saw it when it broke on the streets. And red blood ran down red drains. I take out his things, occasionally, and re-sort them. The clothes he left still carry his scent. The blade is still sharp. There are five bullets. I think about it often, in case they come for me. As they always do, for those few who will not be Red.

One of the neighbours, a lady with dark hair, recently returned from abroad. She wore colours, made no attempt to disguise her face. I saw her come back and I saw her grow fearful. And then I saw her disappear again. Eredicated – that's what they call it.

Yesterday, she was returned home. She arrived, in a top-of-the-range Cinnabar, accompanied by two men in dark red suits. She had been proud of her hair, as anyone could tell from the length of it and the way she would sweep it over her shoulders when she bent down to put the key in the lock. But now she was like a red dummy. Her body stiff, they carried her between them. She glanced up at the building, before they took her up the steps. Red wig, red eyes, red clothes, red shoes. And skin caked in rouge.

I looked down at her and drew the curtains tight but she caught me – she looked at me – straight in the eye. And now, I stay awake, expecting the beat of boots on stairs. The drawer of knives. The knock at the door.

Red was never my colour.

THE BIRDS

My solicitor, who is a moron, told me to write down everything that happened in strict chronological order: how I first became aware of the bird plot; what I did to prevent it. We've been through it countless times already but still he claims he doesn't get it.

It is perfectly simple.

I was raised in the country, where birds behave themselves. They nest in trees. Eat insects and worms. Rise with the sun. Fly on the wind. Hunt by the moon. The males sing for a mate, fluff up their plumage. The females fall for it, lay eggs. And so on and so forth: etcetera, etcetera. This is known.

Then, I moved to the city. Straightaway, I noticed the birds here are deeply confused. They mix up streetlights with sunlight. Sing at all hours. I don't sleep so I don't mind but it must drive other people crazy. And these insomniac birds, driven to distraction, perch on live electric cables: they're wired. Every morning, they make a noise louder than they ever did before. The struggle is quite as cutthroat as that going on below, the commuter battle, to get out of the turnstiles first. Watch the bodies spewed out into the city, the deathless, suited armies of capitalism. Why, I ask, why, does it have to be so bloody?

One night, I was flicking through the TV. The night was coming down. Smoke and hot fumes drifted in through the open window. I was baking under the skylight. Flies mounted a lazy patrol. Cars were screeching over road humps. The little girl who lives two floors down had just started to wail, as she tends to do when threatened with bed.

I was stuck for anything to watch, too uncomfortable to move, flicking through channel after channel, when I stumbled upon archive footage of the First Bird War. I watched it with mounting horror. Put my hands on my head and could not believe my eyes. It showed birds behaving just as I'd started to suspect they might, if pushed too far.

I often stay up late on purpose to think through all the bad things that haven't happened yet. Mostly I worry about breaking my kneecaps, of being crippled on my bicycle the next day. But this notion struck a raw nerve. I couldn't get it out of my brain.

How many birds exist in the sky, and how could we ever hope to fight them? Billions, there must be, millions of billions. Imagine how terrifying, if they took against us. You only have to watch sea birds to see their bitterness. Or witness a storm swell, to see their discipline. Great hordes of them, flying in formation, blotting out the horizon. A murmuration of starlings is beautiful, you might say, only think if it was massed against you. Go outside, see for yourselves the birds that have been radicalised.

Seagulls! The vandals of the avian race. They tear each other apart, feather from feather, beak to beak. Watch as they peck apart bin bags, leave rubbish anywhere they please. And then the ravens and rooks catch on, bombard you from the bridges. At the seaside, women hang out the bed sheets wearing colanders as helmets, they have been struck so many times by the birds. Herons command the rivers and the sea, kingfishers dive-bomb the boats.

Even pigeons, who used to be content, gorging on chips and crapping on Nelson's Column, have been pushed too far. Now, just like the rest of us, they have been maddened by tourists, swoop directly at their massed heads, hoping to disperse them.

First blood to them, I say, but if dogs behaved like that they wouldn't get away with it.

We must examine the cause of bird attacks. What do they want? What do they need? The RSPB ought to know this already. But, instead, its officials march about, very pleased with themselves, exterminating parakeets. Gorgeous green birds who do no harm to anyone, marked out to be purged, because they're not from this country, originally. That's racism as far as I'm concerned. A hate crime if ever I heard of one. I called the police but they wouldn't take any action. Which just goes to show how we discriminate against the avian kind.

So, I started to think. I thought long and hard. How do we discourage the birds from obliterating us?

First. It's obvious. We must apologise. Make amends. They are in the right, morally-speaking, that much is clear. Birds are bold and brave and true. So, we should endear ourselves to small birds, which are harmless, hoping to use their influence with the large birds, which pose a danger.

I, myself, have made serious efforts in this respect. I have many little friends around here.

The bird I got along with best was the one trying to mate with the traffic lights at the end of the road. He courted both at once – the Casanova – and showed no signs of giving up. His warbling got louder and louder, increasingly shrill. His efforts never flagged, no matter how he ached, no matter how he suffered.

That bird is like me. He's a hopeless romantic.

Second. We must undo the damage we have done to their habitat. Forcing all those skyscrapers upon them. Ripping up all the grass and trees. Birds have struggled to adapt in the past hundred years. Great tits have turned pale, trying to camouflage themselves with concrete. House sparrows are addicted to nicotine – they build their nests out of scavenged cigarette butts. Blackbirds are so depressed, I spend a lot of time wondering how to cheer them up, but nothing springs to mind. Three giant blue parrots I've made efforts to console live in Brompton cemetery. They sit on the tomb where the angels weep. They swear and they bite and they bathe in filthy rain, as black tears roll down the angels' cheeks – because they don't know what to do either.

Birds are the natural masters of the sky. We should, therefore, let them have it. Stop annoying them with helicopters and aeroplanes.

In schools, children should be taught about the extraordinary powers of birds. Facts like this: swallows sleep on the wind. Ducks with one eye open. A swan will kill you as soon as look at you. But that's only the half of it. A falcon has reactions so fast its world moves ten times quicker than ours. They have six senses – feel, also, the earth's magnetic field. Albatrosses can navigate by odours in the sea. And flamingos, oh, my favourite bird, I could sit all day, staring at a mere picture of a flamingo. They can sense rain falling hundreds of miles away. It is a mystery, how they do that. Scientists have done all they can but still they can't work it out.

So, you can see what I mean, about the tricksiness of birds. They would be too fast, too small, and too cunning, to be destroyed by conventional methods.

People used to laugh at me when I told them about the footage of the First Bird War. They'd ask me if I'd seen a mental health documentary – shot by the same director – called *Psycho*. Apparently he'd made quite a few. *To Catch a Thief... Vertigo...* Such people wear me out; they are in love with the sound of their own voices. One does not have time for watching old public information films when one is trying to avert global disaster. Only last year, the birds tried to annihilate us with that flu. And no one found that funny. The next virus they come up with could wipe us off the face of the earth. No, I don't see it as a laughing matter. I compiled material about the conspiracy, distributed as widely as I could. It was a job to get anyone to read it. But I, at least, have done my bit.

What should one do when confronted by a deadly menace? Either fight it – in this case, impossible – or try to avert it by peaceful methods. We're all told to recycle, now, to prevent global warming. No one objects to that. If you ask, 'how can the one have the slightest impact on the other?' they can't explain.

This is all about the art of gesture. Every day, for the past six years, I have shared my lunch with the birds. I keep them well fed, I keep them well tended, and, moreover, I drew up a petition against the parakeet cull. But still, that is not enough. There are too many among us who maltreat the birds.

So, last year, I stepped up my efforts. I decided to buy a bird for my house, a canary, or a budgerigar, and care for it superbly. Then I had a better idea. Surely, birds do not wish to be cooped up inside, no matter how well they are treated? Would it not be better to set the captive birds free? My impulse was to buy up birds – birds upon birds – and then release them, so they could fly wherever they liked. They wouldn't have to stay in the city, they wouldn't be tied to it, like we are, putting up with the foul air, the sirens, the never-ending light. The shouts in the street, the cars zooming past, music blaring, all night long. They could fly away from all the rubbish piled up, the drunks fighting at the crossroads, the wretches sleeping rough. That sickly stench that poisons me, floating up from the marijuana farm downstairs.

But then, I thought, how could I afford to buy and release all these birds? Waiting tables doesn't pay much. Naturally, I went to the maître d', to ask for a pay rise. His advice was to put myself out more, start angling for tips. Well, I did just as he said. As I helped the customers put on their coats after a very fine dinner, I'd ask for tips.

I rehearsed it in front of the mirror, until the phrases came out, very naturally, in no way offensive. I've been told all sorts but nothing that will make me much money. 'Never complain, never explain' was one. Another was, 'A problem shared is a problem halved.' Also, 'Never trust a man with a beard.' OK, that last one has proved useful. But still – I wasn't making enough money.

Perhaps I thought too much about it, but I became quite desperate. And then something happened. A very bad thing.

I was a waiter, as I have mentioned, silver service. I worked at a roof-garden restaurant which overlooked the Embankment. It had a waterfall, tropical plants, six birds of paradise, three cockatoos, two macaws and a flamingo. There was everything laid on for a man to fill his belly and pay through the nose. However well you treated the customers, they were rarely happy. In my experience, rich people never are. They bullied the staff, threw hissy fits at the coat check and said please very rarely. And the way they treated the birds, I feel sickened to repeat it… working there, for many years, I did start to wonder if they were in competition to see who could behave worst.

Inevitably, a winner emerged.

I was not actually at work the night one of our regulars

murdered the flamingo. I'd like to think if I had been I could have saved it. Such a fine cluster of feathers. Such a ravishing pink thing. Such a fascinating bird.

Do you know, for example, why they are pink? It is because, for generations, they have eaten too much shrimp. Which might make you think, the next time you eat an orange. But this particular bird was exquisite. Unquestionably the finest bird I had ever seen.

But one day it was there, and the next it was gone. I had returned from a weekend away, bird watching by the sea, and was just putting on my waistcoat and bowtie, when I noticed the absent flamingo and demanded an explanation. Apparently, a row had broken out between two drunken diners: a lord and a judge. One said flamingos could fly. The other insisted they couldn't. One said he was getting confused with ostriches. The other said he knew damned well about ostriches. The pair had already been separated once, and had appeared calm, when the peer, wanting to prove his point, seized the magnificent bird and threw it off the roof.

The flamingo flapped a bit, but did not take flight; no doubt it had forgotten how, during its long incarceration. It fell onto the road below, where it was run over by a bus. A pregnant lady fainted, seeing it, so shocked. The restaurant was shut down, three weeks later, after a thoroughgoing investigation by environmental health. And quite right too.

Still, the recession had hit, I couldn't find another job, which only gave me more time to think. I was thinking all day and thinking all night, without distraction.

Six months ago, I started liberating birds, illegally.

First, I sabotaged the pigeon coop belonging to the man next door. After the birds had flown I set a small fire to cover my track, which was soon put out by the fire brigade. I called them myself.

This was a successful and victimless crime.

Next, I started looking to release birds trapped in people's houses. Well, it's mostly old people who keep birds, so I volunteered for Meals on Wheels. After several weeks, I left and received an excellent reference, which should be among my papers. I later entered the houses I had frequented, under cover of night, in disguise, to release the captive birds. It is absurdly easy to break into the homes of old people as they never lock their windows. I caused no harm to any OAP, nor to any property, notwithstanding birdcages.

I had, by this point, undertaken serious research on birds. I was particularly concerned about owls – which navigate by the light of distant meteors – and penguins – which are decadent and depraved. Of all birds the penguin is the most like a human. Therefore any attempts to start a ground offensive are likely to begin at the South Pole. Down there, according to long-suppressed papers, the male penguin has, for centuries, been gathering in hooligan bands, mounting injured females and misusing chicks. If that is how they treat their own kind it is hardly worth thinking about what they would do to the enemy.

Since both species are captive in our zoos, it seemed necessary to liberate them. We do not want to foster sleeper cells in our midst. We might think birds are content there. But just consider. Penguins live in the frozen wastes. Here it is mild, forever raining. Owls are, by nature, predators. They don't want to be gawped at and petted in an aviary. They want to fly out, night after night, hunting for mice and voles.

I entered the zoo under cover of night. And I got a bit diverted by all the beauty therein. I spent a long time looking at the prisoners, extracted forcibly from their native lands. I deviated from my plan, to head straight for the rainbow lorikeets, and mounted a spontaneous bid to free a scarlet ibis. The lights came on, the alarms rang out, a security guard gave chase and wrestled me down.

That was my first arrest. And I have been a blameless citizen all my life. I was advised they might even drop the charges, if I submitted to a psychiatric assessment. This is how visionaries and prophets are treated in the modern world. What does it matter to me? Sitting in a room for a few hours talking about my feelings with a man who wouldn't know a great crested grebe if it landed on him. But as it happened I asked to go to the bathroom, and, since no one was watching, I snuck out the fire exit.

It was unfortunate that my walk home took me through the East End. I was ambling along, looking in shop windows. Did you know that fashionable people now like to buy lamps made from dead pheasants? Perhaps you have seen them there, standing proudly in the window, with a lightbulb crammed in an open beak? There was a chandelier made from butchered doves. And then, in the corner, an advert for taxidermy classes. Yes, taxidermy… that was the final straw – £200 to stuff your own bird. How to tackle such barbarity? I smashed all the windows and a blade of glass accidentally got stuck in a member of staff. Yet I'm the one in trouble with the law.

One day, there will be a reckoning. When the birds attack and lay waste to civilisation we will only have ourselves to blame…

I'm afraid the only thing I'll be able to do then is snigger.

I hope this statement makes things clear, once and for all. For I am tired – so terribly tired – of constant interrogation. Of being asked, over and over again, to repeat the same details, to so-called professionals, who claim not to understand a word I've said. It's Kafkaesque. That's what it is. Everyone uses the word. But I have cause. The logic of my actions is clear. I am not making excuses. Surely it is axiomatic that I must be set free to continue my work?

Questions must be asked. Can flamingos smell thunder? Why are geese still at large? What makes guillemots evil?

I have requested books on the subject. My request has been denied. I have written multiple letters to each authority. They must have gone astray.

Now, I demand to see the prison governor. For, even here, things are not dealt with as they ought to be. Yesterday there was a bird sitting on my high window ledge. Today, I've climbed up, and with my binoculars, I can see how it lies on the ground. Something ran over it. Its little body is flat and black, guts on tarmac like a smear of raspberry jam.

If I had a camera I'd take a picture for you. For it is a perfect illustration of my point.

The city is no place for birds. Nor delicate sorts of human being neither.

HATS

This week, we're pushing hats, as we do every year at this time. Late May, the world has warmed up, blossom has floated off in the breeze and that heralds the start of wedding season. I had to dress the window – which is tricky because the more a hat costs, the worse it looks.

I was determined to sell the absolute *ghastliest*. To triple my commission, and start paying off the outfits I have to buy to come to work. You must wear the label, you see, to blend in with the aura of impossible fanciness.

Yesterday, I was on my A game. I don't know what came over me, exactly, but I swooped on the ambassador's wife, our very best customer. She has excruciating taste and a purse that bulges like an overdue mother.

I was fussing about in the window, so I saw her BMW mount the pavement and coast into the lamppost. She pulled the handbrake on before she hit it. She can't park there but she didn't care.

She always spends hours in here anchoring herself to the golden display cabinets and emerges cheerfully to a windscreen covered in parking tickets. She will scoop them up and chuck them in the air, like a child playing with autumn leaves. She has diplomatic immunity when it comes to parking charges, she says, and maybe so; the thing I can't understand is how the police haven't stopped and breathalysed her.

Elizaveta – that's her name – Elizaveta is forever getting into scrapes. All the sales girls pretend they know all about her. They say she drinks because her husband cheats. She sits in the embassy, with nothing to do, as he rogers the interns over a desk, with cigars and all that, just like Bill Clinton. And they say he humiliates her in public, keeps putting her down in front of obscure Russians, so she spends her days, from breakfast to tea, utterly sloshed. It's hard to feel sorry for someone so rich. The poor you can cry over, but there's something fundamentally unsympathetic about a woman with at least a million in the bank who spends indecent amounts on godawful crap.

Anyhow, yesterday she staggered in, looking, as she always does, in total disarray. She likes me because I love her. That much is clear. And I was the one who served her the first time she ever came in. I am obsequious with all my customers. The canny ones see right through it and treat me with the contempt I deserve.

Elizaveta and I met during wife-bonus season, which happened while I was still in training. We'd been taken through the day in advance, and we reconnoitered, as before a military operation, positioned exactly, to the right flank, to the left flank, ready to burst upon the bankers' wives, who tend to drift in after lunch, and in she meandered at a quarter to twelve.

It was exactly the wrong time to be humouring some homeless person who'd wandered in to try to warm up a bit before returning to the street and a cardboard sign. And I could see my manager glaring at me as I bowed and scraped before her, treating her like every other woman who came through the door. I did think she was homeless, as a matter of fact, she fairly reeked of booze, but my mother taught me never to look down on anyone.

So I helped Elizaveta cling onto a display cabinet, to remain upright, pointing out the treasures inside, winking at her under the lights, wondering if I ought to point out that the back of her dress was tucked into the top of her see-through tights, and her coat was barely covering her knickers. Fairly reeling from her gin breath, I pulled it down while helping her to the handbag display, showing her this and that, oozing my best oiliness. And lo and behold, she pulled out a credit card, shortly before she was sick on the floor, and wandered out again with a £10,000 crocodile baguette. I was never so happy scrubbing vomit out of carpet.

Yesterday, she was nearly sober, wearing a hat and a duffel coat, although it was thirty-two degrees in the street. I intercepted her, right at the door, I was so quick. It's always freezing in here, so the coat almost makes sense. Bertrand says chic is cold. I gushed at her, telling her how marvellous she was looking, how we've been missing her, why has she not been in to say hello? And she pointed to her foot, which is in a cast, and said she'd had a fall. But right now, she's in a jam, because she has a wedding to go to, she has a dress all picked out, but she'd been flying round Sloane Square as quick as she could hobble and she couldn't find a hat and, she knows it's not our speciality, but did we have anything that might suit her?

It was as if God had parted black cloud and sent sunshine pouring on me. As if a brass band had struck up the 'Hallelujah' chorus with beautiful girls twirling batons. I took her straight to the vilest stuff. The stuff so hideous you wince to look at it. The sort of thing Princess Beatrice would snap right up. The milliners saw her coming, I know they did, I wonder how they concealed their glee while convincing her to clamp a fascinator to the front of her head, which any civilian would tell her looked like a toilet seat. And yet they persuaded her it matched her questionable beige outfit, that she would be the last word in style.

Myself? I avoid weddings. And if I were a good person, I'd have told Elizaveta not to go either. I could see she was vacillating. She had that panicked look – as if she'd dropped her keys down a drain. Weddings cost too much: to the heart and soul. If you're violently unhappy they're the absolute last place you should go. This year I got through spring without receiving an invitation. I hadn't realised how happy that made me until I received one in late June.

My mind started to froth over with excuses. I must not. I must not. I must not… let myself loose on free champagne. Something about the bubbles affects my brain. The last wedding I went to was not my finest hour. The bride doesn't speak to me. And nor does anyone else who was there. It's true, she never liked me much. But then nor does anyone else I've met these past few years.

I don't blame her. I don't in the slightest bit blame her. But neither do I blame myself. Not exactly. Not entirely. What I did – it was unforgivable. But you could also argue that it was an accident waiting to happen, collateral damage, of sorts. I'd bought my dress a month before, it was very pretty, a little too pricey. I was planning to return it to the shop afterwards, only they wouldn't take it, since there were antiperspirant stains on the armpits, which was a shame since I'd only tried it on the once. It cut into my fat underarms, that was the trouble.

In my present state of finances it ranks as a colossal loss: I'd kept the tags pristine, folded it up in the bag it came in, stowed it carefully at the bottom of the wardrobe.

What happened was this. I'd got home at four the night before, or, if you're nitpicking, four that morning, and slept through both my alarms, not hungover exactly, but still drunk, and if the bloke next door had not started screaming and shouting, I might have slept through the wedding altogether and saved everyone involved. As it was I woke up in a panic to these bloodcurdling screams, shot bolt upright, still naked, and ran around holding my head on my shoulders, thinking I should hide from whatever madman was trying to break down my front door.

Somehow, I found my dressing gown, and peeped outside, and when I did, I discovered that our upstairs neighbour had fallen down the stairs. He was lying, crumpled, at the bottom, battering on our door. Kicking it so hard, he was making splinters. So I opened the door, tried to talk to him, to get him to stop, and he started writhing about, since he was deaf and turning blue. I ran for my phone, called an ambulance, they told me to do CPR if he stopped moving.

But he was thrashing about, still kicking hard, which is lucky because I'm not sure I could have given him mouth to mouth, he stank so bad. The ambulance arrived, two paramedics dashed in, got him onto a stretcher, started carrying him out the door. And I'm relieved, thinking God this is quick, the only problem is they were hauling me in there too, seeming to think that we're a couple, of sorts. The man was knocking on heaven's door, so I couldn't object.

I was only wearing my dressing gown but they already had the siren on so I rushed back in, flung open the wardrobe and seized the paper bag with my wedding outfit in it, slung in my coat, knickers, razor, toothbrush, and anything else within reach, and dashed downstairs, to where my deaf and blue neighbour was mid-seizure while half the street gawped behind their nets. Someone must have called the police because all of a sudden the boys in blue arrived and, instead of asking me to get out of the ambulance to unlock the door, took a battering ram to it, rushed upstairs, and, as I watched, came down again with a job lot of drugs, sex paraphernalia and a large machete, which, apparently, my neighbour had stashed above the communal hallway.

It was fortunate, in fact, that I had to go to hospital, because when the police came down they knocked on the side of the ambulance, wanting to take us in for questioning. But at that very same moment they shut the doors, the driver fired up the engine, and with siren wailing, off we screeched, fast as you like, cleaving the weekend traffic in two. Arriving at the hospital, I saw the clock on the front and said, 'Christ, I'm sorry, I have to be off. I have a prior engagement.'

But they wanted me to stick around since my neighbour was in great distress, sobbing, still blue, deaf and now, apparently, blind, so they expected me to hold his hand as they stuck things in him, but he smelled so foul I couldn't bear it. And they were talking, super fast, demanding to know who his doctor was and had he OD'd before?

'But I don't know him,' I said, and they looked me up and down. I did recognise that, as I stood before them, grim-faced, unwashed, reeking of gin, with unshaven legs, dirty dressing gown, no knickers, make-up on one half of my face and hair sticking up on end, so that it resembled, very likely, the nest of a long-dead vulture, I did look like a liar of the very cheapest variety. Quite evidently partaking of whatever drugs had turned my neighbour blue. So I took my coat out of my bag, shook it out and zipped it up to my chin.

'I'm sorry,' I said, imperiously. 'But I have a society wedding to go to.'

My phone was dead but I could tell, by the clock at the gate, that I was too late to catch the train, so I hailed a taxi – hang the expense. And I was so distracted, thinking how I would have to move out, what with the neighbours turning out to be criminals, and the police raiding the premises, and it being a complete shithole regardless of the bankrupting rent... so I was not thinking what I should have been thinking as we neared the church. Instead, I had my eyes fixed on the meter, fretting, 'I'll have to leap out when it gets to £20, will I get near enough...'

So the second I saw a fluttering of bunting I got out and paid, although we were about a mile away, and it was for another wedding. I jogged up the hill, thinking all the time about how much I was sweating, and where in hell I could change. There was nothing to hide behind, the landscape was stark. Just a church, standing alone, and the wedding party assembling like a war camp on the hill. I could see the bridal car waiting outside the church door. So I had to nip behind a gravestone and start struggling into my finery on my knees.

Only the bag I'd picked up wasn't the one that had my dress in it. It's the one I'd shoved in there after the Halloween party went wrong. Well, I had no choice, I had to put it on, I couldn't very well attend a wedding in my stained dressing gown. So I put my Batgirl suit on, for the second time, tied the batmask in my hair, trying to make it look like a fascinator, and made the most of the cape swinging behind me, drawing it round like a cloak, hoping no one would notice.

Capes were in, actually; I'd sold a particularly ridiculous one to Elizaveta, in fact. I had to run the last bit, because the bride was getting out of her limousine, and when the door banged it created a gust of wind, which blew my cape and showed my outfit in all its glory. And it didn't help that the organ struck up and everyone turned round just in time to see the bat sign on my breast and the utility belt at my waist.

I scuttled to the nearest pew as the organist realised her mistake. But the guests on the end were too busy laughing to budge up and let me on the end. So I had to nip round behind the choirboys and sit on a spare chair. And for the whole damn ceremony, there was this girl who hated me at school, in utter hysterics. She kept turning around and practically bursting into tears.

I would have left, then and there, if I hadn't thought it would cause too much disruption. As it was, all I could do was sit there thinking: I want to die I want to die I want to die. I didn't hear the hymns, I didn't hear the vows and when the bride pumped a fist in triumph, I did not cry. Marriage, you see, is an effort of will.

I decided I would leave. Sneak back down the hill. Get home, repair the front door, go to bed. Only Maria spotted me crawling through the gravestones and said I couldn't possibly go, not until we'd caught up, and since my brain wasn't working I couldn't think of an excuse and we ended up in the stately home where they're throwing the ornery wedding breakfast. My head was pounding, I was in no fit state to carry on. So we agreed to have one quiet drink, after which I would leave.

But when we reached the courtyard, where all the booze was, Maria got her heel caught in a crack between paving slabs, fell forward and dashed her head on a stone pillar. I scrambled to help her up, aware that everyone was looking at us, since Maria took a waiter and a tray of drinks down with her. And after that there was no hiding. People who I didn't even know kept coming up to ask me why I'm in fancy dress and started sniggering. So I have no choice, I grabbed the champagne flute thrust upon me, drained it and held it out for more.

When the third successive person came up to me and asked me to take them to the Batmobile, I thought, fuck this, and wrenched a bottle off a waiter, so Maria and I could find a stately cupboard and have a chat in peace.

Of course, I hadn't eaten anything, thanks to my traumatic morning, and I was possibly still a little bit drunk from the night before, so all in all, it was not my fault that the booze went straight to my head. An empty belly reacts to bubbles, and, alas, I suddenly, inexplicably found I was enjoying myself. Maria's a lot of fun, when upright and not reciting her latest beau's godawful poetry. So when the gong went for food, I'd forgotten that I was making a dignified exit.

I found my seat. Or I found a seat. I couldn't swear that it was mine. I talked to the girl I sat next to. I had a feeling I was really entertaining her. I was conscious I was slurring my words, so to conceal this I talked faster. It was quite possible no one could understand me at all. So I did what I always do. I started making my jokes hilarious through extravagant hand gestures.

A hand swept this way. A hand swept that way. I hit a waiter in the face. Entirely by accident. I headbutted him in the groin. Trying to apologise. The plate he was carrying landed on my head, the fish got caught in my batmask. I laughed, much too loudly, at whatever it was I was saying. And then, finding that the seats next to me were both empty, I renewed my attempts at conversation with the people opposite. Whatever response they made profoundly bored me. So I got up, and moved on, to congratulate the parents of the bride and groom. I spoke to everyone. And delighted them all. Elizaveta and I are well aware of how you triple the gaiety of nations by hitting the bottle.

And then the gong sounded again and someone put their hand over my mouth, which helped me understand that it was time for speeches and we were all to be quiet, so everyone could hear. I felt a surge of energy, a wish to dance. Silence was the one thing I was in no condition to join. And, alas, the best man's speech was a dismal mess. There didn't appear to be a punchline to whatever it was he said. No one tittered, no one laughed…

So I heckled, I couldn't help myself, I heckled. Only small things. A few 'Boos!' and a 'Ba Boom Tish!' Then the bride took the microphone and started singing to the bridegroom and dear lord that was so funny it made up for everything. An agonising performance, and everyone trying to keep a straight face. I was laughing uncontrollably, I couldn't help myself, what was there to do, she couldn't hold a note. One of the bride's cousins dragged me from the floor. He wasn't at all nice. Threw a glass of water in my face and told me to calm the hell down. So I started crying instead and rolled around on the floor. Well, what an embarrassment. I wanted to go home. But, unfortunately, I found I'd lost not only my batmask, but my utility belt, my bag and my shoes.

So I climbed out of the window of the little room I had been locked in and went off to find my things. My vision was unreliable. And my stomach was causing me all sorts of trouble, unsure of whether it wanted to expel its contents or take in more. I felt a terrible thirst for water. I couldn't go back into the hall to get some. So I wandered around the grounds looking for a tap or some sort of sprinkler.

I got lost in a hedge maze, had to climb up it to get out, and from the top I spied, like an oasis in the desert, a fountain spurting forth in the middle of the park. I crawled towards it and found it covered in moss, and cascading green: but water is water, I inched towards it, it was so very hot, I hadn't the energy to walk. I put my head under the water and opened my mouth. And then, since it felt so very pleasant, and since I hadn't had a shower in forty-eight hours, I thought I'd take off my bat dress, lie down and cool off.

I felt pretty splendid, floating, as the sun sparkled at me through the water, beautiful rainbows cascading over me, I felt free for the first time since I'd woken up. And inevitably, with my head propped up on a stone shelf covered with antique slime, I fell asleep.

It was unfortunate – and not at all my fault – that this was where the bride and groom were having their pictures taken. And it was unfortunate – and not at all my fault – that the photographer didn't notice my naked appearance until afterwards. And it was unfortunate – but not at all my fault – that a dance floor had been erected between the stately home and the fountain where I slept and that the wedding party all emerged for the string quartet. A tiny page boy pointed me out, where I lay so tranquil. And there was quite a hoo-ha about me being unclothed.

In my view, it was body fascism. I'm sure if I'd been some slip of a thing I would have got away with it. But they took one look at my white belly, my great dimpled haunches and – I'll say so myself – my absolutely enormous breasts, and rushed over with a tablecloth to wrap me up. And I was told that if I didn't leave immediately, they would call the police.

'Call the police?' I said. Much too loudly. 'CALL THE BLOODY POLICE? I'll have you know I've been invited.' And then I pointed at the groom, who had, it's quite true, asked me, apparently as a last resort. And he looked away, as if he hadn't a clue who I was.

'We have known each other,' I said. 'For twenty years at least. And we were *carnal lovers* right up until last weekend.'

Well, that's friendship for you. Not for the first time, I was dumped by a friend. It's lucky I'm so good at making new ones, because I'm an absolute expert in getting rid of the old. People are so fussy these days. Bursting with indignation. As my sister said, 'Who doesn't get drunk at weddings? Why, if only you were drunk and naked, it can't have been much of a bash.' I think the trouble was I did it at three in the afternoon, whereas at midnight, I might have got away with it.

But I'm supposed to be telling you about my triumph yesterday. And this hideous hat that I persuaded Elizaveta to buy… hideous, hideous… how she picked up one hat, utterly hideous, very like a beige squid. And she picks up another and tries it at an angle. Even worse… an alien appendage made with pipe cleaners. How she looked a complete sight. Her hair dirty, the smell of vermouth, faint, almost imperceptible. She picked up and tried out another. Two fleshy, taupe testicles dangled each side of her brow. And I was standing there trying not to laugh, as she turned her head this way and that, as they shook and nodded.

And what I should have said was, 'Elizaveta, take my advice. Do not go to this wedding at all… save yourself the embarrassment, divorce the philandering rogue…'

But I'm not a good person. So I sold her that damned hat, for all I was worth. The ghastliest, the very ghastliest of all!

DARLING

Darling shoots out of the house – no coat, no shoes, and it's freezing out. Face white and wet, she runs straight into a car, slams her fists on the bonnet. The driver starts cursing at her and she runs on into the alley.

Two seconds later 'B' comes out. There's the kid wailing behind her and the man trying to calm her down but she's howling and bawling, fit to wake the whole street, demanding to know where Darling went. Then 'B' swings round to me. I hit my head on the hanging basket, stub my toe on the boot scraper, all the while attempting to shrug. I meet her gaze. And her eyes are slits.

Frankly, I don't care for any of them. When 'B' lived in that house I know what she did to my cat when he went in their back garden. So now, when the kid kicks a ball over the fence, I never throw it back. I can hear the man complaining about Pushkin, the balls and the state of my garden. He says it's a mess. He says it's not right. He says something ought to be done about it. And he doesn't keep his voice down.

Darling has heard it all fifty times and more. At first, she said it was none of his business how I leave my garden or treat my fence. Then she said, if he was so worried, maybe he ought to invite me around for a drink. Perhaps, if we all got to know one another... the man snorted, started sawing more wood.

I don't know what their real names are. Honestly, I'd prefer not to know a thing about them. The young girl – who ran off down the alley – he refers to as 'Darling'.

The older woman, who chased Darling out of the house, I call 'B' because he refers to her, always, as 'that B**** who claims to be my wife'. I'm a lady, so I won't use that word. His voice rose in volume, all summer long, eviscerating 'B', his list of grievances lengthening, rising and drifting over the fence. There was no escaping the racket. But there's no point getting upset about it. There isn't anything I can do to make it stop. So I make myself as comfortable as possible and try to enjoy the drama vicariously.

Every morning, come rain or shine, I recline in the garden on my sun lounger, under the beach umbrella, feet up, a thick blanket over my legs, to see what drama the new day brings. Whatever the season, fresh air is good for the lungs. I'll try to read the papers or a magazine in my lap, while I drink my morning tea. And it used to be very relaxing. But all I ever hear these days is his stupid voice calling out next door, to the girl who's much too young for him, who's always running round after him: 'Darling this, Darling that, Darling, Darling, Darling.' Before ranting and raving, whingeing and whining, on and on and on, about: 'that B**** who still claims to be my wife'.

They look very similar, 'B' and Darling, like two versions of the same machine. It's all very confusing, to me. The same limpid smile, auburn hair and aquiline nose. 'B' sees the resemblance and doesn't like it. But I don't see that she has the right to object. After all, she was the old model, the one that malfunctioned and had to be replaced.

I had been living in this house almost fifteen years, undisturbed, when the man and 'B' moved in next door and the whole neighbourhood went to the bad. From the second they moved in I could tell they were trouble. The man introduced himself by insulting me, repeatedly, because my car was in the way of his removal lorry. My car had been parked in that spot for the previous six years at least, without once causing offence.

But I moved it, to be neighbourly, for the whole afternoon. When I came back he didn't thank me and 'B' stared straight through me when I introduced myself. It all deteriorated from there. They sniped and carped and caterwauled at things too petty to mention. They didn't like my car, they didn't like my cat and they didn't like my face. They spent a year convincing me they were the vilest couple I've ever met. They seemed so well suited – I don't know why they split up.

And, frankly, I don't care. But something must have happened, because 'B' started going out every night, on her own, and didn't come home until the early morning. Of course, he called *her* 'darling' then. She only became a 'B' later. The kid was crawling at that point and had trouble with his teeth, poor mite, and the man couldn't stop him screaming. So when she came home, just after the boy had drifted off, the man kicked off about it, and the awful time he'd had, which woke the boy again, and only encouraged her. I lay in bed as the walls shook like paper and my furniture started to dance across the floor.

'B' liked throwing things that smashed impressively and she loved slamming doors in his face. The crockery dwindled, the doorframes splintered, the garden filled up with china fragments and furniture snapped in two. On the weekends, he'd get drunk and lock himself in the bathroom. She'd be hammering on the door, demanding he admit to his ever-accumulating failures, and he would shout back.

Then, around 2 a.m., having finished the bottle, he'd start singing that he was sorry. 'Darling, don't leave me, darling, don't leave me. You can't take' – whatever the kid's name is, it sounded like Marvin, but that can't be right – 'away from me.' Then she'd yell some more, at an animal pitch, insults I couldn't quite make out. And that only made him furious. He reverted to taunts and vitriol. Night by night the repetitions of 'darling' dwindled, and she hardened, for him, into a 'B'.

So the fights got ever fiercer, the reconciliations ever rarer, and I was so sleep deprived I had to crawl under my desk every afternoon to take a secret nap. Every night, I'd stuff my ears with cotton wool in preparation, hugging the blankets, willing myself to drift off. And either they were already at it, and I wouldn't sleep at all, or else the arguments would start later and permeate my dreams. Every night I'd have a nightmare more savage than the night before.

Finally, they had a fight so bad 'B' walked out on him entirely. I was so relieved I felt quite giddy. She took her clothes and shoes; I watched her out there on the doorstep, with overflowing bags. Another man was there to put her stuff in the boot of a car and drive her away. Later I learned she'd shacked up with some driving instructor she met salsa dancing. They have their own little love nest around the corner now. She took the kid with her but sends him back on weekends to barrage me with balls.

There followed a delightful six weeks of such peace and quiet. I slept and dreamed quite wonderfully.

But he got over it, I have to say, very fast. 'B' moved out before Christmas. All January, he was out, carousing, combing the local bars. Occasionally, he'd bring a woman back. Most of them left, straightaway, never to be seen again. But a few of them stuck around, as he tried to expand his vocabulary. The nights were punctuated with 'babies' and 'sweethearts'.

Some 'dears'. A smattering of 'loves'. Once, on the full moon, there rang out in the stillness, a single, ecstatic 'honey'.

But by Easter, the vocabulary was narrowing again. The woman he now addresses as 'Darling' made her first appearance on Shrove Tuesday. He tossed her pancakes, the old wretch. I recall all the details because I met him that day at our respective front doors. He was laden down with carrier bags full of flour and lemons, and a frying pan poking out of one. When I smiled at him, quite by accident – thinking I'd make pancakes too – he asked me if I wouldn't mind turning down my television, because he was entertaining, and did I really need it on so loud? I was so appalled by his cheek, my brain failed my lips and I found myself apologising.

Under the circumstances, I don't think I can be criticised for taking a closer look at what was going on. I recognised at once that this new 'Darling' was much too young for him. She stood there in patent black boots, slender and sweet, her auburn hair twisted up, neat as a ballerina's. I felt, instinctively, that she'd be back. No doubt, she reminded me of someone.

And so it proved. She soon became a regular fixture. They played music late and went out on the motorcycle he bought at New Year. Then she moved in. I thought at first she might be penniless, and had identified him as a sugar daddy, but I understand that she was paying him to live there. So he's a skinflint, I thought, as well as the rest. But that's beside the point. Overnight, she was transformed. She lost her name, whatever it was, and became his current Darling. And the old Darling became 'B'. And they all settled down, to share the kid and live happily ever after.

That was when the ruckus started.

Now, I blame him for not preparing either woman. He can't have explained his situation in any detail. Neither of them can have been anticipating the shock. 'B' and Darling were introduced to one another, quite by accident, one Sunday morning. 'B' knocked at the door, to collect the kid, and Darling opened the front door. I happened to be on my way out, to buy a croissant at the bakery across the road. So I saw 'B' coming, passed her on the pavement, turned and hurried back. I snatched up the binoculars I bought for bird watching, and raced up the stairs, just in time to see 'B''s eyebrows shoot up and her mouth scrunch up to form a point. As if she were trying to embody a question mark with her face.

What would you do, when confronted by your doppelgänger? It's the sort of terrifying thing that never happens in real life. But I can tell you what happened in this instance. 'B''s nostrils flared, she put all her fingers in her hair, and, withdrawing her hands, had several strands caught in her nails as she and Darling shook hands.

'B' likes to dominate. That much is obvious. She thinks herself superior to her estranged husband – and I can't disagree. But Darling is so sweet-looking, she has such a young face, in certain lights she looks like a child. If only she were, one call to social services would cut off all this nonsense in its prime. As it is, the council couldn't give a damn about my noise complaints. 'B' saw Darling had assumed her recent title. And she didn't like it one bit. I'm pretty sure she decided, then and there, to get rid of Darling.

It was an inventive campaign. First, 'B' started coming round on Saturday nights to watch them all through the blinds. The reddish head outside glared at the reddish head inside, laughing with the kid, watching television. 'B' watched it all with mounting rage, as Darling sat in the sitting room that 'B' had painted a hideous yellow. Darling's feet luxuriated in 'B''s fake polar bear rug. Darling's face was illuminated under 'B''s Scandinavian chandelier. 'B' apparently forgot how happy she was with the driving instructor, in their little love nest round the corner.

As a woman, you might expect me to take Darling's side. After all, she hadn't asked for such shenanigans. But, actually, I don't feel a shred of sympathy for either woman. It makes no sense to be fighting over that slab of lard. His conversation revolves around wood-burning stoves, famous people he met in the eighties and the latest BBC paedophile enquiry, none of which he knows anything about.

When he's trying to suppress a belch, he moves his head from side to side, like a greedy snake trying to swallow a piglet whole. He's potbellied. He eats in the most disgusting manner. And afterwards he uses his shirt to wipe the fat dripping from his chin. You'd think, at least, he'd have a bulge in his pants, but my binoculars are yet to distinguish it. All summer long, he sat out there, practically naked, eating meat he burned on the barbecue. Calling for Darling, simmering in red wine, playing the soundtrack to *Oklahoma!*

In fairness to her, 'B' did not want him back. She simply wanted, much like her namesake, to piss all over him, mark her territory and walk on. So I rubbed my hands and limbered up for the showdown. I went out every evening for the first time in years. I took to clearing up the patch out front, put up hanging baskets, watering them, pruning them. I pulled up all the weeds that were breaking through the concrete, planted a sunflower in a tub, took recycling seriously. I watched as 'B' turned up, whenever they least expected it, and raised hell.

'B' found out Darling's phone number, at work. Kept calling her and threatening her, left voicemails, wrote emails, turned up whenever she pleased. 'B' let herself into the house, when Darling and the man were out, to take back her furniture. One day, she packed the sofas and the blinds in the back of a removal lorry. Well, he called 'B' up and started shouting at her again about that. So 'B' upped the ante. Accused Darling of mistreating the kid. Engaged lawyers, sent threatening letters. And this is the point at which I got annoyed. For, regardless of how little I care for Darling – she's wet through and she's a fool – suggesting she hurt that child was downright cruel. She ran around after him like a damned au pair.

In my opinion, Darling needed to have it out with 'B' directly. That woman was taking the mick. But all Darling did was sit there, wringing herself out like a damp rag. Trying to get the lump of lard to help her out. Curiously, it was on the matter of curtains that Darling finally made a stand. She said she was fed up of being watched through the living room window, by 'B' and anyone else who might care to take a look. In the dark, when it was impossible to see out, she had the unmistakable feeling that half the street was looking in. Since 'B' had removed the blinds, couldn't he put up some curtains? She stamped her dainty foot.

Well, that was asking far too much of him. He didn't see why such expense was necessary. He didn't see her problem. True, she was paying him a hefty amount in rent. He couldn't deny it. But still. And so they had their first fight, which went along these lines. She shouted and he shouted. But this time, he won. He slammed the door, in triumph, and played the soundtrack to *Oklahoma!*

After that she stopped calling him 'darling' and started calling him David.

So all through that winter... déjà vu. There was rowing, plates smashing, footsteps thudding – only not so many and not so hard. This time, to his own amazement, David found he was winning. It helped that when the kid came round, Darling made no noise at all. She just went up to the attic and whatever she did up there she did it in silence. To my certain knowledge, she has not seduced any driving instructors. She does not rush out in stilettos or come home after three. She does not play Latin music or practise the limbo in the back garden.

And then, this morning I heard screaming out the back. I ran to get there, just in time to catch 'B' struggling with David at the garden door. He wasn't a match for her, never was, never will be, so 'B' got into the back garden, where Darling, it appeared, was cowering behind the shed.

'B' was practically upon her when Darling, with surprising pluck, scaled the collapsing fence and tumbled into my garden. She started off apologising about crushing my dead plants, and panting something about how she had to get out my front door. And before I could answer she had run into my house, was grappling with the locks, all the while muttering, 'OhDearOhDearI'mVerySorry.' And out she shot.

I followed her, just in time to see how it ended: slamming into that car, disappearing down the alley. A right little sprinter, Darling proved. If she has any sense she won't come running back again.

'Love,' someone sang, 'is a losing game.'

Now I sit here, thinking it all over, watching the steam rise off my cup of tea. I'm sitting in the garden, just in case something happens, on my sun lounger, with a thick blanket over my knees. I really think we might have reached the end. And I have to admit I've had my fun. It's been more amusing than the trash on television. But I could do with a rest, before the next one moves in. As I peer through the slats, watching him simmer, I can tell it won't be long before he finds his next 'darling'. That's the joy of an all-purpose term.

BAD ROMANCE

Once upon a time, there was a girl called Zlata, who foolishly believed in fairytales. Her mother had read them to her every night before bed. So she knew that a prince would find her, fall madly in love, and make her the queen of his faraway kingdom. And when, after years of patient waiting, no hero had come to claim her, Zlata had to modify her search criteria.

Six months later, she met a man on the internet. Robert Filigree was a three-time divorcee twice her age, but he was damned keen. He made her an offer and bought her a plane ticket, which is more than any other man had done. So when he met her in arrivals, with two dozen roses and an array of compliments, Zlata tried her damnedest not to notice how he limped. Nor that he was balding at the crown, bulging at the waist and kept repeating himself.

At the end of their two-week trial, Mr Filigree, sensing success, took Zlata to a dimly lit restaurant on the King's Road. And she cried real tears when he got down on his good knee, to flourish an antique diamond in a velvet box. She was staring so hard at how it flashed in the half-light, she tried not to notice the stench of the cheese course, nor how her fiancé demolished it like a bulldozer.

Zlata and Filigree were not engaged for very long. It was not so much a whirlwind as a hurricane romance. Of the wedding, she remembered the polished panels in the waiting room, waiting nervously in case it all fell through. She chanted her husband's unpronounceable middle names over and over under her breath. She did not want the registrar to suspect her motives.

There were four in the congregation. A friend she'd made on the plane who left straightaway, two of Filigree's colleagues and his ancient mother. Afterwards, they went to dinner at the Endurance. Zlata kept squeezing her husband's hand, hoping that he would make a speech and break the bread. But he was talking, very earnestly, to his colleagues, on matters of business, leaving Zlata to his mother, who talked much too fast, and pulled a face whenever Zlata replied.

At half past nine, the elder Mrs Filigree left and, for the remainder of the evening, Zlata sat and drank. As the evening wore on, the pub became hotter, and the talk more intricate, so she sat and watched the sweat build up on her new husband's nose. She had no idea what they were saying, so she spent a long time in the ladies, holding on to the sink and talking sense to herself in the mirror. She could not remember getting home so Zlata did not know if her new husband carried her across the threshold. All she knew was that she woke up on the sofa, under a blanket, her head roaring vowels.

For the first three months, Zlata tried, very hard, to call her husband Robert. She practised it, over and over, both silently and out loud. But in her heart he was always Mr Filigree, the man who had messaged her pretending that he loved her favourite novels, the unlikely hero of her future life.

Zlata learned how he liked his shirts ironed and which dishes he preferred.

And then, one day, Filigree announced over his breakfast tray that he would have to leave the country for a little while and that, as his next of kin, they would have to agree on a set of kidnap questions, just in case he was taken hostage abroad. He talked far too quickly for Zlata to do more than worry. When they had agreed a simple word code, he sat flicking through the news channels, searching for gunfire, for the rest of the day. That night, he fielded one phone call after another. Zlata stayed up and, when Filigree finally came back inside, asked him to show her, on a map, the small African republic that had plunged into civil war. The next morning, he got up early and told her to get into the car. He would have to go into the office, he said, to get some injections, and they could buy some plants together on the way home, as she'd long requested.

Later, when he was all packed, they waited for the taxi to come, holding hands, at the bottom of the stairs. When her husband left Zlata sat down and cried. She had wanted to cry – for such a long time. She started to fret about what would happen to her if Filigree were kidnapped or killed. If he were captured she would have to spring into action. Remember the right codes, make his company pay the ransom; get the government to organise a transfer of hostages. But how could she make them when her English was so bad? And if he were killed, how would she live? She found it very difficult to sleep. It was so lonely during the day. The phone never rang. The postman hardly ever came to the door.

But Filigree may have indulged in a little drama of his own. He returned after a month, with a deep tan, duty-free Scotch and a kiss for both her cheeks – without any fuss. He showed her the contents of his digital camera, of himself smiling in a flak jacket, between men with Kalashnikovs, sitting on top of a tank. Filigree, pointing at unreadable graffiti, posing in the rose-gold bathroom of a tyrant's palace. Outside, artful photographs of reddish water running into drains. Looking at her husband grin, Zlata was reminded of how her friends were always pictured in their holiday photos: posing under palm trees, smiling beside waterfalls, pointing out famous landmarks, and larking about.

Zlata practised her English, intensely. When they sat down for their meals, she would name every item in the room. When they used the bathroom in the morning, she would decline her verbs. They spoke, over and over, on the same subjects, simply at first, and then in greater detail.

All through the spring, Zlata found her husband would gladly talk, well into the night, of his previous wives. The first: that broke his heart. The second: that took his money. The third: who should be certified insane. She had been very beautiful, and young like Zlata, but she used to hit him in bed. She was prey to her own frenetic enthusiasm and had been through many fads in the short time they were married. She had been fanatical about dance competitions in particular. Eventually, she forced him to attend classes. He waved his hands about and made the face that indicated when he was telling a funny joke.

But Filigree's eyes looked sad and he had salad oil on his chin, so Zlata put her hand on his knee and poured him another whisky. After he had told each tale of woe, over and over, word for word, Zlata understood completely. It was lucky, she thought, she had married a man so very much older. It was very good for her English. And their marriage, on the whole, she thought, was also very good. She had gone into it with great hopes, romantically, of course, and it was all working out just as she had planned.

Already, they had drifted into a happy routine. She would work very hard in the house for two weeks, and then he would be sent to some trouble spot for a month, and she could relax. Sitting in the garden. Tending to her plants. Trying to read the books she knew best, in English translation. And she was in England. The place she had read about so often when she was a child. The land of Dickens. And Galsworthy. And Byron. In her husband's absence, she visited museums and galleries, wandering around in the damp air, trying to feel at home.

When the summer came, Filigree started to talk about having to take his annual leave, which, he said, he did not like to do. The moment he stopped work he always came down with a nasty virus. He'd rather battle through. But the company heads were insisting and he would have to take two weeks off, at some point. He hoped it wasn't a prelude to forcing him out.

Zlata was rather excited by the prospect of travelling. A honeymoon had never been suggested. But after saying they ought to go away Filigree made no further mention of it. Communication in relationships, Zlata had read, was mostly about body language. But it was hard to tell what he was thinking when he spent all his time at home doing nothing at all. He slept, he worked, he ate: stolid as a vegetable. He watched television and they went to bed.

Mainly, he enjoyed eating her meals, mewing like a cosseted cat throughout. Zlata ate less and less, took pleasure in the washing up. The water running off her shining spoons, curving up and spraying, the bubbles popping with curved and winking rainbows; the bowl drained, she went at the tap with an old toothbrush to make it shine. She watched her tiny face bend out of shape, a tired circus trick.

Zlata was finding it difficult to sleep at night. Filigree was putting on weight and his bulk on the mattress made the bed roll, as he turned to one side and then the other. And Zlata would dream, every night, that she was floating on crashing surf. When cast on the rocks she would sit bolt upright, alert, only to lie down again, trying to slip off, her mind full of thoughts. After a while, sleep stopped coming at all. So she would sit in the kitchen, early each morning, listening to the house in the dark. The beating of the rain as it fell, all July; the scratching of mice beneath the floorboards.

On the first day of August, Zlata smashed the plate with Filigree's dinner on it and said she would cook nothing more until he paid her some attention. He glared at her, asked what had got into her, slammed the garden door. Zlata threw the rest of the food she had made in the rubbish. Left him to burn his own toast and moved into the spare room.

A night alone had its effect. In the morning, Filigree told her that when his next foreign assignment came up, she could, if she liked, accompany him. He would book a hotel, in whichever country was nearby, and safe, and they could have a holiday before or after he did the job. She would see the sun again and he could claim her fare as a legitimate business expense. Zlata lit the gas and rummaged around in the fridge. For breakfast, they had blini and the beluga she had been saving for a special occasion.

When a coup was launched in an African state, the Filigrees made hasty arrangements. Shortly after crossing the equator, they kissed goodbye. Filigree would be smuggled across the border and a taxi was waiting for Zlata, to take her to a luxury resort. After a forty-five-minute drive, her car pulled up at an old colonial hotel, bullet holes in the perimeter walls and brown stains running from the doors.

Zlata checked in, unpacked her bags and went for a walk. She went to the beach, sat on rocks in the drizzle, staring at the green waves as they lapped in. Every morning she went back, counted the cigarette stubs that floated on the water, went for a swim and caught up on her sleep. For at night, the half-built hotel next door put on a light show for an empty dance floor and turned up the music, which drilled straight through her brain.

When Filigree joined her, he was displeased. He could not bear the hotel – which was manifestly not the five-star resort in which he had stayed twenty years before. He was horrified by the weather. He bullied the staff but refused to leave tips, so it had no effect. Their room was neglected. Zlata's husband went to bed early, sleeping straight through the noise from the hotel next door. Zlata took to sitting on the balcony, massaging her temples.

When the sun came out, the locals went to the beach to play. Zlata spent a whole day watching a young couple with their little girl. She toddled along faster and faster, before her chubby little legs failed and she fell into the water. Zlata couldn't bear it. And she couldn't bear either, the teenagers, playing in the sea. Zlata tried splashing her husband, where he sat, struggling through an Italian newspaper. But her husband only frowned. He would not come into the water. He sat under his beach umbrella, writing postcards.

One night, after he had fallen asleep, Zlata went through her husband's luggage. For clues, she told herself, as to what might cheer him up. In his suitcase, buried under all his shirts, she found three postcards in envelopes, which was curious. One was blank. One was addressed to the UK Border Agency and, judging by the indecipherable scrawl, had been written very drunk. He must have written it as a joke. He could not be so cruel, nor so preposterous. And the third was addressed to a woman in England, saying that he missed her, quite desperately, and could not wait to return. If she wanted dance lessons, he would give her dance lessons. Plus several other obscene things. Zlata began searching through the pockets of his jackets and his shorts. She went through his phone. She examined his crossword puzzles. Her chest was tightening and her eyes were stinging.

Zlata returned the postcards and went to the empty hotel bar. She tipped the barman heavily and started drinking through the cocktail list, from Absinthe to Żubrówka. It was very expensive. She made sure it was all added to her husband's tab. She thought she would give him a little surprise before they went home.

The staff began to warm to her, now she was spending money. For the final stretch of their holiday, Zlata veered between profound insight and a vicious headache. In the morning she floated in the sea and in the afternoons she flirted with the barman. She no longer made any effort to speak to her husband, let alone do anything else with him. The rooms had started dancing round her. The streets shook and the lights blurred. She went out for air. Couples surged all around her. She sat down in the sand and fell asleep, feeling so very ill.

The next morning Zlata woke up to find her husband staring at her. He had had a call from London. His mother was gravely ill and he had to fly home immediately. He would cross the border, he said, get the final signature on the contracts and then take a helicopter to a specially chartered plane. Zlata would have to wait, pack up their things and take the flight they had booked for the end of the week.

He had never liked holidays, he said. Really, he was just a man who lived to work. Zlata wondered if Filigree was making some sort of apology. She let him kiss her and said she was very sorry about his mother. He seemed quite happy as he climbed into the back of the taxi. And she wondered if the departure had the slightest bit to do with his mother.

She watched the taxi disappear down the dirt track. He didn't turn around so she didn't wave.

All alone, Zlata started to enjoy herself. She slept during the day and went swimming at night, in the empty, moonlit pool. She began to think, properly, for the first time in months. She decided if he made a guarantee not to mess up her citizenship, she would ignore his taking up with his former wife again. Waiting for the taxi to take her to the airport, checking through their suitcases one last time, Zlata rehearsed what she would say to him, how she could explain it without damaging his ego, when she heard a car cut its engine just outside the door. She zipped up both cases, put a call through to reception and dragged one of them behind her. But the taxi had not arrived.

Waiting on the concourse were three men, in desert camouflage and dark glasses, demanding, very urgently, that she get into the back of their blacked-out SUV. Zlata hunched up, as if refusing, so they started to ask her questions where they stood. Was she the wife of Robert Filigree? Zlata said she was. Was she aware of the kidnap protocols of AZ Oil? Zlata frowned. Was she aware her mother-in-law had passed away? Zlata said her husband had gone home because he had been told his mother was very ill. They asked her, once more, to get into the car. Zlata put her hands to her head and wished she had not drunk so much the night before.

Inside, the vehicle was icily cold and smelled strongly of leather. Zlata could feel sweat forming at the back of her neck. One of the men took off his glasses and presented her with a piece of paper. The words waltzed before her eyes. She stared at each man in turn hoping for help. They watched her carefully. And when the tears, in crystal chunks, landed on the paper, they took it away and handed her a scarf which her husband often wore.

In trying to stop her tears, she succeeded in getting hiccups. And in trying to stop her hiccups, she held her breath so long she couldn't feel her legs. She opened her mouth, to tell them the kidnap codes, for her husband was very obviously still alive. But a wave of sickness flooded through her and she felt a desperate need for air. Opening the door of the car, she tumbled out face first and split her head open on the concrete.

By the time Zlata woke up, three weeks later, extremists had long ago beheaded her spouse. The company paid her a large settlement, to keep her quiet, and her husband's life insurance paid out an exorbitant sum. Zlata found herself appreciating Robert Filigree much more, now he was dead. Her marriage, she knew, had been a grubby transaction, a bore and also a sham. But to be widowed, by Somali pirates, when so very young. It restored her faith in the fairytale ending.

And she lived happily ever after.

DEATH OF A LADIES' MAN

I was sitting outside Gregory's suite, watching the buildings turn from pink to grey, trying to empty my head, when you strayed back into it, just as you tend to, every day between one and five. The sun fizzled out, it got so cold, a band came and played carols outside the station.

The wind got up, snatched the hat off the trumpeter, blew it maliciously, every time he stooped to catch it. The snow fell in swerves. Still the wailing came through the glass. Gregory kept me waiting another hour. He might have hoped I'd give up and go away.

The sky went dark; yellow squares appeared in the buildings opposite, one by one. Matchbox figures moved around, like live toys in a doll's house, multiplying under mistletoe and tattered tinsel. Down below, the snowflakes were whipped into fury under the streetlamps. The Christmas shoppers zigzagged across the pavements, buffeted from side to side, abandoning, in sheer frustration, their dead umbrellas.

And that was when I saw you, hurrying to the Perseverance, just like always. Your great camel coat gaping open, wrestling with itself. I knew it was some other portly man, struggling with his collar up. But still I had that prick of recognition. Skin tricked into goosebumps again.

So my head was full to bursting, and I was stiff right through, by the time they called me. There was nothing I could do. I handed in my letter of resignation. Stared hard at Gregory's mouth, watching as his eyes scanned through my careful phrases. I couldn't trust myself to look him straight; my eyes always give me away.

He asked all the questions you would find in the binder. Why – but why? – did I want to leave? So I told him about all the pressure I've been under, trying to clear up the mess you made. And I did not mention that I keep seeing you in the halls. She should have been fired, I said, it's a disgrace, an absolute disgrace, that after the way she behaved, she's still with us. Gregory sighed and bit his thumb, as if considering what I said.

Then he rushed through a torrent of lies, each less convincing than the last. He offered me a pay rise, along with other blatant bribes. I was in line, he said, for several bonuses and perks. But I told him money couldn't possibly cover it. So he offered me his ski chalet for the month of February. I didn't know what to say to that, so I just sat there, staring at his mouth.

I went back to my desk and started packing up my things. If I were you I'd have telephoned reception, demanded they keep a driver waiting. In my opinion, and I've gone over it and over it, your first mistake was getting hooked on the company expenses. I see that as the crest of your slippery slope. I cleared out all my drawers. Took down my photographs. And then I took one last tour of the floor, to say goodbye.

I remember when I first got this job, how I couldn't believe I'd finally managed it, how I wandered around, breathing in the atmosphere of power. But here I am forced to leave, through no fault of my own, in incomprehensible defeat.

Often, at night, you and I were the only two here. You used to sit so still the lights went out. If the cleaners came past and made a noise, you'd shoot both hands up, startled. Waving with all the enthusiasm of a drowning man. I always assumed you were catching up on sleep, relaxing there in your air-conditioned cell. Like a monk with nowhere to go. But not a bit of it. You were lackadaisically embezzling tens of thousands of pounds in between games of solitaire. You had so much time to conceal all the wrongdoing. I can't understand why you didn't manage it more intelligently.

You took such risks, without any research. Even your win rate, at the card game, was pathetic. It was all so unnecessary. You bought her a car when she cannot drive, jewellery she says she lost, and commissioned a painting of her nude which still hangs in her apartment, because we can't get anyone to buy it. I found a card from her, underneath your keyboard, with suggestions quite revolting, I had to burn it then and there. Only later did I think that I should have preserved it as evidence.

I wonder what it was about her that made you lose your mind. I look at her and I can't see it. But then I have never seen the appeal of any woman who made a man lose his mind. I suppose it's because I'm the sort of woman who helps him find his keys.

The deeper I had to go into the whole sordid business, the more I wonder how she encourages all the pawing. For she does – unquestionably – she does. She dresses in bright white like she's auditioning for a Daz commercial. In winter it's all furs and peplum skirts. In summer, dresses in broderie anglaise, so tight and small she looks as if she's wearing a few strategically placed doilies.

Her limbs stick out, I suppose like a model's, tall and thin and gangling. But she never opens her mouth except to say something stupid. And then she laughs that awful laugh of hers, that unbearable noise, half cackle, half sneeze. She snorts her appreciation and then hawks back all the phlegm in her throat, as if gargling with the joke. And that, apparently, is what men find not merely attractive, but devastating.

Her laughter has got even louder of late. Vacuous, unceasing giggles. They let her keep her job. I couldn't believe it. I got quite angry. She is the most useless operator on the floor. But it turns out you wrote her a lot of emails which could be construed as evidence of sexual harassment. And so she had them exactly where she wanted them. If I were in charge I would have taken it straight to tribunal. Put that nude picture to some use. But no one here has any balls.

There are many things I wish I had done differently. If I had my time again, I'd pay more attention. I'd have started with her evident sinus trouble and moved on from there. Apparently, your fling with her was all anyone else was talking about. But I was too busy, doing my job, making vast amounts of money, to engage in petty chitchat. I didn't look at you as a man, only as a rival. And as that, I dismissed you on sight. You sat in your side office, looking increasingly like John Major. Sinking into your dull grey suit, your shirt tucked into your underpants, pretending to work as late as possible, fiddling about.

You were perfectly polite, never tormented the secretaries. You did not march around, cutting the graduates' ties in two. You got your own coffee. Smiled at the interns indiscriminately. The closer it got to the weekend, the more frequently you nipped out to the Perseverance and came back smelling of beer and cigars. But I happen to like the smell of beer and cigars. So even the smell didn't bother me. In short, you did not interest me in the slightest.

And that's what's truly hilarious, isn't it? Considering that I see you, now, at least three times a day. Disappearing, just ahead of me, at the end of every corridor, the back of your head bobbing up in every crowd. Straight after you died, the very next day, I knew you were dead, but you still walked the halls. No one else can see you. I've made enquiries, and it's only me. And I've exhausted myself trying to discover why. I've been to the doctor, who says it sounds like a stress reaction. A psychiatrist who made distant surmises about my absent father. A psychic medium who patiently explained that we have been lovers, tragically separated, for several centuries at least.

According to her, the rash, which I get on my neck, is not an allergy to angora. It is an indication that, in a former life, I was guillotined. 'Well, it makes perfect sense,' the psychic said, stroking my hand, as her tapered white cuffs trailed in her cup of tea.

After that, I looked into hiring an exorcist. You can see what nonsense I've been driven to. Why can't you just die, like everyone else?

I blame myself, of course. I blame myself. The whole rotten business I've recast as my fault. It must be, else you wouldn't haunt me. I keep thinking if I'd never said a word to you, you'd never have found out and then you'd still be alive, perpetrating fraud. I'd still have a job, perfectly oblivious. And we both of us would have been spared all this bother. But try as I might to think myself out of it, this is what I dream, over and over, about that party, a year ago today. How I emerged, from the cloakroom, flustered and embarrassed. How you were standing beside the door, on your own, a pint in hand.

And you said – only I don't remember what it was you said – a pleasantry, something bland. I was trying to get my breath back, I wasn't thinking straight. And then you said,

'I'm so relieved to be at a party where I don't have to lie about what I do for a living.' So I asked you what you told people you did. And your standard reply was so uproariously dull, and, consequently, so very mendacious, that I burst out laughing.

And this, I think, is why what happened next is so very unfair. For it was in a spirit of camaraderie that I told you what I saw. It was because I was laughing, and you were laughing, and we were sharing good jokes, that I giggled my way through the distress I felt, right there in the pit of my stomach. That I rehearsed, in graphic detail, the grotesque scene I'd just uncovered in the ladies' cloakroom.

You stopped laughing immediately. But I didn't notice that, until I thought it through afterwards. I wasn't alert. I was a little too drunk. I should have taken the hint – tried to backtrack. Recognised the error. Said it was a crass joke. I should have said anything – anything at all – to get rid of the piteous look which was spreading all across your face. But on I went… trying to sound amusing… with the tale… of how I'd gone to get my coat and she'd been there, both her stalk legs wrapped around Gregory's middle. Her little white dress hitched up to the hip, the mistletoe falling from her tangled hair, her lipstick smeared across his neck, like juice from a pierced raspberry, his whole face a deep maroon, as if about to have a coronary. How they tugged at each other, cloaked in fur, like a pair of grooming baboons. I'd turned around, straightaway, abandoned my coat, since it was irresistibly caught up in the melee. I decided I'd take a taxi home, collect it in the morning, I'd send Gregory the bill for my drycleaning. But even when I finished my tale, noticed only I was laughing, still I didn't understand. I thought it was the way I told it. That I'd made it sound too foul.

And because I was laughing, as I so rarely do, I found, to

my embarrassment, that I couldn't stop. I laughed on and on, louder and louder, trilling up and down, unable to say a word. So I launched myself at you, in a goodbye bid, left the last of my lipstick, a slight bruise for your cheek. I saw the rebuke in your eyes. But departed, laughing still. I fell into a taxi. Regaled the driver, too.

I got home. Went to bed. And slept – like I hadn't in years.

There were very few people in the office next day. You weren't there. She wasn't there. Gregory stumbled in sometime after lunch, shambolic, and still the wrong colour. She was always taking sick days and you, well, back then I rarely thought of you at all. It was a good day to do business so I only read about what happened on the journey home. I picked up the *West End Final*, half a mind on finding my gloves, to find the headline: TOP BANKER DIES IN TUBE HORROR.

Even then it didn't occur to me – because you were not and never would have been a top banker, but you know what newspapers are like, always trying to cheer people up with a sensational tale. Bystanders had reported that a man in an expensive suit, carrying a large camelhair coat, had been behaving erratically, straying across the platform, shouting. One of them said you'd been swearing, described you as 'very hyperactive'. That must be a polite way of saying 'drunk'. No names were mentioned. There had been an argument, on an overcrowded platform, and a scuffle, in which a man, fifty-two, had fallen on to the tracks. A couple, at the scene, had been taken in for questioning by the police.

She must have spent hours at the police station explaining herself. I know she kicked up a fuss because they put her in a cell overnight and sent her off with a caution. No one seemed entirely sure what had happened. Had you fallen or had you been pushed? I'm still confused. I've even been down there to have a look. I thought, perhaps, you might be outraged, because there had been some miscarriage of justice.

But the facts are these: the station was full, too full, of people, drunken people, all wanting to cram onto the last train home. The line had been disrupted by an earlier signal failure and the concourse had not been properly salted. Your shoelaces were untied. The ground was slippery with ice. Standing there I could see how it happened. Your foot twists, your head turns, and you fall. The train catches you; your body is dragged down the track. It ends up a misshapen lump of suit and coat, bleeding on dirt. She faints. Gregory catches her.

So why do you keep appearing before me? For me, it's as if you never died at all. Your presence has been constant. Ineradicable as a faded tattoo.

Early on, I went to your funeral, thinking it might help. I suppose, in my heart of hearts, I was hoping for objective proof that my mind was playing tricks. At that time, I thought I was hallucinating. I thought if I could see that you were cold and dead and since cremated, that that might help unpick my delusions. So I saw your dust buried in a hole in the ground.

I drove out to the small church, in a hamlet near enough the M25. My breath made tiny clouds, and the pews were three-quarters empty. The priest couldn't pronounce his r's. It was all so impersonal. As if your relatives didn't know what sort of funeral you'd prefer. Traditional readings. Dirge-like hymns. At the front there was a lady with a black veil and a tiny child, who clung to her like scaffolding.

Your wife, I thought, since you always wore a ring, and your little boy. I'd seen his face in a photograph, on the wall behind your desk. And then on the other side of the church, at the back, there were several other mourners, beautifully dressed, sitting apart, dabbing their eyes occasionally. The singing was faint, all you could hear was the organ. When the service was done, everyone save for your widow and son stood up and, one by one, hurried out. They kept their eyes on the floor and moved quickly and nimbly, like children who have dared each other not to tread on pavement cracks.

I thought I'd stay for the wake, do my bit, since no one from the office had made an appearance. I lit a candle, said a prayer, and was already leaving when your wife came rushing towards me, all at once. She had this look in her eyes, and I thought – that's how I must look when milady does her cackling. Not annoyance, exactly, more a deep, abiding hate. She pulled her child with one arm and walked quicker than he could run, his blond curly hair so long he looked like a girl. He began to cry and dropped the toy he was holding.

She dropped his hand and pressed her nose right into mine, standing up on her toes, like a lady boxer, ready to trash talk me into submission. I started to tell her she had got the wrong idea. All her insults tumbled out, one after another, each dirtier than the last. I was shocked, that she could say such things in church. And perhaps she heard me, as I jabbered on with my explanation, for her words trailed off and she looked at me, as if prepared to let me speak.

Her eyes are very beautiful, the Scandinavian kind that are so pale and clear, they are like ice. But all I said then was – I'm so very sorry. And she hit me hard. A sharp, smart slap with the flat of her hand. My eyes filled with tears, as she pulled my hair and ears, before rushing off in pursuit of the other women who had been in the church. And, for whatever reason, she had at them with her rolled-up umbrella.

I sat down and your boy stood staring at me, unsure what to do. So I told him that I had worked with you, that I was very sorry that you were gone. I told him you loved him very much, and all the things you're supposed to say at funerals. All the things I would have told your wife, if she had stopped to hear them. Platitudes, endless platitudes, one after the other. I'm good at that sort of thing.

I tried to take your son's hand, but he wouldn't give it to me. Still, we walked together to the church door, just in time to see his mother chase the mourners out of the churchyard, slashing her umbrella this way and that, knocking off their little hats.

I left straightaway. No point in hanging around. But, privately, I felt ecstatic. I thought, 'Great! That must have done it!' For I'd not only seen your casket, filled with the ash of your conflagration. I'd made what amends I could to your wife. It would be natural, as far as ghosts may be considered natural, that you would need someone to take responsibility for your death.

I've even spoken to *her* several times, on your behalf. I actually told her: the least she could do is attend your funeral. And, indeed, I only took it upon myself to go after she refused. Each time I've talked to her she's had nothing to say for herself. Do you haunt me because she's so tough and insensible? Maybe that's what it is.

But now I was done. I felt satisfied. Tranquil. Relaxed, for the first time, almost like my old self. When I got back to the office, to finish the day, I deliberately passed your office, several times. Delighted to find you did not appear once, not even in the corner of my eye. That evening, the lights were back on, as a promising associate unpacked his things. I recognised him as new – not you – immediately. He turned and saluted when he saw me coming. That's the effect I tend to have on the young men. I sat at my desk, until I'd made the time up, until the building was perfectly empty. I called a cab and went down in the lift. Just in time to see you disappearing before me, down the stairs.

Short of calling for a priest and holy water, I don't know what to do, anymore. You have terrorised me ever since, for a whole twelve months, off and on. I live in constant dread that you'll appear. I began to think I was losing my mind.

It was not a sudden decision, calling Gregory, and telling him I had to leave. I loved this job, before you made me afraid to even enter the building. And Gregory has done what he can to keep me. Even today, making me wait the whole day. It was a compliment of sorts.

There isn't any going back. My boxes are packed. I'm waiting for security to escort me downstairs. And right now, I've started to think I must do something extra, make some last gesture, to make sure you stay here, and leave me alone.

I feel I should cry for you. But the tears never come. I close my eyes, try to speak to you, but that isn't right either. Then I remember something I read somewhere. Ghosts only want to scare you. So I open my mouth and I try to scream. But no sound comes out either. Oh it's cruel, so terribly cruel, I can't help it now. When you are punishing me, so vindictively, for that single peal of laughter.

NOTES ON THE UNDERGROUND

Let me tell you about the day I fell down and died.

First of all: no one noticed. I was walking along the street. Stressed, and talking out loud, as was my habit. My good side and my bad side were having a debate. What about? I don't remember. The point is, I wasn't concentrating. So when the precipice materialised, I fell off it.

What was it doing there, in the middle of the street? It's a question without an answer. I always put one foot in front of the other. It is a habit you must adopt to win the human race. For me, it was a matter of professional pride. Some go quicker than others, I moved faster than most. I was an expert at weaving through crowds and at jumping onto trains as the doors were closing. I always stepped off the carriage first. I'd sprint up the steps to get through the turnstile first.

You see, only a fool would walk to the office voluntarily. If you start to think about it – sitting there all day, doing whatever it is you do – your legs revolt. They tremble and shake. They won't work for you. It's a problem. So you've got to keep yourself distracted. You have to go as quick as you possibly can, your eyes reading all the signs. Your ears crammed with nonsense. Run across moving traffic; make sure you catch that bus. Stop only if you hear a siren. You have to keep your feet on track. And you're thinking all the time…

No pain. No gain.

It's not me. It's you.

(Please place the item in the bagging area.)

That morning, what had I done? The same as any other: I'd got up late, turned the alarm off more times than I can remember. I'd raced for the tube train. I'd even got a seat. I closed my eyes straightaway so I wouldn't have to give it up. Not even if a pregnant woman stuffed her belly right under my nose. It was a normal day. I can't distinguish it from all the other mornings I spent like that. I flicked through the free newspaper before chucking it on the floor.

Fox eats baby.

Woman wears dress.

Head of Jesus burned on toast.

Before I knew where I was, the train rattled to my stop, I sprinted on and up.

Out in the air, I scaled the streets, onwards and upwards, to the beat of my clicking heels. Never once did I tread in the trails of dog piss that meander down those pretty, pristine pavements. Never once did I pause to admire the ornate house fronts, like giant slabs of wedding cake you could eat with a gigantic fork. The crocuses were coming out. There were snowdrops in the churchyard. And the pavement disappeared.

One foot was in freefall, my body toppled after, and that was that. At first, I tried to kick and punch, to grasp hold of something, to get back up. But I was flailing in broken concrete. It was hard to hang on. Through sheer determination, after several hours, I managed to grab hold of a street corner. I got one arm hooked around a lamppost, bit down on a grate with my teeth.

Of course, all I needed was a hand to pull me up. Any passerby would have done. But the crowds, when they came, parted around me. Occasionally, if someone were in a real hurry, and walking too fast, they might tread on my head, accidentally. A convenient stepping stone – that's what I'd become. No one thought to look down.

I can just imagine their appalled faces – if they did!

Here lies a woman, drowning in tarmac. Mouth full of asphalt, choking on dust, face smeared with grit and dirt.

(It is impossible to look one's best, under the circumstances.)

I was awake all day and awake all night. Trying desperately to cling on, hoping, sooner or later, to be retrieved. I was never at peace. Even in the hour before dawn, when the city went to bed, I could hear the cars on the Westway, ebbing and flowing like the waves meeting the shore. The suck and the drag. The spit and the sigh. As the shingle struggles to hold on to the sea.

But then, one night, my body protested: argued, viciously, with my brain, as to what to do. My legs were still kicking, my fingernails digging. But my heart had had enough; it knew its utter stupidity had got us into this mess. And there was no hope of resurrecting us. So my heart packed up and left. My ribcage said good riddance. And I was left with an empty chest, a blouse over breasts. I lost my ballast, gave up the fight. My iron will had its way. Seized me by the left ankle, dragged me right down to hell.

My eyes closed. My mouth shut. My hair flew upwards. I let the rest of me do whatever it liked. I no longer had any right to tell my organs what to do. I had failed them, and no mistake. I was in such a pickle!

And a voice in my head said: 'Is your manicurist a sex slave?'

How long ago was that? Three years or ten? You lose track of time when you're stuck underground. Down here we exist under fluorescent light, rattle from station to station. We can get off any time we choose, change lines, wander down every tunnel. Wait for the train to rush onto the platform, as the wind frisks up our tights, we just can't get back up to the surface.

I love the lifts at Russell Square. For a minute or more, I delude myself; I'll be spat up to the surface. I love to walk up the 193 steps of Covent Garden's spiral staircase. A third of the way up I can almost feel the fresh air reaching out to touch me before I'm knocked back down.

I think, one day, I'll get back above ground. When I was up there I didn't appreciate it. Now, I know, it would be so nice, just to walk among the living, for an afternoon. Down here, I co-exist with devils, who never speak. A fat man, who jumps, endlessly, in front of trains at Bank, trying to retrieve a sandwich he dropped on the track. A girl who sits busking, spitting pomegranate seeds in an empty cap.

But what I like best is to sit here at Angel, for days together: watching Sisyphus as he rides the escalator. All on his own, with a gigantic briefcase, that could, at any moment, crush him flat. He climbs, up and up and up, he never stands and rides. He reaches the top, and each time he does, he knows he'll go free, to see the dear earth again. Only he plunges back down again. Knocked down and down and down.

And that is the great joke: his eternal optimism. It reminds me of what I was like, before.

It is cold down here and it's lonely. There's nothing to do but laugh.

But what I want to know, before I close my eyes, is this: 'Why was I the only one who fell and died?'

DOUBLEPLUSGOOD

3 October

Today, at last, something remarkable happened.

And to think I almost didn't go into the office at all. The alarm failed. The shower broke. I had no clean clothes. The rabbit had chewed through the handbag I'd left in the kitchen. And if I'd known the reception I'd get, I would have stayed in bed. The manager glared at me through the glass, called me in before I'd taken my coat off. 'That's the third time you've been late this week,' he shouted. 'Stop rushing about like your skirt is on fire and show some bloody commitment.'

Well, he has a damned nerve. No one here works harder than I do. Of course, he's jealous. Last Tuesday, the personnel director asked me if I 'had the time' as we were going up the escalator. The comment must have got back to him. My talents have at least been noticed by someone in the building.

Lately, I have been getting the hang of things.

When I first arrived, I'll admit, I didn't know what to do. The position I thought I applied for was perfectly straightforward. A call operative, in sales. Well, I want for nothing more. Hand me a headset, I'll sell surplus straws for the backs of camels. But they steered me past the banks of phones, the endless desks, the great open field of steel and glass, and had me sit outside an office, in an air-conditioned waiting room, surrounded by orchids and fish in tanks.

When my name was called, I sat in front of three suits, all asking questions. Whatever I said must have been impressive. They took me out, had me sign a few documents, and told me to come back the following Monday.

So I've sat here, ever since, on my swivel chair, staring at this computer. No one has told me what to do and I certainly don't want to let on I don't know. Everyone lies on their CV. It's the only way to get a job in the current climate. But I had the feeling I'd gone a bit far. Unless it was a mistake, and there's some woman sitting in sales, with no idea what she's doing either. I assume I am supposed to be supervising something, writing copious reports. Certainly I'm a paper pusher. Everyone else here spends their days typing, so I do quite a lot of that.

I sit at my desk, for days together, and drink a lot of water. If anyone looks at me I smile at them in a winning manner. (In such circumstances you should always show your teeth.) I already had a mobile but they gave me an iPhone, which is constantly going off. I take calls, I receive emails, exchange texts. It's all bollocks to me but I reply to each enquiry with whatever occurs to me. I take great pleasure in my own efficiency. The messages come through at all times of the day and night. When London starts to idle, New York perks up, and so on and so forth. Last month, since I'd stopped sleeping anyhow, I started replying to each enquiry the second I got it.

My operation is 24/7, 110%, 365.25 days a year.

The last place I worked you made your calls. Totted up sales. And if it wasn't for my bad luck I never would have been fired. It's true the job wasn't really right for humans. If you ask me, it's a job for cyborgs that haven't been invented yet. For instance, in training, the first principle is: the customer is always right. But anyone with half a brain knows that the customer is invariably wrong. And that's only the most blatant example of how everyone, in the corporate culture, says the exact opposite of what they mean. In my third disciplinary hearing they told me I had to go because I 'had an established record of behaving in a non-positive manner'.

Well, I'd love them to see me now. A junior account manager, if you will, with embossed business cards, premium grade card, my name in a beautiful copperplate. I am fourth floor. Corporate Compliance. American Success. I couldn't ask for a better place to work. The only problem I have, really, is that no one ever talks to me. My colleagues sit at their computers, typing, and if they see or hear anything I do or say they show no sign of it.

At first, I did try to attract attention, but that didn't go well for me; they got quite annoyed.

The money is so good, I didn't want to jeopardise things. So I kept schtum and started to copy them, on the sly. They spent their days typing, so I started to type too. I didn't have anything to write so I began composing emails to several old friends I don't see anymore, apprising them of my situation. Then I deleted them, one backspace at a time, inventively, tip tapping, so it sounded like I was using the whole keyboard.

You can't be sure who is monitoring your inbound and outbound communication. It's hard to know what they think of me; they don't give much away. There are CCTV cameras in each corner of the room, keeping four eyes on us. I know, from experience, you should never deal with personal matters on company time.

Soon enough I realised I might need something to show my manager, in case he asked what I had been doing all day, so I began to write long, detailed memorandums instead. I'm pursuing blue-sky thoughts and thinking outside a box of monolithic proportions. I have come up with some excellent ideas. My eyeballs ache from exhaustive research.

Of course, when it comes to productivity in our office, I would thrive, if the boss gave me a shred of work. But there seems to be a hierarchy when it comes to doling it out. The woman who sits next to me gets given all the tasks. I make myself useful to her, go and make her tea. But nothing ever falls in my lap. Sometimes I think I'm just making up the numbers. That the boss requires us to sit here, to bolster his ego, make him look more important. The idea struck me that none of us, perhaps, are here for any reason at all.

But that can't be right. For the first week, I went out every day at one o'clock, for half an hour, to eat my sandwiches, on a bench across the road. There's a nice sort of wilderness there, in between the skyscrapers. On the Friday, a note was left on my desk while I was out, asking me to see the manager, since he had a bit of work for me. When I went to see him, he had gone and he hadn't left a message. So I stayed late, so I could speak to him on his return, show my enthusiasm, to get cracking.

When he finally turned up, past nine o'clock, he told me that it was far too late, he'd given the work to one of my colleagues – who always exhibits the dedication our job requires. I went home, feeling very dour and determined never to leave the office again during daylight. Of course, as soon as I abandoned lunch, I discovered that no one else takes it either. They eat at their desks. They sit there, frowning at their screens, chewing, and clicking furiously.

Say what you like about me – and people do – I never repeat an error. I learn. I adapt. These days, I sit so long in my chair, I develop muscle spasms. In life, no one hands you anything on a plate. If I am to thrive, get to the top, I must find out what I'm supposed to be doing and do it excellently. So I started to pay attention to the others – to learn from them. They don't move much – but whenever they do, they take care to roll across the room on their chair wheels.

In the evenings they do their nails at the desk. They get out their perfumes and fire them at their wrists, making the whole room smell like a rotting flower arrangement. Their phones ring, their iPhones ping, they get out their pocket mirrors and make every one of their eyelashes stand out like tiny toothpicks. Their lips get redder and redder and their cheeks shinier and shinier and then, finally, the manager appears and tells us we can go home. It's so late, by then, I overhear them moan in the toilets about the places they could have been and the people they could have met. Then they all go for a drink together, at a bar across the road, never once asking me to join them. Judging by how green they look next morning, I'm glad.

I can count myself fortunate, for I do not have much of a life outside of the office. I go home and have my tea in my room. It's a grotty little place and I can't stand the people I live with. They spend half the time screaming at each other and half the time cooing at each other, squelching in one another's saliva. And I'm never sure which is worse. Their rabbit is systematically devouring anything I leave on the floor. When I get home, I don't have much to do. Sometimes, in the evenings, when I don't watch myself, I sit here, drumming my fingers on my knees, just like I am typing, only I am not typing, I am just making the movements. It's like my fingers need to keep going. Here I go, tip tap tip tap tip tap. Such a pleasurable sound, such a pleasurable feeling. Fingernails on letters, racing across the keyboard.

It reminds me of the first job I did, the start of my shimmy up the greasy ladder. I was so dedicated, I couldn't answer a phone without saying 'Hello, Crème de la Crème customer service, how may I assist you today?' – even when I wasn't at work and received a phone call that couldn't possibly have been related. It was automatic, a phrase drilled in my brain and left there. The problem I have with colleagues, at whatever place I work, is they're jealous of my efficiency and drive. I know that is why they never ask me out for a drink.

After all, I'm no teetotaller. I sit here, late into the night, drinking alone in my room. I need to these days because my thoughts have got so quick, I can't get them to halt long enough to allow me to sleep. I'm so supercharged. It's not that I mind it – most of the time it's quite exhilarating. But some days I do feel exhausted, and that's when I drink. I dope my mind until I slip off into dreams. But even then, I don't exactly sleep. My mind is stuck whirring away until morning like a computer, caught on blue screen, that won't shut down.

All in all, I have to say, I prefer work to home. I never get bored in the office, and nor am I lonely there. I can see five televisions from where I sit. They are all on different news channels, so information floods to me from every corner of the room. When there has been a school shooting or a terrorist attack all the others stand up and stare at the one nearest the water cooler. They cross their arms and mutter. I prefer to stay where I am, keeping an eye on them all. You can't trust newsreaders indiscriminately. Some of them are more interested in their own outfits than delivering up-to-date news.

My latest innovation, for keeping my mind active in the absence of all work, has been to record what other people are up to in the office. I make detailed notes on their behaviour. Who whispers to whom. What they eat for lunch. I now use my trips to the water cooler to look at their computers. And to my horror, I find that they don't appear to be doing any work at all. They just sit there typing words into search engines and buying new shoes. They spend hours filtering through dieting tips and sending long emails to each other sharing their feelings. With links to videos of cats falling off radiators. Or the head of Jesus, as it appeared on a bit of burned toast.

Our manager sits in an office with glass walls, surrounded by pot plants that are waxy and green, watching us surreptitiously. He keeps his office very cold, to help him stay awake, he says. Also, I suspect, to burn calories. For he sits there, stuffing his face with cakes and biscuits, to cheer himself up. He is visibly expanding, bulging out of his suit and tie. Most of the time, he leaves his door wide open and my desk gets enveloped by the icy draught. I sit there shivering in my office attire. Every morning he tells me I have to take my Puffa jacket off, he says it doesn't look professional. But what am I to do? I don't want to catch a chill. I live in perpetual fear of coming down with a cold because it's not done here, to take a day off. So I sit and I watch them, as they develop the most horrifying diseases.

One day, in my memorandums, I recorded all incidents of coughing, and was kept busy all day. A concatenation of hoarse rasping spread out, in diagonals, from his cubicle door. It seemed to me they were infecting one another with a slack attitude. They cough, they get up, they have a glass of water, they sit, eyes watering, sniffing on their screens. They do even less than usual, wheezing into tissues. But then it struck me that they might very well be coughing in code. As I sat, making notes on it, I could sense certain vibrations, travelling through the air. They are communicating... plotting... somehow.

But I have wandered off the point. I must get down to what happened today. For I feel ecstatic just thinking about it...

To punish me for being late, the manager made me run all his errands. Punishment, ha! I didn't mind at all. I had so much to do. I watered all his plants. Cleaned out his fish bowl. Picked up his drycleaning from the laundry around the corner.

I was taking the lift, weighed down by his gigantic suits, trying to push the 'up' button without dropping his ugly ties, when I saw, out of the corner of my eye, the CEO's Rolls-Royce draw up outside the door. Quick as you like, the CEO himself bowled through the revolving door, skidded to a halt in front of the lift, and looked me up and down.

He pushed the button twice, and, when the doors parted, actually stood back to let me in the lift first. He must be nigh on sixty but he's still a very handsome man. He smiled at me, a broad, bawdy grin, and asked me my name. I told him, showed my best teeth. He asked me what floor I needed and where I worked. I told him and he nodded. Then he ran his tie through his fingers, checked the cufflinks on both wrists, sweetly nervous. He stood back to let me out, coyly saluted, and carried on up to the thirtieth floor.

I checked myself in the mirror afterwards and I wasn't looking at all bad. So it's not so surprising that he was so taken with me. I went back to the office and threw the manager's drycleaning across his secretary's chair. They were out again. I have no idea where they go. But the whole afternoon, for the first time in years, my heart was seized by a tremendous optimism. My thoughts were spinning. With love hearts and sequins. Saying, this could be it! Everything I have waited for – so long and so patiently – I must grasp on and hold tight!

10 October

There has been a miraculous change in the last week. I am under bombardment. I have no doubt as to what it is due to… the CEO is trying to test me, to see if I am capable of handling the pressure which would fall to me as his consort.

I now receive hundreds of emails a day. My desktop is always dinging. My phone is always singing.

Now I can see everyone eyeing me jealously and wishing it was their device going off. It can be dangerous, I find, being busy in the office. So I've switched all my machines to silent and now I go by the signs: the winking lights, the constant buzzing. They'll try, even harder, to give me an illness if they recognise how well I am doing.

It's been raining non-stop and the damp seems to make their diseases more virulent. They sit and splutter over one another, getting worse by the hour. Sometimes I wonder if they're holding a contest to see who can drag themselves out of bed in the deadliest state. Hacking up bits of lung. Sneezing yellow projectiles. It's like they're sunk in a stagnant pond.

Yesterday, I caught a pain in the head. It struck me unawares on the way to the water cooler. I had to sit down on the nearest chair, which wasn't mine. The manager saw immediately, stared at me through the glass. I winced, visibly, as he came out and started speaking to his secretary. I dragged myself back to my desk straightaway. I must work through the pain. Now is not the time to be ill. However much they wish it on me.

I haven't seen the CEO again since we met in the lift but I have employed my time well. I have been researching him diligently. His name is William James Ogle. I think it is a wonderful name. So dignified. So intelligent. He is fluent in French, Spanish, Italian, Portuguese and has 'sufficient German to get by in Swiss nightclubs'. He has not been round to see me but I imagine he doesn't want to make a move until his divorce comes through. It might complicate things, legally speaking, if his wife found out about us.

He will expect to run into me again in the lift. He won't want to make his approach too obvious. He's a gentleman of the old school.

The internet has started teaching me how to look amazing for our next encounter. It seems to know, instinctively, what clothes and shoes I ought to buy to impress him. I have taken out a couple of credit cards to cover the extra expenditure. (You must speculate to accumulate.) And I have started writing everything down, longhand, in a notebook, making sketches and placing orders. I am overhauling my life, wholesale.

11 October

I went into work early today, on purpose, to get ahead of myself. I sat down, printed out all my memorandums and filed them in chronological order. It's clear that Mr Ogle will expect me to get to grips with every aspect of his company. In the course of my research, I have discovered that the company seems to be in some financial trouble. My solution is simple. We must fire my manager, first and foremost, and then his underlings, one by one, until the work we are supposed to be doing is revealed to us all, and a few of us can get on with it.

I have developed an elaborate system of colour coding to define who ought to be fired and in what order. Imagine if the state of affairs in this office were replicated across the whole building! We could save thousands, if not millions, sacking all the managers, and the creeps who prop them up. Mine, of course, has started spying on me, even more than usual. He has obviously heard about Mr Ogle and me, and is worried about what I'll say, for he has started acting nice all of a sudden.

This lunchtime the manager asked me what the weather was like outside. I googled it, without looking up at him, and said:

'It'll be fine until three p.m.'

In fact, there was an 80 per cent chance of rain. He left his umbrella and came back very wet.

I carried on typing.

5 November

I have been furiously busy for the last three weeks and have not had time to keep up my diary.

Tonight I went to the company bonfire party. I was looking forward to seeing Mr Ogle, as they say he always attends, makes a speech and lights the first firework. I made sure I got there a little later than the others and was wearing my new Mulberry jacket and boots. I had my hair blow-dried and got a manicure while pretending to be at the dentist. It was a great shame it was so dark out as I looked stunning. I was counting on the full moon to show off my hair. It is so shiny. But I found I had to rely on the bonfire to cast an alluring glow, if only Mr Ogle would step near it. Unfortunately he spent most of his time in the cricket pavilion.

At nine o'clock they handed us all sparklers and had us draw circles in the air. Then some suit made a speech about how this represented the need for employees to work together, during the tough times ahead, how we had to sprinkle our sparks of inspiration onto the future of call-centre operations. Blue skies may well turn black, he said, but we must keep thinking, cloudless. Now, whenever I close my eyes I see the circles of light, leaping about, as one. Very clever. Mr Ogle must have thought it up himself.

I went over to his little coterie in the cricket hut. The caterers were handing out baked potatoes in tin foil. I was watching him very closely and got near enough to hear what he was saying. Suddenly he turned around and brushed my sleeve.

He said, 'I'm so sorry.' And I said, 'Not at all.' And he said, 'I hope I didn't get any potato on you?' And I said, 'Oh no, sir.' And he said, 'How is it going in accounts?' And I was confused. But then I understood, and said, 'Very well.' Giving him a meaningful look, followed by my best teeth, which, I had already checked, had no food stuck in them. He smiled straight back at me and then he said, 'So Mart, you were saying…' I stood there for a while looking at Mr Ogle and then turning intelligently towards Mart, and nodding where appropriate. 'The problem is, Jimmy, the staff aren't fired up enough. As I said to Geoffrey, OK isn't good enough, good isn't good enough, great isn't good enough. They must be ubergood, supergood, hypergood…'

'Doubleplusgood!' I cried. This man was on my wavelength. Ogle turned and smiled. And it struck me that this was not the time for flirtation. So I gave him a significant look and retreated to the bonfire.

I could hardly stop myself from dancing. Ogle must have instructed my manager to transfer me to the accounts department. And that bastard has thwarted it. That fat lump is seething with jealousy, anticipating my magnificent future. I had long suspected it!

6 November

At home I am persecuted, at work I am persecuted.

I am furious with my so-called 'manager'. This morning, when I came into the office, he spoke to me so rudely.

'What the hell are you up to?' he shouts, so loud his wax plants quiver. 'Do you think I don't know what you're up to? Mooning after the CEO. It's inappropriate. He's old enough to be your grandfather. And where did you get those clothes from? They look absurd. I don't know why we keep you on, I really don't.'

A month ago I would have locked myself in a toilet cubicle, clamped my head between my knees and sobbed for half an hour. Or I might have gone up to HR and showed them the dossier of evidence I compiled on how he bullies me. But no longer! Am I some nobody? Some low-level employee? Not a bit of it. His mask of professionalism is slipping. He's seething with bitterness and envy and can no longer hide it… in years to come I'll laugh at him. The silly little man. His face looks like a mouldy beetroot. His body, in that suit, looks like a sack of mouldy beetroots. And he thinks he can tell me what to do?

I did not enquire as to why he had not transferred me to accounts. I would not give him the satisfaction. He'll feel the fool, next decade. Like the caretaker who told the janitor, Albert Einstein, what to do. Or the modelling agent who told Marilyn Monroe to give up and go to secretarial college. I wouldn't be him for anything. For the rest of his life, everyone will ask about the time he spent with me and he'll have to make it all up. First I will become the head of this company and then when Ogle and I are married we will take over the business world.

My manager is a bug I will crush.

Although, unfortunately, I see he does have a point about my clothes. That is the nature of high fashion. One day it's chic, the next day it's deranged. I looked in the mirror this lunchtime and discovered I resemble a dinner plate. Of the cracked willow-pattern variety.

I spent the rest of the day ordering more clothes on the internet. Ogle was wearing a purple tie yesterday. I ordered everything in purple. Violent violet. The indigo of power!

8 November

I took a rare night off and watched a movie on TV. I was surprised to learn the whole thing was about me. There I was in the office. There was my manager. Making my life hell.

There was Mr Ogle. Trying to seduce me. I had to turn it off. It made me agitated. Just then the phone rang. It was my bank, asking if my card had been stolen. They read off all the transactions I made this month.

And since it did all seem a bit extravagant I agreed that my card must have been stolen. This morning, my flatmates informed me, a lorry blocked the street while the man inside it insisted that someone in our house had bought a grand piano. Even he could see there was no way to get it through the door, so he took it away again. A strange joke these fraudsters are playing.

I have so many things on my mind. I must try to make time. I went to the doctor yesterday on account of the pains in my head. He asked me if I felt OK. I must have looked a little stressed. Taking time off for doctor's appointments is frowned on in the office. He asked all sorts of questions. What I eat. How I sleep. And so on. Well I haven't been doing much of either lately. Since I really don't have the time to spare. When I close my eyes, my mind pulsates. He had me fill out a questionnaire – which I really couldn't see the point of – and then gave me a prescription for sleeping tablets.

They knocked me out straightaway but they give me odd dreams. I woke up, bolt upright, at 3 a.m. this morning, with a complete plan of action. I reached for my note pad. Wrote it down and conked out again. In the morning, I was so excited, remembering how inspired I'd been. But, on the pad, all it said was: 'CS gas. Crumbling floorboards. Rats. Let off with a caution.'

I can't make head or tail of it.

11 November
Today I finished my files. They are ready, now, for Mr Ogle. I got in three hours early to print multiple copies. I took

an envelope and addressed it to him, careful to disguise my handwriting. It contains all my brilliant ideas. Of course, he will know it was me. But he probably won't want to tell anyone, just yet.

This is how it began. 'Research shows, throughout their entire working lives, office workers spend an average of five years sat at their desks without getting up. That is five years of life spent without moving. In our company, according to my calculations, it'll be closer to ten...' And then I go on, explaining their laziness, and what should be done. My best idea, I think, is the introduction of treadmill desks and computers powered by cycling. I read about them in *Vogue*.

The idea is to work out while you work. Firstly, it will eliminate all the disease in the office, if they were healthy they wouldn't get ill. Secondly, it will combat obesity. My manager, for instance, could do with losing five stone. Thirdly, it will stop employees spending an hour at lunch, going to the gym. Plus, we could be the first company in history to go completely carbon neutral. The lights could be powered by one work-cyclist, the air conditioning by another.

Employees could hot desk, from cycle to treadmill, and do their work. As a solution, it's utter genius, if I do say so myself.

I took the lift up to the thirtieth floor and went to enjoy the fancy bathroom. The decor up there is extraordinary. The sinks and the floor are made from marble and there are two huge mirrors opposite each other. You can see your head from every angle, and then smaller versions of your head, repeated again and again, getting smaller and smaller, in squares. I gave myself, and all my little selves, a strong talking to in there. 'This is your chance,' I said. 'Don't blow it.' Then I stared at myself, very hard, as my head disappeared and I took seven deep breaths.

I was just coming out when Mr Ogle walked past with his secretary.

It wasn't supposed to happen like that. My tongue wouldn't work for me. So I let him go past and enter the lift, slipped through his open door. The opulence of his office is something else altogether. I walked straight in and put the files down. Then I had a little look at his cushions and his trophies. It was all very tasteful, in silver and purple. In the corner, there is a stuffed leopard, which looks ever so lifelike, and a coffee table manual on jujitsu. I decided, on impulse, to rearrange his in-tray and put my report at the very top. I had tied it up beautifully, with a mauve ribbon.

I snuck out again and went back to my desk for the rest of the day, a little downcast but determined to persevere. At half past twelve I went outside to call my bookie. I just knew that I was going to win the 3.20 at Cheltenham. But the sun was glinting right in my eye and I must have been crying because I could shoot rainbows off my eyelashes and straight into the clouds.

Suddenly I had all these thoughts, chattering away, fighting for space in my brain. And I realised I would have to get them down on paper. I decided to head straight home. There was no point going back into the office, where the manager might intercept the flow of my thoughts. As I hurried along the street, the lampposts and the trees and the telegraph poles were all stammering at me. It was a struggle to remember every suggestion.

Everything came together, for me, this afternoon. I knew what it felt to be electricity. I could understand the beating heart of a telephone. God, I saw, staring through the eyes of a white Pomeranian. I sat down in the street, worrying I'd forget it all. I scrawled the main points down on my arms since I hadn't any paper.

When I finally got home, I lay down in the empty bathtub, where it was cool, to transcribe my notes. I was sweating cats and dogs. The words had smudged, the ink was running down my hands and ankles. I closed my eyes and saw the fireworks, leaping and skipping round in perfect circles. At some point, I must have fallen asleep, for when I came to, staring at the grubby enamel, the wretched rabbit was pounding her head against the bathroom door and the windowpane was dark. The rabbit burst in. Trying to get at me. That wretched little beast is my nemesis.

And then, just as I was thinking about running a bath and washing my hair, an email came through to my iPhone, saying the company is going into administration and we'll all be made redundant, unless a buyer can be found. I'm not sure I trust my own eyes.

3 December

It's all LIES! The newspapers made it all up. Even in newspapers I read that newspapers make everything up. Tissues of lies, that's what all newsprint is, tissues of lies. The journalists invent facts, disseminate them online, they get printed in the newspapers, spew forth from the mouths of newsreaders. We know this. It is a conspiracy.

I didn't sleep a wink. I'd run out of tablets. I felt wretched, so I called the doctor's surgery first thing, to get a new prescription. The bastard wouldn't give me any, said they were 'habit forming' and accused me of finishing a month's supply in two weeks. I got into the office, thirty minutes late, and my manager came down on me even harder than usual. He said I should see the doctor on my own time, not when the company was in crisis. For medical emergencies, he said, I could see the nurse on the fifth floor.

My colleagues are now talking about me, quite openly,

in the ladies. Their breathing is so pronounced now, they are making me ill. They know about what's been going on, between me and Ogle, they're jealous and bitter and cerise with rage.

When they retire they'll look back on their working lives and wonder why they spent so much time in the office. Just before they die, all they will have to think on is how long they sat, pointlessly, in the one chair. Not having children, not travelling the world, not creating anything at all. They will wonder what it was all for. Their graves will join the uncountable other graves of every other person that time and humanity forgot.

But I wish they would stop sneezing at each other. And I wish the walls would stop humming. And I wish the newsreaders would stop arguing with each other. I've started wearing headphones but it's not helping much. All the noise comes right through the padding.

Even when I'm alone, sitting at home, the whole room chatters at me, only it isn't loud enough that I can hear what is being said. It's driving me up the wall.

5 December

Yesterday, I indulged myself, gave up for the day. But today, I redoubled my efforts, determined to regain control.

I spent the whole morning preparing for action, reading and doing my researches. I set the rabbit free. It was gnawing on my shoelace while I was making my porridge and I'd had enough of it. So I picked it up, opened the front door and pushed it out onto the street. It twitched its nose and started chewing the pavement weeds. It would not be free. So I had to carry it to the park and let it loose among the bushes.

This may be important. The masses will not free themselves. They may even resist. We must imprison all the

driver was very difficult. I had to look at him sternly. If he doesn't watch himself I shall have no choice but to take away his licence. I wrote his name down and put one strike against it.

I didn't go into the office... why would I? They cannot expect any boons. There is nothing for me there now. I don't even want to see Ogle. I'm not sitting at a desk all day, betrayed, abandoned, typing, typing, typing.

And typing what?

V-Day

Today my manager turned up at my house, demanding to know why I hadn't been at work. He made all sorts of sounds with his mouth but I managed to block most of them out. The gist of it was something like I can't just take three weeks off because I feel like it. Today, apparently, there was to be an audit of employees and I couldn't be absent unless I wanted to make him look incompetent. There are plans to get rid of our department or the customer care department. How he can care about such trivialities I don't know.

Well, I followed him as a joke. I was already dressed in my beautiful diamanté suit – which I have not taken off since I assumed power – so I got into his car, communicating only with my eyebrows. As we drove across London I nodded at the crowds as they surged around the windscreen, quietly acknowledging their tribute. They must have thought it very funny to see me in his decrepit little hatchback.

When we arrived in the office, I made a show of taking off my fox-fur cape. I was very curious as to what they would do when confronted with my majesty. They all just sat there, as if they hadn't even noticed. I looked at them all and thought – how typical. You'd think they had candyfloss for brains if you didn't know their skulls were empty... the sheep! The goats! The bovine bores! If only they realised!

Yes, they would all be bowing and scraping and begging for their lives...

I sat down, crossed my arms and stared straight ahead. I didn't turn on my computer. I didn't touch my keyboard.

The manager summoned everyone into his office to tell us what lines to parrot at the CEO if he asked any of us a question. Mr Ogle had already been spotted in accounts and would, presumably, be with us shortly. All my colleagues filed back to their desks, to smooth their hair and puff powder on their faces. It was a pathetic sight. I crossed my legs, stretched out my elbows, and cast a casual eye over the mendacity we call 'newspapers'.

I started to ponder, once again, whether my suit made me look like a disco ball and was quite lost in my ideas when the manager came over and bundled me into the crowd.

'Take your filthy hands off me,' I shouted. Everyone turned and stared. So everyone was looking at me, and not Mr Ogle, as he came through the door. They all rushed forward, like peasants in a charge, but I held back, proud, holding to my strategic position. He shook hand after hand and then he reached me. I stared directly in his eyes, bored into his soul and marvelled at how his love for me had turned so sour.

'How dare you?' I demanded, with a quiet dignity.

And then, since he made no reply, I repeated the question, more loudly. And since he still had nothing to say for himself, I lunged.

I'm pleased to say I got him before they got me. He'll find it extremely painful to walk for quite some time. The manager held me by both arms – he shall not be forgiven – and my co-workers all leapt on me. I think I must have had some sort of fit because everything suddenly went black and I woke up, strapped down into a stretcher with some fool asking me who my next of kin was and who my doctor was – of all the impertinences. I screamed at them to let me out.

The entire state is rudderless. I'm furious with myself for having gone into the office. That place is my nemesis, not the rabbit.

Xxx

My rebel government has been... destroyed. The Queen has resumed her position as head of state... it was not an ambulance... it was a Black Maria... and now here I am. Peeling walls. Stench of geriatric piss. Disinfectant. Germolene. Banana flavoured stainless steel. White sheets, white bread, white lines, they pump me full of stuff that makes me so tired.

All sorts of people come to see me. The interrogation has begun. I pretend to be asleep. Then I am asleep. They put things in my food to make me drowsy. I am so tired... so tired... and thirsty. They bring water in a cup. More pills. The bastards got me. So tired. So very tiring.

Xxxx

Today they gave me a book and pencil. Said I should keep a diary of my moods. But I will not record my thoughts in anything anymore. I will not record them in anything but fire.

Xxxxx

The office sent flowers.

I decapitated them.

Xxxxxx

Too tired.

Xxxxxxx

Every five minutes I am spied on. I could set a clock by it.

They keep asking me what I am doing. Writing this on toilet paper and stuffing it in my bra. If they must know.

Of course I do not tell them.

Xxxxxxxxx

I am forced to sit in a group and discuss my 'feelings'. They talk about the importance of breathing. Fools. If I didn't know how to breathe, I'd be dead.

That much is clear. It doesn't help that I'm surrounded by dangerous lunatics. There are the kleptomaniacs – who steal everything – and the pyromaniacs – who set fire to everything – and the egomaniacs – who just go on and on and on about themselves. On and on and on. I'm so fed up.

I demanded my release. They said it wasn't possible. So I demanded access to a lawyer. And we had a little row. Three nurses sat on me. And they gave me an injection. Bastards.

Xxxxxxxxxx

The doctors say I have 'no insight' into my 'condition' so they will not let me out. They will not even tell me when they might let me out. Fools. There's nothing wrong with me, besides being held here against my will and force-fed drugs that make my head full of pap and my eyes shut like traps.

In the evenings, I have to sit in the social room and play board games, among other damn-fool pursuits. Filthy cheats. I dig my nails into my knees until I draw blood. That will teach them. Now I spend half my time awake I've started to look for an exit. I need to get out of here. All night, the egos wail. All day, the kleptos watch you. I've joined the pyromaniacs. We smoke cigarettes and talk bonfires.

Xxxxxxxxxxx

A new psychiatrist has arrived. He is very intelligent. At

first, I couldn't say anything to him. Or, I mean, I tried to say things, but I was bamboozled by his impossible attractiveness. He smells like all seven types of heaven. Wears nicely cut suits. He asks very rude questions. But I bat them all back at him. After our first meeting I took a good look at myself in the mirror and demanded access to tweezers. I look a state. I need to get out of here and find a hairdresser.

Xxxxxxxxxxxxx

I absconded from the secure unit, and the police were sent to find me. I was just on the high street, having a cut and blow-dry. Fools! I was brought before the psychiatrist. He'd clearly got worried about my leaving him. Which of course I would never do. I asked if he liked my new hair. And he looked sheepish.

Xxxxxxxxxxxxx

I spend my time agreeing with everything my doctor lover suggests. This means I get on much better with the nurses and everyone else here. I go to groups. I paint my nails. I trade all my food for beauty preparations. I look fantastic. I find myself laughing for absolutely no reason these days. I could swear these pills are making me high. But Dr Handsome says he has faith in them.

Xxxxxxxxxxxxxx

They are releasing me tomorrow. They say I'll probably be all right, if I keep taking the tablets, and at any rate they need the bed. They had cleaned my suit for me. It has come out quite well, although it's bald in places and has an Ogle bloodstain. I put it on and it felt very tight.

I will go back home, have a nice bath, and then go back to the office, make up with Mr Ogle, tell him about Dr Handsome, no hard feelings and all that. No doubt they'll have been struggling without me. The company was on the brink. And then I was incapacitated. Which can't have helped.

I feel nothing like myself, of course, I'm so full of positivity! I feel I could do anything – if someone would just give me the chance! If I was doing everything again, I know I would do it all differently. I have so many thoughts that are unlike my own. It's as if they are emanating from a foreign brain which just happens to have been implanted in my skull. It is a nice, clean, happy brain, so full of the joys of spring. It is full of love for a beauteous world. At first I felt afraid that my brain was crammed with these strange, Technicolor, bubble thoughts. But I am out and I have a new love and…

I forget what I was saying.

Xxxxxxxxxxxxxxx

I got the taxi to take me around the sights. Since it was a sunny day. The sky was pink. The buildings grey. The grass was brown and dead. I went home. My key wouldn't fit in the lock. I hammered on the windows but nobody was there. So I went to work. My pass wouldn't work on the revolving doors. I asked the security guard to let me in and he said he couldn't since, apparently, I no longer work there…

Well, I was so full of inexpressible happiness, I turned around, got back into the taxi, and decided to go back to Dr Handsome, reveal that I secretly returned his love, and did he want to get married at once or should I go back into the unit and we would continue our relationship there? The taxi driver became very aggressive about my paying him. Which I couldn't do since the holes in the wall won't give me any cash.

When I got back to the hospital they said they couldn't let me in and Dr Handsome was not available. And then I figured out what had gone wrong. It is Ogle, taking revenge on me. For moving on so quickly. I must return to the office, confront Mr Ogle.

I cannot let him get away with wrecking my life like this.

Xxxxxxxxxxxxxxx
... I'm not taking these tablets...

Xxxxxxxxxxxxxxxxxxxxxxxxxxxx
One evening, I was sat, in a huddle, on the pavement. Watching the light glint off the revolving doors. The sun sat down. A red haze of flames across the sky. My bones ache. My teeth clench. There is this pain in my eye. As I watch a small figure, reflecting the light, like a tiny disco ball, turns up outside the building.

She has this sort of watering can that she took out of the taxi driver's boot while he was paying for petrol in the garage just around the corner. She carries it like it's too heavy for her, but she needs to feed the plants and flowers outside the building where she lavished her youth.

She does it so well, the water drips down, splashing everywhere, it soaks the mats and the steps, and then she starts to cry. Well I may be ill, but I'm not done yet. I lit a cigarette, to keep calm, and went over to help her, when all of a sudden she turned around.

And I saw then that this woman was me. And the petrol ran off my tights and my shoes. So I threw the cigarette, as far from me as possible, as the world began spinning, all on its own. It span and span and span.

Image shattered. Thousand pieces. As the flames shot up and merged with the blood-red sky...

Xxxxxxxxxxxxxxxxx
Now I'm on remand. Imprisoned on false charges. Arson

with intent, they say. And make me take my medicine three times a day. I've nothing to do now but sit and wait. Bored out of my skull. I've exchanged one incarceration for another. Which is worse? It doesn't matter. I learned how to cope in the office.

My mind stays strong. My thoughts all wrong. And now I have to tip tap tip tap on my knees.

My fingers flying. My thoughts firing.

Tip tap tip tap tip tap.

SUPER-LIES

A friend of mine caught you in the lingerie department at Selfridges feeling up the panties on a mannequin. She said you saw me drifting off the escalator, panicked, dropped to your knees, tore at the bows and off they slipped. Crawled flat, towards the fire exit, your mouth stuffed and scarlet. Oh, scraps of sheer silk: sufficient to choke on.

This friend of mine, she's not very bright, so she saw all that and rushed straight over to turn a coincidence into a joke. 'Oh God,' she gasped, 'they looked so whorish, you've got to promise me, when you unwrap them, you won't scream.'

Then she tried to frown, a feat that failed since her features have been very carefully frozen. Her beauty now so petrifying, her face scares off death.

And since she was so concentrated on making her own expression, she can't have noticed the look of utter dismay on my hot cheeks. Because whoever you're buying underwear for… it's not me.

And so I smiled at her, nodded at her, raised my eyebrows, shrugged my shoulders, willing her to stop talking so that I could kiss her twice, embrace her tightly and ask, incidentally, where had you gone? But I suspect she'd already had a lonely consolation drink since she pointed so imprecisely. And by then I was so mad to find you... damn her if she saw me run.

I thought I might yet catch you hiding somewhere. Under a cash register, behind a pillar, stuck explaining to a salesgirl why the knickers you wanted to buy were soaked in saliva. No such luck. So I tried your number again – again – from my phone and when you didn't answer, I asked to use the Selfridges line... then the pay phone in the Underground station.

But I'm such a fool. You'll have known it was me trying to call...

And if you'd picked up what would I have said?

'Happy Valentine's Day, baby...

'... scarlet lingerie?...

'... you really shouldn't have...

'... I'm so sorry I didn't get you anything...

'... but while I have you on the line...

'... I just wanted to say...

'... I hope...

'*you rot*

'*in hell.*'

But you didn't, so I sat on a kerb in Bond Street and cried. What to do, what to do?

Because it never occurred to me, in all the months since you left. It never occurred to – why didn't it occur to me? – that you'd simply replaced me with someone else.

I went back into the store to take a look at the mannequin, standing knickerless still. I don't know why. Perhaps I was studying the bra that remained. Or, more likely, fretting as to how you must have replaced me with another model. She's exactly my size, and no doubt – no doubt – two decades younger. Fresh and new. And to think how, when you left, I feared... idiot and fool... that you might be dead.

My darling, when you leave a woman, you ought, at least, to let her know. As it is I was surrounded by all your things, quite as if you would walk back through the door.

My darling, my darling: when you break a woman's heart you ought to tell her so.

So I went back home. Took a pair of scissors and a knife, ripped apart the silk shirts you left in all their manifold colours. Cut your ties in two, sliced through your suits. I ripped your affected books to shreds, made confetti of your papers. Disembowelled that enormous animal you won me at the fair, pulled out the stuffing and dumped the remains in a cardboard box. I tossed the whole lot out of the bedroom window, hoping to cheer myself up. But all I felt, staring down at my work, panting for air, was sweaty and breathless, miserable but warm. And I watched it there, in the shrubbery, through the intervening weeks. The box became sodden, an unsightly mess. I started thinking maybe I ought to bury it, for appearance's sake.

Meanwhile, my hands trembled and my head ached as if my nerves had been shattered by thinking of you again. Since you left I'd been working on my issues, which are deep-rooted and obscenely expensive. I'd been sober and almost sane. Sleeping, with the aid of pills, although now, no matter how many I take, I can't rest, so I go to bed and lie there for hours; it's as if I am vibrating.

Later that afternoon I went back out, bought a bottle of whisky, squinting so I couldn't see the love hearts in the shop. I had that pain in my throat that comes from staving off tears. Back home, as I opened the bottle and drank, I found myself staring at the chill, empty streets, before walking in the sad rain, determined to find you. I followed the river as it snaked silver in the low, greyish sun, walked until I was soaked to the bone.

Ten years ago, a man like you, I'd have eaten for breakfast. Yes, I'd have eaten you for breakfast, thrown you up by lunch. Feasted on a boy at dinner. But, instead, I fell in love. I don't think I need a reason for falling like I did. It was not my fault. The body concludes before the brain gets a vote. Love, when it comes, comes too quick for us to concur. And my heart was inflamed for a man such as you. Years before you arrived.

You're a little too short. You're a little too fat. But lying down in the dark something in me came alive that I'd thought long dead. For decades love had only visited in sleep. You were a waking echo of all I'd lost. The dream from which I used to wake and could not return no matter how I closed my eyes and prayed. And that's a better excuse than any I've heard. For falling in love. With a man like you. Better, I think, than lust. Better, I think, than boredom. Better, I think, than any of the excuses I've conjured in the past.

I don't know how long the binge lasted. I lose all track of time when I'm drunk. I consumed the best booze first, until I was numb, and then the bad until I slept. Always, when the alcoholic tingle reaches to my fingers and toes, my spirits rise and I am seized by the insatiable urge to dance. To 'Danke Schoen'. To Sinatra. I went out a lot, fortified by all the wine I had been saving as an investment. I had a lot of people around to drain the last of the champagne that I had reserved for victory and defeat. And when there was no one around, I danced with my mannequin. The best parties we had, she and I, playing all the records we liked best, discovering every ancient bottle, finishing every dreg. And when it was all done, I put her back in the corner, and went to bed to sleep it off. (To sleep you off.) And spent a fortnight there, holding my neck, crying.

So that is why I'm not sure, exactly, when the robberies commenced.

I'd been invited to a fancy-dress party. It is my rule to always attend a party, else one day they'll forget to invite you. And I felt I'd spent sufficient time cataleptic. I would pull myself together, try leaving the house. So I went to take a look at my bunny outfit. I wasn't intending to wear it. I just felt like reminiscing. About the days I went to parties dressed like that, if I wore anything at all. Perhaps I wanted to check if I could still get into it. That's a thing I like to do, from time to time. My confidence may be shot, but my body is as bold as ever.

So I pulled open the armoire, went to shake it out of the tissue paper, to find a drawer that was empty of anything save old cashmere cardigans. I pulled out the next drawer; also gone: my strawberry-patterned kimono. I used to wear that quilted Chinese silk kimono when recovering from the shows. Lying absolutely flat to stop the world convulsing, I would concentrate on the cool silk against my skin, avocado on face, cucumber on eyes.

After the accident, I didn't take it off for six months, which was why, when I recovered, I packed it up carefully, and consigned it to the back of a drawer. I pulled the armoire apart, to see if it had fallen down the back, but still couldn't find it.

One should never search for anything when vilely hungover. But I'd started and couldn't stop. It became clear that my house had been ransacked, peculiarly and subtly.

At first, I thought, it must be my fault. I'd rearranged things, drunk, and forgot; that sort of thing had happened before. I was always losing things. So I went through the attic, went through the garage, to see about the rest and found my most prized, irreplaceable possessions were missing... I felt very disorientated, since insomnia had me in its maniac grip. I wandered around the house all night, unable to sleep, admonishing myself to keep calm, keep calm, keep calm. And I began to notice that every room was curiously disarranged. Lighters, cigarette cases, sunglasses, handkerchiefs, all removed. My costume trunks pulled apart and everything gone: my mink, my sable, my chinchilla, the ocelot collar, the ermine wrap. The things I'd hidden, in improbable places, the Bulgari brooch in the cigar box, the golden salamander with an emerald tongue in the glasses case behind the books on the shelves. Oh, oh, oh, and all my Cartier pearls. My handbags. The lacquered Louboutins. Each and every suicidal stiletto. The too-high heels Ferragamo named after me.

I hate to go on… but even my scents that I kept at the back of the fridge, which I use like smelling salts to revive my feelings when I go dead: the smell of the night in Paris or Rio, what was tangled in my mother's hair, Eau Sauvage, Deci Dela… and this is when I screamed: my Schiaparelli lobster dress, the Lacroix matador jacket, the Sorbet dress Erté illustrated – each pressed and preserved professionally, and stored in the wardrobe in the basement – my Hermès scarves *and* the bloody Birkins.

I'm missing belts, corsets, stockings, suspenders. My shoes, my boots, my goddamn lingerie: each and every knick-knack of my brilliant career. My whole damn life in exhibits A to Z.

I didn't expect it would be Marzena, who comes to clean, but, callous as I am, I asked her anyway. She flew into a tantrum, bit her lip until it tripled in size, demanded to know: 'Vat vaz I implyink?' She smashed a glass and packed her things. I had to double her wages to get her to stay.

And that has made my life so very much worse, because I feel how she watches me now, with those petulant pinpricks that masquerade as eyes. As if she's poisoning me slowly with each coffee she makes and leaves, steaming, beside me on the windowsill.

I keep her every morning in my empty house, inventing jobs on purpose to annoy us both. Today, clean the back of my divested fridge. Tomorrow, polish the invisible artefacts that once adorned my bedroom. And, as there's nothing else to do, please polish the kitchen tiles so furiously that my silhouette may keep me company through these cold, sun-drenched, empty days.

One final hypothesis, before I confront the truth...

Yes, I thought of another explanation! My hands had trembled, incessantly, since you'd gone. My head was aching without cease. I got so lonely, I started to hear your voice, quite clearly, wherever I went.

And I've been talking to you, like this, constantly, ever since. I explain everything to you, although I know you can't hear. My memory has always been lousy but it's been getting worse. Perhaps, I concluded, there was something amiss with my mind.

Yes, that would explain why I spend all my time berating myself out loud.

So I called my doctor, diligently waited for an appointment. And, on the day, arrived much too early to sit in the waiting room as inconspicuously as I could manage. I flicked through the magazines, gingerly, with one finger, until disgust overcame me. Then I fixed on a sign on the wall that said 'one person, one problem' and cackled at the very idea.

The other patients glared as they sat there, pale and seething with germs, and when the doctor finally called my name I'd had enough. I refused to fill out a questionnaire about my mental health on grounds of irrelevance and demanded blood tests. Then we talked about what I ate and how I slept and how I felt: which is nothing, never and bad.

A few days later, I was summoned back to hear the worst, face-to-face. Convinced, absolutely convinced that I was dying, as the doctor lectured me, on and on, about all my filthy habits. Before breaking the news I'm in perfect health.

Underweight, alcoholic, chainsmoker I may be. But the moral of this story is (don't) eat. Drink and be merry.

And it was that day. That very day. The day I got back from the surgery, feeling – God help me – almost jaunty, that I discovered my mannequin was gone.

I went into the bedroom thinking I'd put my lucky dress on, go out for one, carefully chosen drink. I affirmed to the mirror that of all the men that have plagued me in the past, you are by far – I know it! – the least worth crying over...

And I was half-dressed already, one leg into a daring contraption by La Perla, just getting to grips with the hooks and ribbons, when glancing in the wardrobe mirror I noticed the bare wall behind me.

A blazing, an infuriating omission. I swung around and looked at the floor. Two dark green footprints on the sun-bleached carpet – and no mistaking it.

You had been here pilfering while I was out being told there was nothing wrong with me.

So I have to tell you honestly now. (For you are the one that lies.) That was it for me and you.

For this is the final loss I will not stand.

So I phoned the police and reported you for breaking and entering. Also for burglary, and fraud.

My darling: I have to admire you. How vicious and how clever that you should know exactly how to break me. For I've never broken – never broken once – since I was a child. As revenge – by God – yours is complete – for whatever it was I did.

But...

...I'm afraid, my dear, I can't let you get away with it. The police wouldn't take the matter seriously.

They made the whole affair ten times worse. I called up, explained the situation, and if they heard it was by a miracle because I'm sure they didn't listen. I was only half done going into the specifics when they cut me off and said you can't be charged with breaking and entering if you have a key to my house. They said it wasn't an emergency – in fact I ought to try to 'resolve the issue' myself.

Well, how is that feasible, I demanded, when you've gone, without telling me where you went?

How is that feasible, when you never, but never, answer your phone?

How is that feasible when you hide from me on sight?

Should I hire a private detective? (Yes, perhaps that's what I ought to do…) Or maybe I ought to leave a wheelbarrow outside the front door, just in case you fancy coming back for something you forgot?

And then the voice no longer sounded bored and started addressing me as 'madam', which only served to remind me, even more…

I hung up the phone, called the non-emergency number, and, rehearsing all the details again, in a tone of indignant rage, got results: a sore throat and a couple of young police officers dispatched. But even then they wouldn't help me. I had to drag them round the house, to the site of each theft, as they made notes and prepared to do next to nothing.

First, I took them to the pale rectangle on the living-room wall, where my Helmut used to hang. I was halfway through explaining how it was shot and what it would fetch if sold at auction today, when I could see in their faces, hear in their voices, that they were smothering laughter.

Well, no doubt it's quite preposterous to keep a portrait of your splendid flesh on the living-room wall. And a life-sized model version of yourself in the corner of the bedroom, oh,

yes, it's very comical, to live with your fibreglass doppelgänger.
I smiled, pretending to be in on the joke.

But I don't find it funny at all.

So I had to suffer the indignity of standing there, in the
middle of my living room, clinging onto the back of the
rattan chair until my knuckles turned white, trying to work
out if I were hallucinating.

What is the point of having had a career such as I've had
if one cannot display the fruits of it, prominently, in one's
interior decor? Personally, I would think it odd if, possessed
of a face and body like mine, all tributes to it were kept under
lock and key. People might assume portraits of me were
degenerating like the picture of Dorian Gray.

As it happens, my morals are perfectly intact, just like my
beautiful face. And this particular photograph, the notion of
which so amused the officers, was on billboards worldwide.
It was forty feet high, unveiled on Times Square. Here, the
press blamed it for traffic accidents in Piccadilly. They said I
caused men to lose all sense of direction.

And my mannequin, I refuse to be embarrassed about her
either. She is integral – absolutely integral – to my home.

An outfit, to be appreciated as it ought to be appreciated,
must be worn. Even a Galliano can't speak fully on a
coat hanger.

Over the years we have lived together, my mannequin
has been a great comfort to me, and a constant companion.
She has helped me cope with many of my most devastating
outfits. One only has to look at history to see the countless
women murdered by their own clothes. I dare to think how
much worse my life would have been, in all respects, had I
not had my mannequin to share the burden.

But I didn't know how to explain all this out loud. I
did not want them to snigger. I could just imagine, from

their half-smirks, how they'd climb into their squad car and start guffawing. So I said nothing, and watched as all chance of help receded, much like your hairline – and quite as inexorably.

All I could do was take them to the space where my mannequin once stood and conceive of sentences I failed to enunciate:

'I don't know how they make mannequins these days: no doubt in a factory, very cheaply, very shoddily. But when I was at my peak it was the done thing to make copies of real girls.

'And that decade, we weren't straight up, straight down like the models of today.

'My body was a wonder to behold. I was preserved exactly. 34-18-34. Lying on my side I was a rollercoaster ride.

'Now, I am a connoisseur of mannequins. I pause and reflect whenever I see them in the store. And they are never anything in comparison to mine.

'There are symmetrical dips where there ought to be eyes. A protuberance where there ought to be a nose. They are an assemblance of angles, in shining white plastic. That's all they are. Often nothing but a torso impaled on a metal stick. Each time I catch sight of one of those, I feel bereaved.'

But I didn't mention any of that.

All I managed to stammer was: 'This mannequin... she is my replica. She is, therefore, irreplaceable. This man' – *this man*, I said, I could have called you so much worse – 'has stolen not merely my possessions but an integral part of myself.'

So... let them laugh at that.

I ran out of inspiration, was defeated by their complacent faces.

Gathering themselves up, they repeated all the things I'd been told over the phone. They appreciated my distress – such a lovely phrase – but could take no further action. And since I myself admitted that you had a key to my house... since I myself admitted that I had not changed the locks... since I myself admitted that I wasn't a hundred per cent sure ...

(Although, I am, I am damn sure, that it was you.)

I don't know what came over me. Some surge of hope. I ran into the basement, and found the strips of sticky tape on which I had captured what I presume to be your fingerprints in talcum powder. And they stared at me as if I were insane.

All I could do, then, was show them to the door.

Thank them for their negligible efforts.

Watch as their car drew away.

And so I was left to wander around my empty house again, brooding over what to do.

I walked for hours, unable to settle. And since, by three in the morning, I'd still not reached any conclusion, I went back into the bathroom, and took the last of the sleeping pills, thinking it was time to go to bed.

I drew the curtains, switched off the light, lay there shivering in the dark, waiting for the drugs to do their work.

But I needed something stronger.

I had no peace. I couldn't rest. I got up.

Turning the lights back on, I took off all my clothes and retired to the corner, to stand with my feet on my mannequin's footprints, filling the emptiness.

And I tried to stay as serene as she was,
        as my tears dripped onto the floor...
                ... like when I was a girl.

I seemed to spend all my time hiding in corners. I'd close my eyes and pretend to be a model: perfect, pristine, inviolable. I'd practise being peachy limbs and silken hair, no way to get inside, no heart and no mind. If I was perfectly still, my stepfather might fail to find me. But my lips were always moving, murmuring, moaning. And my eyes always leaking as my mother lay, pale and weak, dying in a bed upstairs. She did not know. What happened in the dark.

That's when I learned to lie. I learned to lie early and I learned to lie well. That was when I first decided that I would, one day, not have to be like that. I let the tears dry on my face. I stood, made up, with unflinching gaze. And that's called lying by omission.

It's a rare talent, a fantastic skill, being able to lie so well that no one can ever tell. The trick is to make yourself believe it. Even you, who are so practised at it, look nervous, obfuscate and perspire.

But you're a man of means. I don't imagine you've ever had to alter your fate. You weren't born to one life and interfered with but determined to enjoy another. You may have seized your chances, but I'm sure you never had to make them out of nothing.

I don't like to talk about, and I don't like to think of, the time before I escaped the house of silence in which I grew up. But that is where my discipline grew.

It was a boyfriend who found the magazine competition. Not the first of his sex, and not the last, to stick to me like thunderflies in sweat. They knew, somehow, how did they know, that all my innocence had long been stripped? I wish, one day, you'd tell me how they sense it, smell it, breathe it. Whatever it is that marks me out.

So this boyfriend, a little rich boy from the valley, took a picture of me with the camera he'd been given at Christmas and said we'd split the money if I won. If I lost, he said, I had to stop staring at myself in the mirror. I had to stop behaving like I was so much better than I was.

I could tell he thought I hadn't a hope as he laughed at *me*, a species of joke. Repeatedly, ceaselessly, laughing through the day, laughing through the night. And he was still laughing, I imagine, right up until I won.

But I wouldn't know. Because I left him. The moment I seized the envelope.

I was waiting for, expecting that letter. I knew it was coming; I knew that the magazine would select my face. I'd known it immediately, looking at the photograph. For my face appeared so startling. Impossible to resist.

I was obsessed with the comings and goings of the postman. Until one Saturday morning that pristine envelope dropped onto the mat.

I was there, ready to tear it open, run upstairs and pack. I'd been waiting for the slightest excuse. But this was better. And I sat, calmly, in the corner of my mother's room, telling her what I'd done. Since she made no sound at all, I lay down beside her for the whole afternoon, holding her hands and breathing in her hair. She did not know that her husband would never have let me alone. And if she had, she would have wanted me to go.

Still, I know there is something very wrong with me to have left her like that, not quite alive and not quite dead. A ruthlessness, a callousness, a coldness: to have taken all her scent, her best clothes and her best shoes, together with all the money that was hidden in the house. But back then I felt I couldn't keep myself together. I thought, one day the truth would get too much. And in that quiet house I'd scream and scream and never stop.

In London, I knew, I could erase all of that. Devise a new name, a new age, a new personality. And I thought I'd change it every decade to amuse myself, to fit in with the friends I had or the lover I enjoyed. I laugh, looking back, at all the lies

I told. I see them, standing out like the scars that map the veins on my wrist.

I don't remember much of the magazine luncheon.

It was the first time I drank alcohol. It tasted foul but I liked it right away, for it mended my nerves until sure enough all the other guests' heads swam and blurred. I wore a tight pink satin dress I'd stolen from my mother and her heels, which pinched. I had grown too tall. Halfway through the dinner, the dress split at the back as I bent over to retrieve a knife I had dropped on the floor, and I had to hold my seams for the rest of the evening. I felt their eyes constantly turned to me, as if trying to fathom a mistake.

It was all I could do not to cry. I sat and ate nothing, hid the food from my plate. Dug my nails into my palms until I drew blood, and since that made me calm I did not disappear. Long after everyone in the room was filthy drunk, it was, apparently, time that I was shown to the woman who had chosen me. They told me – in what they believed to be whispers – that she had an all-presiding gift. But now… she didn't have long to live. We went up three flights of narrow stairs to a tiny room at the top where a fire was raging in the hearth and it was hot as all hell. I had to shrink to fit.

Lying on a couch, covered with a blanket, was a woman in miniature. They told me to sit next to her so she could look at my face, but she only took my hand and turned it over as if reading my palm. She was as shrivelled and dried up as a long-dead leaf; she looked as if she would crumble into dust if I touched her. And when she'd finished peering at me all she said was 'yes, yes, yes' and seemed to turn to the rest of them as if wondering why they weren't in my thrall. And then she started cackling as if she were mad.

I thought they would throw me out then and there; she wasn't in a position to dictate terms. But the shoot went ahead, according to her instruction. And since they vehemently disagreed with a decision they considered crazed they turned it into an exercise in humiliation. The sort I was to endure, over and over, in my early years. I stood in the centre of an opulent room, with Louis Quinze chairs, half-naked, as they debated, quite openly, what they considered my defects as if I were deaf, pointing and sneering as if I were blind.

All they agreed on was how very wrong I was – and they kept muttering: to think *I* was the last *she* picked… my face was too smooth, too plain, too blank: they couldn't see what she saw in it. My eyes too perplexing – changing with the light, having no colour of their own. My hair too anarchic and wild, while my body, which ought to have been as slender as a blade, swelled, alarmingly, at the hips and the bust.

I was tall enough and thin enough, but it was as if I was cursed: I could not smile. They'd tell me to – such a simple thing – and tears would come instead. Oh it was my fault, my grievous fault, but there was nothing I could do.

I moved from place to place, a precarious sort of life I lived, always struggling. Doing anything I could so as to accumulate money. I washed dishes, waited tables, cleaned rooms.

I worked hard to get my tear sheets and test shots. I laboured on and on, no matter how I failed. I went to every casting, regardless of whether they asked for me. I grew even thinner, eating next to nothing, living on tinned pears, tomato soup heated on a Primus stove.

I tried to attract the right men. Men who would help. But whatever I felt for them, none of them stuck. I secured a few catalogue bookings, since there was no faulting my never-ending legs. But I wanted to be more than that. I had ideas…

Other girls gave up, got married and fat, but I persisted. At the castings, when I wasn't booked, I'd hang around and make myself useful to the models. I started to revenge myself upon them by appropriating any pretty things they left lying about.

If you saw pictures of them, you would think their lives were so very glamorous. You wouldn't be able to tell that they found their days so very dull. A model's main duty was to wait and repeat. It was partly the boredom that led them to drink and do all the other things that they shouldn't have done. Because after a while they got to like it like that. After a while they were too stoned to know where they were, and that played into my hands…

It was useful, having me around, seemingly sane and sober. A regular Cinderella, sweeping the floor, always ready to make good the carnage the girls left in their wake. To style a shot with the props I had to hand. I learned how to set their hair, apply make-up, and then I'd lend out my pilfered jewels to add a little depth. To set off a collarbone, flatter a wrist. They tolerated me if I was helpful.

All the time, I kept my mouth shut and my eyes open. As the other girls enjoyed themselves, unthinking, squandering their gifts, luxuriating in their own radiance. Radiance – I could have told them – wouldn't last. And I shudder to think at how those girls ended up. The ones I hated with all my heart. Puffy all over, faces lined. The legacy of all those days we spent together. When they never once went home to stare in the mirror, despising their own face, thinking, always thinking, how to fix it so they would be beautiful. Forever.

At the shoots, I'd lock myself in the bathroom, climb into the empty bathtub and clamp my head between my knees. That was my technique for when my head wouldn't stop roaring. It was a talent I developed, pulling myself together, persisting. I concentrated on the cool porcelain against my skin, concentrated on the pattern, whatever it was, that spread all over the bathroom wall. I bit down hard on my knee and counted out the breaths until the tooth marks faded.

And I'd ask myself questions, until I found answers. I read so many books. I came to understand that the stories we tell about ourselves are vital. That our lives are shaped, for better or worse, by our own narrative. So I told myself that it was good to be overlooked and ignored in the ranks of the adored.

I started to believe that, one day, I'd get my reward. All those days I spent, walking home alone, a dismal shadow in the late-evening sun. Or sitting and watching, appalled, as the successful models made love to the camera without ever feeling nervous or embarrassed or ashamed.

For that was my problem: the thing I could not do. No matter how fiercely I tried I could not stand in front of a camera and smile. I would stand there trying to make myself, but the second I managed it my whole face turned livid. I blushed, madly, from head to toe. I tried. I tried so hard, spent hours practising; I so desperately wanted to emulate the other girls. To outdo them all. But my lips would not turn up at the corners. The only way I could work was to stand, hand on hips, and scowl.

I was full of rage.

Beauty, most people think, is a blessing one is born with, but that's a lie, like everything else. Beauty is a matter of willpower. As a man, I don't expect you to understand. How I had to spend all my time coming to terms with the fragile glow of my face, marvelling at how my colouring altered with the light.

Back then, I assumed my beauty would fade same as any other girl's. That my skin would crease and my cheeks wither. So I was haunted by the knowledge that, if I could only get my picture taken, I'd never die at all.

It's there in the Old Masters. A woman alive, her beauty

still ablaze when her billion sisters merely died – as if they'd never existed. I knew I had no discernible talent. I could not paint or write or think. I had to be preserved by other means. And so a photographer becomes not a man but a god, annihilating who he pleases and creating who he wills. And since it seemed I was heading straight to hell...

Naked, I knew I was as close as a flesh-and-blood model would ever get to a blank canvas, with my clear face standing out like the moon on a clear frosted night. And since I already knew that if you want anything in life you have to connive at it relentlessly, I was tired of hoping to be discovered. I set out to find my fame.

I scoured every magazine, every newspaper, every party, every show for an artist. The search was long and hard, but – for you, my dear – I'll cut it short.

I stumbled across Frank's pictures in a dingy little gallery in the East End. What I was doing there, I don't remember; I was very probably drunk, but if I close my eyes, that first sequence still stands out clear in my mind.

It was six Polaroids of a concrete building. A girl was climbing up the sheer face, God knows how she managed it, in a swimming costume and red lacquered heels. In the fifth shot she had reached the top. In the sixth, her body lay back down on the pavement. The colour of her shoes matched exactly the blood that spilled from her mouth.

Seeing it, my hair stood on end, a coldness shrieked up my spine, and I came alive. This photographer, whoever he was, showed the world as I knew it to be: at once doomed and sublime. I questioned the attendant who stood, yawning, in a corner. He knew nothing about the show, was apparently only there to ensure nothing was stolen.

So I lay in wait for the owner of the work, who, when he finally appeared, told me he had found the collection, as it was, in Paris, in the studio of this mad little man who looked like a peasant in the background of a Bruegel painting.

And when I had Frank's name it didn't take me long to find a newspaper report about the death of that girl who'd scaled the concrete building. Shortly after Frank had sold the Polaroids, she had plunged from the open window of his fifth-floor studio. When questioned, her relatives said she had disappeared altogether, several years before. They hadn't known she'd been with Frank. And his only comment struck them as strange. He said, of her death, that she'd believed she was a bird and she'd flown. She had landed on the cobbles below, not for lack of trying to take flight, the blood streaming from her head, but her lips too pale to match.

And since he claimed this vision was so much more beautiful than he'd imagined, he was arrested and questioned, then and there. No defence wounds, no signs of interference, were to be found on her body. A post-mortem showed she'd been high, while Frank was clean. And after that there was one further reference to him, before all mentions stopped, describing how he had gone back to the police station after he was released without charge, demanding to be interned again. For he was treated like a murderer, wherever he went. His work, he complained, had suffered, since everyone shunned him and no model would pose.

And since they refused to detain him on these grounds, he took off all his clothes, and made such a scene someone took a picture of *him*, which I still have, in a cutting…

The article was dated half a year previously. But I saw my chance. All I could do was pray that he was still alone. I made my preparations. What I needed was the right dress. And I found an emerald green Dior gown on a bedroom floor upstairs at a house party I'd not exactly been invited to in a mansion block in Kensington. It fitted like a dream.

I fled, I raced, I ran to get to him before some other girl had the same idea. I spent most of the money I'd saved on a ticket. I tramped around Paris with my faltering French, utterly determined to find him. And then I sat in the café he was said to frequent, waiting to see if he would appear. I would sit all day in my unconscionable dress, as the waiters eyed me with derision.

I bought coffee and sat before the cup for hours. It was too cold to stand and wait outside. But it didn't matter how long I spent waiting for him to appear… I asked the staff, sought directions to the studio he was said to have, but they shrugged, nonplussed, claimed not to know, asked, in their best French way, if later I'd care for a drink…

I was in a phone booth studying the telephone directory, searching again for his name, when I found at my feet a shrunken catalogue – watermarked, no cover – and on the first few pages unmistakably his Polaroids, reproduced, and an address printed in tiny letters on the back. That is how I found and set siege to his door.

I absconded from my hotel, took a room opposite so I could study him, analyse his movements, as he came and went. I'd connive at a meeting, make it a happy accident. But from the first he wouldn't play along. I'd waited for days, I'd waited for weeks – I'd waited for months, waited for years…

My assessment of time has never been accurate, so I can't say exactly how long it took.

I can tell you only how it felt when I determined to break in. I took my precious dress to the dry cleaners, put it on one final time, made up my face, lingered, very unobtrusively, outside the fire escape, and when the door opened for the couple who came out at eleven each morning to share a cigarette and kiss, I slipped in and up the stairs.

Five flights, and at the top his door, where I knocked, tentatively at first and then desperately and incessantly, as he didn't answer. I sensed, somehow, that he was standing behind the door, his interest aroused by my distress and, further, by the rage he could see flare within me. As I thought of how I had spent all my money, of how I had eaten nothing in days, of how I had worked so very hard, and got nowhere. Of how I had been alone, all my life, of how I had allowed myself – so stupid – to hope, and had those hopes smashed every time my fist failed to rouse him to the door.

And as I fell to the floor I knew, in that moment, I'd reached the end. That every effort I'd ever make would fail. That soon I would fade. That soon I would die – having accomplished worse than nothing – and no one would ever remember my name. And to stop myself crying, I thought how to end it all. How pretty I'd look in my final dress, standing on the Pont Marie, plunging into the Seine.

And that, of course, was when he let me in. Frank spoke no English; I spoke appalling French. But he held a hand out and made a show of wanting to see my identification papers. I didn't understand until much later, when I realised how superstitious he was, that he wanted to check my birth sign. He entertained about a thousand conflicting suspicions and exercised them all at once. He would have thrown me out, then and there, if he'd not found what he wanted. But this… this was my first and last piece of luck. He held open the door and I walked through.

Frank's studio was completely black: the walls, the floors, the ceiling, the windows. Everywhere there were half-built sets under pools of concentrated light, a mannequin posed wherever he lacked a model. And these enamelled dolls arrogantly flaunted the latest fashions, quite exactly as if they were real. Gold was the colour of the season, and so they shone like angels, their faces he'd made up so cleverly – if you had only half an eye on them, you'd swear they were looking at you.

In the centre of the room there was a vast trestle table on which papers, notebooks and Polaroids were scattered. Each picture was planned to an infinitesimal degree. With canvases, too, which he'd attempted to paint, stood up on easels or ripped apart and discarded on the floor. The whole place was a violent mess. I didn't see how he could live in it, since there was nothing to sit on, no comforts at all. No telephone, no television, nothing but sets and lights and mirrors. A stove in one corner, but no fire in the grate; it was so cold it hurt to breathe.

There was another tiny room at the back, with a bed stripped down to a single white sheet, a wash basin concealed by a curtain, a vase of long dead violets, petals dust on the sill, the scent so faint, almost imperceptible. To the other side, there was a sort of kitchen that served as his darkroom, in which he looked like a grinning devil, bathed in its dull red light. And in this gloom I stumbled over the half empty bottles strewn across the floor.

Frank went to the bed. He didn't talk or offer me a drink. He simply looked at me, as if half-starved and shown a feast, and opened a box that lay underneath, withdrawing a necklace that he drew around my throat. He told me to strip and lie down on my back. His eyes explored me from every angle, searching my body, and when he found the constellation of Capricorn, charted by the moles on my back, if any doubt remained in his mind about my suitability for the task, it was vanquished forever. He swept the mannequins off his sets, and instructed me how to pose as they turned their disappointed faces to the wall.

It all went so fast, I couldn't stop to think. My breath made clouds and I lost all feeling in my fingers and my toes. When the cramp came, I could have cried out in pain, but he ordered me to hold still. All he took was Polaroids, hundreds and hundreds, before he took me to bed. And when it was all over, and I lay shivering, he suddenly started to talk. He talked and talked and talked. And, however hard I stared at him, I couldn't understand.

Later on, I'd try to recall the phrases, willing myself to translate in retrospect. I thought he'd told me something vital, then, that I'd missed. He ran a bath, to warm me up; sinking into the water, my skin was set on fire. And as soon as I was clean, he made me dirty again as with his camera we did it all again: endlessly, endlessly, endlessly. For days and weeks and months. Every minute spent taking my picture and doing whatever else he pleased.

He was so happy looking at me through a lens; it was all he would do. He pored over every bit of me as a scholar obsessed by some indecipherable text. He took me just as I was and made me better. He told me what to do, and seemed to approve of me because I always did as I was bid without complaint. He looked at me with that hunger of his, as I had prayed, long ago, the man I loved would. And all the time we worked, he never once asked me to smile. Nothing would be faked.

Even later on, when our pictures were published and he became the most famous, the most celebrated, the most sought-after photographer in Paris, he would refuse to look at – let alone photograph – anyone but me. I had appeared to him as a thing of wonder, and he would not give me up.

His lust for me was insatiable. I scarcely deserved it, in those early days, when he was still teaching me what to do. As we worked out how to speak to each other. He picked up my English, better than I did his French, thanks to that irritating habit I still retain of talking to myself, non-stop, out loud.

Once, when he was a little drunk, after we'd had published

our most extravagant, exuberant, exotic shots yet, he acted out a little charade, with broken phrases, as to how, when he saw me, through his camera, he got electrocuted. Not a static shock but the kind you'd get if you scaled a telegraph pylon and hung yourself from the wires. Volts shooting through your skeleton, frying your flesh, incinerating your bones.

Frank taught me how to turn it on. He transformed me, exactly as I needed to be transformed. He kindled whatever spark was in me into total flaming beauty. My skin, so very pale, he made like milk; my lips, so delicate, he made like blood. My eyes like preternatural water. My long, wild, colourless hair he dyed a deep red, so it blazed around my head as if I was burning at the stake.

He shot me to excess. Nothing was left to chance.

The images we made together were like nothing anyone had ever seen. Not mere photographs, they were artworks – and they caused a sensation. But we didn't care about that, we continued because we were obsessed only with making more. All the magazines and designers started to send us clothes, commissioning Frank to shoot next season's look. But though it was said they went into paroxysms over our work, if I wore the clothes at all, they'd end up on the floor. We experimented relentlessly. I knew when I realised I'd not seen another soul in so long, and didn't in the slightest bit care, that we were lost to the world.

But that is what it is like, falling in love. A perilous, unnatural state. And ever since, I look at anyone I meet, wondering if it ever happened to them.

In all the years since, I find it so odd… How everyone talks about falling in love. And never once does anyone tell you… how to get out again.

I was in love with a madman, that much I knew, from the very start. There was a wildness in his eyes I couldn't mistake.

But I was so consumed by him, I didn't care. And he was so pleased with me, then, that it wasn't so bad. He'd been longing for a girl to arrive, and he was so delighted in me, couldn't tear his eyes off me, he kept repeating, *ma femme, ma femme, ma femme*. Naked to his whim, we plunged into a sort of ecstasy. Oh, it was all so perfect, so neat, so symmetrical: he'd waited quite as long for me as I had for him.

He had planned out the tableaux we staged meticulously. Somehow, we knew instinctively when a picture worked. And we'd retreat, to stand in the darkroom, waiting for the magic arrival of my face on paper. And then such pleasure was ours: we were so impulsive, our madness spread, we knew we'd made it...

But, even in the halcyon days, I could trace his tendencies.

Too often, he'd push me a little further than I could go, for the pleasure of seeing me snap. And then he'd come over, so extraordinarily sweet, trying to cure me, making me cry, making me laugh, all at once, until I was so bewildered I too went half out of my mind. Under his kisses, my body experienced such frissons and spasms and shocks.

And I'd taken such pains; I was desperate to please him. I forgot. I lived for my man. Oh, it would have been fine if only he'd been good. But he was a sort of demon, always changing shape.

I could, perhaps, have learned exactly what he liked, if only he knew. But what soothed him one moment enraged him the next. He was consistent only in the way he liked his tea. That was all I managed to get right. And even now I make the same foul brew. I make it precisely as he showed me, leaving it to stew until the water was black. I make it and I still don't like it, but I drink it all the same, a habit I can't break. As the steam rises, he materialises in the next room, only to dissipate when I walk through the door.

I expected us to be content when he became famous and celebrated and adored. I thought that's what we were working towards. But success only seemed to bring Frank a pressure he had never felt before.

One day, Frank will be acknowledged as a genius. I know he will, for he elevated photography to an art. But he was never satisfied. The more we accomplished, the more disillusioned he became. Always, always, there was something wrong that worried him more than he could bear; like a single speck of cloud on a horizon that must be clear. He wanted to rival Leonardo or Michelangelo, and since he couldn't, he began to despise what we *could* do.

He wanted to create mythic, fantastic scenes: the martyrdom of St Catherine, body broken on a wheel; the rape of Leda, Eurydice lost like a ghost in hell. And, having decided in advance that it could never come off the way he wanted, he put a sort of hatred into our work. I came to dread his books, for I played all the parts.

I know that muses must bear such things, that this is the price we must pay. It's true: 'a beautiful body perishes, but a work of art dies not'. I wasn't the first woman made physically ill, having to lie seven hours a day in a freezing bath while my man made me Ophelia, drowned. But he abused me, vilely, when I didn't come off as ravishing as a Pre-Raphaelite.

Afterwards, he'd sulk – superhuman sulks. He'd not speak to me for weeks, labouring over his sketches, tearing up paper, screaming that he had no ideas left. He worked himself into such a state he couldn't eat, couldn't sleep, couldn't breathe. He'd fly into incoherent, inconsolable rages, take knives from the kitchen and saw at his wrists, bleeding and drinking and howling. And then, once, he turned on me, held the blade to my throat, and for the first and last time I was so frightened that when he relaxed his grip I fled.

And running down all those steps on my weak, bony legs, feeling the savage sun on my thin papery skin, I became so dizzy and so disorientated, in the heat and the dust and the noise, that I fainted, and a doctor was found for me, and I was taken back inside. The doctor took one look at the both of us, sick in heart, sick in mind, and prescribed tranquillisers and sleeping pills.

I never took mine, for when the doctor left Frank ate them both, and slept, and was restored.

We got back to work. Pictures, more pictures, more pictures. Such beautiful things. Such beautiful things. His inspiration returned and we carried it off better, spread after spread caused a sensation. And, for a time, we had success, until... until... once more the herograms overcame him, and he got desperate again.

So we summoned the doctor. That damned doctor, with all his pills. Frank had a liking for them. Always doubled his dose. When his waking mind was empty, he took sleeping pills and the ideas came to him in dreams. So he started to take them all the time, and, pursued by images all through the night, he'd have me wake him up and talk to him, so we could make notes.

And in the morning I'd make his cup of tea, leave it by the bed and bring him round, enjoying his scented flesh, our shadows kissing on the wall. Often I felt as if we were, so very nearly, returning to those early days of rapture. But when I read back through the scrawled notes, and saw what we were to do, I felt a slow sort of horror.

He had me reconstruct the suicide of his mother. He shot me, in the night, lying naked on her grave. He wanted me mutilated, bloodied and bruised; the dead girl at a crime scene. I didn't like it. He dreamed, always, of death and decomposing flesh, of rats and fleas and lice and wasps. Of bile and bones and gore. In the notebook he'd dreamed of an explosion – the leg torn clean off, still wearing its beautiful shoe.

So I'd portray the leg, would have to hold my breath and sink down in the bath, which had been filled with black stage paint, and he'd shoot my bare white limb, sticking out of the gloom. He'd wrap my head up, tight, in plastic, have me breathe through a straw as I shivered and felt so unwell. And afterwards we'd find the paint had seeped through and there was no getting the enamel out of my hair.

There was nothing for it – he shaved my head and then remarked that without my hair I was nothing at all. Forced me back in the bath, and photographed my bald, dirty, disembodied head. Even then I didn't complain, not even when he started to taunt me, not even when he told me I was getting ugly. Ugly and old. Muses suffer, muses die – and their image is immortal. That was the deal I made. All the while his camera was infatuated with me, I let Frank do as he liked. He was less, and much more, than a man. To me, he was a kind of god.

I thought, I felt, I knew… he was about to cast me out. That I was finished. Over. Done. So I was surprised, but, of course delighted, when he proposed. Past the point where I was sure – so sure – he was tired of me.

But I was a woman in love with a man. Not one single part of me said no. We were married in the dead of night, in the studio, by some obliging priest and two drunk witnesses, summoned out of nowhere, and, after they left, he took our picture under the lights as we drank champagne and danced. And I was so happy, I should have known it couldn't last, I threw my head back and laughed. I fell asleep. And my mouth… was *smiling*.

Only, I woke to a bitter headache, as he announced that my modelling days were over. No wife of his would make an exhibition of herself as I had up to that point.

That morning, Frank sent the word out that he wanted to use other girls. And they came in their hundreds, they came in their thousands, stampeding our door. Imploring him, begging him, promising to do anything, if only he would take them, each knowing that he had the power to make them a star. Suddenly, the studio door was opened up, not our private space anymore, as they auditioned, one by one. I made my excuses, went to sit in the bedroom, but Frank made it clear: I was to watch while he ordered them into one position after another, just as he'd done with me.

In the summer, he dressed them in leather, had them wilt, desperate for water, burning under the lights, wrapped up in vinyl, roasting in their own sweat, to enjoy the sight of them slowly passing out.

In winter, he'd audition them in their knickers and have them dance about for him with violet nipples. He stretched them until they split.

He had two types he liked. Those who cried were booked and subjected to further cruelties on an actual shoot. Those who concealed their discomfort were afterwards treated with courtesy and respect, but he rarely gave them any sort of role.

He refused to hire assistants, didn't want anyone else around, so I was to apply the paint and strip them of their clothes. I despised myself but I was complicit in it all.

Another English girl, like me only five years younger, came to sit for him. He asked her questions very quickly as he played about with the lights. Her age, her star sign, what she wanted for lunch, as if he had no interest – was not even listening – to her answers.

So she rambled on, so enthusiastic, trying to sound better than she was, lying about her age, rattling on about the sign of Aquarius, how she'd been reared a vegetarian. He had her wait while he auditioned the other models, and then, after making her stay three hours more while he fiddled about with his set design, Frank said he wanted her, she should come back the next day. She was thrilled, so happy, and no disguising it. And I hated her because she looked like me.

For these new shoots with these new girls, Frank overcomes his agoraphobia, arranges shoots outside the studio, and makes all kinds of effort he never made for me. So for this job we meet in the street, just after sundown. It's a hot evening, and sticky, we walk for half an hour or more, up and down tiny cobbled streets, searching for the right alley, and then, when he finds where we're meant to be, we walk up a sharp flight of stairs, straight into a butcher's shop. She starts to laugh, a little nervously, thinking it must be a joke.

But we go inside and he insists she take off all her clothes, tells her to sit on the counter, legs parted and dangling, to display the high-heeled shoes as he'd shown her the day before. She is a tall girl, almost as tall as me, so her head is level with three skinned calf heads strung from the ceiling above. Live, their lolling tongues would be licking her hair.

Frank is very busy, talking to the butcher, ignoring the little sounds she makes, the little sniffs, the slight expressions, and I keep my eyes firmly on the ground. Frank is still talking to the butcher, who, as he makes to leave, puts his hand behind the counter, draws something out, and slaps a slab of rancid liver between her thighs.

It's hot the way Paris gets hot in July, so hot and stifling. And it stinks, all this meat, and seems to attract every fly in the whole city. She tries very hard as they gorge on her lap. She tries to hold the pose. And she almost manages it; I can feel her struggle as I stare, stubbornly, at the floor, her neck contorting, exactly like mine, as she tries to swallow her tears. Her eyes stinging as they start to trickle in two lines… and that, of course, was all he wanted. She can't read him, but he's snapping away, thinking: *magnifique*. I can tell, just by looking at him, that he's got the shot. But he continues to take her picture, pleasured by the scene.

She stands up and throws the meat at him. Her aim is no good. She misses. But then she yells the type of yell that, even in heat, makes you go cold all over.

And runs out of the butcher's shop, naked except for her high-heeled shoes, not stopping to collect her clothes.

Frank starts laughing. He never laughs at anything, but he laughs at this, shakes his head, starts packing up.

Then he turns to me and says: '*Ces modèles sont inutiles. Elle a un visage comme une tarte.*' And that, I think, is the closest he ever came to saying: *ma femme, ma femme.* I love you like no other on earth.

He auditioned hundreds of red-headed girls after that. Not a single one showed anything like my talent, my devotion, my skill. Naked, cradling a giant rat, I didn't sob. Dangling from gymnast stirrups for hours in suspender belt and stilettos, I never whimpered. Boiling alive under hot lights in a leather catsuit. Handcuffed in a back-bend for the best part of a day. Recreating the crucifixion. The burning of Joan of Arc. Every inch of my skin covered with glue and sequins until I felt like I might die of asphyxiation because he'd had some nightmare in luminescence.

I collapsed, many times, and it was up to him, if he chose, to bring me round. He could have killed me at any stage, and admired the deed. There was, for Frank, a perfection I could only achieve if absolutely dead. But, by this point, he said barely anything to me at all.

The sleeping pills were making him sluggish. He piled on weight, which slowed him down. So he had the doctor come again, and prescribe more drugs – to wake him up – and since this doctor was so obliging, Frank soon became dependent on the very worst sort of stimulant until his nightmares continued whether he was asleep or awake.

Once more, he retreated into the darkness of his studio, the only place he felt safe, and I'd find him talking to himself in the bath. Unable to recognise me at all, he was convinced that rivals were crawling into his brain and clearing it out. I tried, I was desperate, to persuade him otherwise. But it was true: the other photographers had seized on his techniques, were producing work as bright and bold as Frank's was now dark and artificial.

With every effort I made to pacify him, he became more frenzied, accusing me of betraying him, of sleeping with other men, and since he'd reached that conclusion, he wouldn't let me out of his sight for a second, followed me wherever I went, watched me while I slept. The shoots became rarer and rarer, but when they went wrong – as they always did – he turned on me, rather than the model.

For the September spread, the pinnacle of our year, he planned to reconstruct the beheading of Mary Hamilton. An awful tale about a Russian emperor whose mistress killed their child and so he had her put to death. But spectacular, there was no denying it; the dresses we'd been sent were breathtaking.

So the Tsar, he kisses Mary Hamilton, before the swordsman cuts off her head. And everyone agrees it was the most gorgeous head they ever saw. And then the Tsar, he holds it up, severed and bloody, and he kisses her again. Drops it, and leaves.

The model Frank had chosen took one look at what she was supposed to do and walked. And Frank was in such a rage, he took the sword and destroyed the set, and, beating me with his bare fists, dragged me through the streets by my hair.

I knew, then, I knew very well he was going to kill me. I knew very well it would only be a matter of time. And I became exhausted waiting for death to come.

He was still dreaming, still striving for the perfect shot, the shot that forever eluded him. But the models wouldn't work with him anymore. And he wouldn't use me, no matter how much I prayed to him. For a while, he returned to his old dead dolls that he had used to stage his inventions before I arrived.

The September spread was a failure. Every frame was scrapped. And when Frank received the news he couldn't seem to take it in, continued walking up and down the studio, up and down, up and down, waiting for the customary praise. When the plaudits failed to come, after a while he seemed to forget what agitated him, and went back to his camera.

Pictures, so many pictures he took. Directing new models that cavorted before his eyes. But even they would not take instruction. The air was made of curses as he worked and worked. I couldn't watch him, I went into the bathroom, climbed in the tub, and bit my knee. I listened as his voice faded away. Feeling how he relaxed as he came to a climax, got the shot. And then his footsteps on the bare boards as he went into the darkroom, anticipating the delicious aftermath: his ideas made real, with chemicals and paper...

And then the howl, the raw mad howl, as even Frank could see that all he'd shot was an empty room.

That was the night he set about destroying my image. Convinced, utterly destroyed by the fact, that everything he had ever produced was worse than nothing and therefore that it should not exist. He was haunted by my face, the way it used to be. He needed to clear it from his mind, to start again, afresh. And perhaps then he would be free. To take a picture which was perfect, that would be printed so everyone, everywhere, at last, would see...

All the time we'd lived together, I'd kept Polaroids, photographs and negatives, magazines, adverts and posters, preserved and catalogued exactly and discreetly amid the chaos in which he liked to exist. Frank, I knew, hated that, and I'd had to be clever, to keep it from him, moving it, always, out of his reach if he descended into a rage. Screaming about how he had wasted his time, how he had failed God, offended mankind, because his work was never of the quality it should have been. And now, and now, I could see, by his crazy movement, he was fixated on the one thing I had left. He had found matches, had found oil, and was limbering up to burn the lot.

So, for the first and last time, I hit him with one of his books as hard as I could around the head, and then I dragged him – somehow I dragged him – into bed. And when he came round, he complained about the feeling in his skull, so I made him a pot of foul black tea and gave him tranquillisers, telling them they would help.

If there was one thing Frank loved, it was pills in every colour, so he was pleased enough to drink them all down with his tea. And I watched him – God knows how I watched him – as he fell asleep; the occasional starts as he fell into the deep. And I told him – God knows how I told him – that tomorrow everything would begin again. That when we woke up all the best of us would survive. And all that was rotten would wither away and die...

And then I drank his foul black tea and took the pills that he'd left. And I held him – God knows how I held him – as I went the same way, slipping, inexorably, into nothingness.

Next morning I woke, very much later than usual, exhausted still, and dead in mind. And then I did what I always did every morning of my life, I got up and I made some tea and I left a cup by the side of the bed.

And, confronted by the wreck of the day before, I went into the studio to clean up the mess. I picked up all the negatives Frank had spilled on the floor. Made good with the photographs, filed the magazines, the adverts, the posters in a new place that would take him time to find. And then I took every pill and powder he had lying about and flushed it all away, every trace. I took all the knives and put them in a bag and threw them away.

And I knew when he saw what I'd done, he'd scream and scream, again. And I started to laugh – God, how I laughed – a terrible laugh, thinking of how, just lately, he'd told me I must stop thinking for myself. Because he could hear all my thoughts as I sat there silent, in the dark; my very presence was ruining his life… my thoughts were poisoning him… I had to stop. He'd had enough.

And, pretty soon, I found I was cleaning up the whole filthy studio… thinking I might as well be hung for a sheep as for a lamb… and after an hour I found nothing I did helped disguise the squalor. And, having failed to improve anything very much, I gave up and went to run Frank his bath.

I think all the time, yes, I think I knew, all along… that Frank was dead. I think I felt it in the night, when he stopped breathing. I think, when I woke, I sensed somehow – he smelled different to the night before. Yes, I think I knew, before I made the tea.

So, you see, my love, why I'm telling you this.

You see, don't you, what I need you to know?

How I have survived.

So much worse.

Than you…

*

Frank hadn't made a will. But I was his wife, and he had no other relatives, so I inherited everything. At that time, it was mostly debt for all the drugs and props and kit. His grand concepts laid waste to money, but he was so disordered he never kept track of what he was paid. I needed to fight to get everyone who'd commissioned him to pay what he was owed. But I didn't have the strength for it. Not then.

Without Frank, I collapsed altogether, couldn't function at all. I drank everything in sight. I ate everything too. My stomach swelled up like I was pregnant. I went to the inquest, rotund and tragic. I met a man there who said he wanted to represent me, who helped me escape from the press who were hounding me all the time. He said he could get me work, as soon as I was ready.

He was a charlatan, like all the rest, but clever as the devil. He sent my stock soaring, told the reporters I was carrying tragic Frank's baby. Then he dispatched me straight to a spa to lose all the weight. They struggled with me for months for I'd stuff myself with fistfuls of anything I came across. I hadn't eaten properly in years. It became a sort of compulsion. I was devious and determined.

Slowly, very slowly, by a process of trial and error, the clinic managed to whittle me down. They discovered horses were the only thing I loved, let me ride about on horseback as much as I liked and then presented me with horsemeat for breakfast, lunch and tea. And I was so hungry. I was so lonely. I was so lost without Frank. I got thin again and my agent said I'd lost the baby.

Every day, for a year, I'd fall asleep crying and wake up crying, and cry through my dreams. The doctors gave me pills, which alleviated nothing. My agent started to play Frank's role very poorly, screaming and shouting and saying I'd miss my chance if I didn't start work soon. Once a week they let me out of the facility to place flowers on Frank's grave. And one Sunday, as I lay among the azaleas in deep distress, in dread of life, thrown flat on the ground, sobbing so loudly since no one was around, a man came and put his hand on my shoulder. And that was how I met Paul, the great designer (which is not, of course, his real *name*) who had known Frank once, long before I met him, when Frank, he said, almost passed for sane...

He invited me for tea in his atelier, and he told me that the times were changing. That soon, pretty soon, a figure such as mine would be back in fashion. That he wanted me to model for him and, not just that, demanded half a dozen of me, for the Paris shows. Oh, what a day it was, the day we made my mannequin. Standing like a statue, centre stage, in a room as vast as an aeroplane hangar, as his assistants scurried around me, remaking me exactly.

Paul asked me to stay with him while the mannequins were made, to check the accuracy. Day after day we sat in a little heated room at the very back of his atelier, Paul amusing me with all his tales as he set about his collection. There were windows on every side so he could keep an eye, at all times, on everything going on around us.

At eleven and four we took tea with slices of lemon, sitting in armchairs either side of the gas fire, and watched my fresh limbs dangle from the ceiling, strung up on meat hooks. Complete 'me's were hung by the neck. Half assembled 'me's stuck out like frosted lollipops, ending in a foot, or a hand.

When complete, I was sprayed pure white all over. Given full red lips, glass eyes, a flame-haired, silken wig. Two fine brows, a light blush on the cheeks, long, thick lashes. And then these 'me's were sent out to work in the stores.

Later, when my mannequins wore Paul's designs, there were complaints, which amused us both. They were too perfect, too real; certain clients claimed to be frightened of them, since my mannequins had such attitude. Even then I was overly attached to them, almost as if they were a part of me. I insisted on going into the shop to see. As a joke, I played the *vendeuse*, and Paul and I laughed.

A succession of women rang the bell, I let them in, helped them enjoy, vicariously, all the jewels in the showcases, showed them hairpins and pendants and brooches. I demonstrated how to wear that season's hat. Forward, to the left – *et voilà*! But they just looked at me, and looked at my mannequin, as if pinned between two evils, stared at their feet, then shuffled off without buying anything.

Oh yes, I said, sarcastically, as they wandered off down the street. It must have been my dummy's fault that none of them bought a thing. Not at all to do with their profound lack of *chic*.

It was Paul, I suppose, who helped me believe that I could really be something – with or without Frank.

So I went back to work and, second time around, no one complained about my blank face and non-existent smile. My talent was not in doubt. I was no longer an insignificant nothing. I was a great man's one and only muse.

That decade fashion went crazy. It was as if the whole industry had been infected by Frank's disease. No request was too outlandish. No idea was too eccentric.

Since you stole my portfolio, along with everything else, you can take a look, if you like, and bear witness. The economy was booming. Money was on the rampage. Photographers with massive budgets endlessly regurgitated Frank's ideas and made them even more vibrant and spectacular. It would be difficult to explain to the models of today how incredible were the demands put upon me.

There was no time to breathe, let alone think. I took any sort of pill or powder: first to stay awake, then to fall asleep.

If I ate anything at all, it was the little fruits served in my drinks. I flew across the world, spinning faster and faster, whole countries spread under my feet. As I – who had once stared so long and hard into mirrors – was proclaimed the fairest of them all.

The only time I ever stopped was when I was arrested by the sight of my dear mannequin. For a decade and more, I'd stumble into a version of her wherever I least expected it. I'd be hurrying, in my murderous heels, down Fifth Avenue; Bahnhofstrasse; the rue du Faubourg Saint-Honoré. My head full of where I was going, what I was doing, all the crazy things that were happening. When suddenly I'd feel a presence to one side, stop dead and turn, to find I was staring right at myself.

Standing, so very pale, all velvet skin and piercing eyes.

Even when they got rid of her in Paul's stores, replaced her with a less disconcerting model, I would still, occasionally, run into her on a back street somewhere. Demonstrating there whatever they forced her to, looking vicious and discontented in second-hand clothes. Once, when I found her posing in a Milanese junk shop, I felt the need to rescue her altogether. For she was stuffed into a window crammed full of crap.

Her head poked out from an orange turban, with an astrological scarf dangling from one thumb. Oh dear, dear, dear, how she had fallen, her face a picture of despair. I dashed in and bought everything she wore. Carefully rearranged the window, made her more comfortable. And left.

Of course, I was a monster. That is not in doubt. That whole time I was in a haze of highs. And they allowed me my fun, no one stood in my way, because, however unbearable I was, I worked like a slave, just as I'd been taught.

The photographers waited for me as I recovered, mauve and bilious, in the morning. They knew I'd do my job in the afternoon.

After Frank, I acquired a certain reputation for always being game. In point of fact, the crazier their demands, the more confident I felt.

So when, one day, a particular photographer, shooting swimsuits, complained that the sea was entirely the wrong kind of blue, I didn't flinch, only helped the startled assistants find exactly the right kind of turquoise dye. Then I lay about, patiently, for hours under a palm tree, as the photographer grew more and more furious at the time it took for the tide to come in.

Then I stood, as desired, while his assistants poured the dye around me, fast as they could into the swelling waters. I stood, exactly as I was instructed, while my feet became stumps of agony as the cold water did its work. And I stood fast, still, even though it was clear that with every wave the dye dissipated into the ocean.

I was blue with cold, and blue with dye, and blue, right through, with disaster, as the photographer bawled, incessantly, at the waves, the waves, the waves. So stubbornly, so wretchedly, the wrong kind of blue.

They always sent me out on those jobs, the ones no one else wanted to do.

What was the worst shoot? That's obvious – the bridal special.

They had the notion of a wedding dress that had been hewn from cloud. So they had me parachute out of a little plane on a particularly cloudy day, upside down, my parachute billowing out like an extension of the dress. I was tangled up in virgin silk with white tulle, struggling to pull the parachute; everything slowed down as I plummeted and knew I'd die.

And then somehow, the cord released and I went twisting around in the air, landing in a tree. I'd plunged down too fast for the photographer to catch me enveloped in the cloud. It was all over in a minute and a half. Success relied on pulling the cord simultaneously with him. But by this time I was in no condition to cooperate with anyone. I wasn't sleeping. I'd snatch five minutes here, and five minutes there.

I was drinking to steady my nerves. And I had to get drunk to leap out of that plane. I couldn't have done it any other way. When they extracted me from that tree, they hoped to make good, try it all again. But I started vomiting uncontrollably.

Frank, of course, would have loved that. It would have made his day: a bride sicking up on her dream dress. I missed him savagely at such moments. As it was, they were furious. The photographer, a tiny Italian, cursed me in three languages, called me a bitch in six. He reminded me, as if I didn't know already, that skinny girls are ten a penny. And there were *milioni* younger and prettier than I.

I wince to see those late spreads because I remember what I went through to get the picture. I should be proud of how I looked, divine in nine-inch stilettos and a string bikini, teetering on a mountaintop, glaring imperiously down a 300-foot drop. There was nothing to stop me tumbling over the edge save my own iron will. I should be proud of myself, so ravishing in a zebra-hide poncho, lying prone on the rocks as the mountain lions prowled just below.

Even in the close-ups, all you'll see on my face is that expression of blank-faced torpor, which *Vogue* preferred that year.

The editors always wanted me for the most dangerous shoots when the other girls baulked at the very idea.

I took particular pride in that because my reputation for fearlessness was something I'd built myself. It had nothing to do with Frank; it was down to the fact I never smiled. By that point, no one knew I couldn't do it, they just thought I was serious and original, so exceptional and defiant not to grin and simper.

The legend they all talked about was the shoot in Chicago, when the earthquake hit. The whole hotel rolled, the very marble rippled, and what I wanted to do was run screaming into the street. What I did was freeze. I sat there as chandeliers fell around me, as vases shook and toppled, mirrors cracked and smashed, and I held my pose all the while, with my usual snarl.

The photographer, Babe – because she too was a genius – also stood fast. We got the picture, then drank the bar dry.

After that, it was swimsuits in the Peruvian rainforest. They wanted me in a river that was absolutely green. Whether it was stagnant water or the reflection of jungle leaves, they didn't care.

It was a ridiculous shoot. I trod water in a dirty river, pulling a yak, which we had hired from a zoo, on a raft behind me. My legs were caressed by sly, slithering things, as a swarm of gnats nested on my face. The yak didn't like it anymore than I did, and became very agitated, causing the raft to buckle. I swallowed great gulps of rancid water, trying to reach the surface.

In a suicidal bid for freedom, the yak jumped on my head, and we both should have drowned, had not the photographer wrecked his camera jumping in to fish me out. And he was furious, since we'd failed, and he'd lost his vital equipment, and wouldn't say a thing to me in the car, as he drove away at ninety miles an hour, even when I was desperate for water, running a temperature of 105.

By the time we arrived in Lima, I was totally delirious, complaining of scratching noises in my head. I was put to bed in the hope I'd sleep it off. And all I could think was, 'This is what Frank meant. They really do climb into your brain and steal your thoughts.'

Two days later, I was taken to hospital. A mass of flesh-eating maggots were discovered chewing through my ear canal. I lost so much weight, I was put on a drip. When my agent arrived to pay all the bills, he heartily congratulated me. I'd never been thinner.

He dispatched me straight to the Paris shows. I'd been working non-stop for far too long. I was spent. But he said if I just finished the spring/summer collection, afterwards he'd let me take six weeks off to rejuvenate in Rio.

But, of course, the second I stepped off the catwalk, a call came from New York. Diana was thrilled: carmine was pervasive. She wanted a montage of matadors and flamenco dancers for March. When Diana says, 'Go', you go. So we all piled in a van and set off for Madrid, with bottles and pills and blankets, playing cards in the back. We took turns to drive and slept in shifts. We checked into the hotel, threw a party while we waited for the clothes to arrive. They were accompanied by a telegram from Diana. Two words: BLOOD RED.

The bull was supposed to go for the matador, sweeping a *muleta* beside me, but my skirt was just too much. I was tossed up by the horns and landed on my head, woke up when it was over. Somehow they'd got the bull away. But the pain was indescribable. I started yelling for help. They dusted me off. Said they hadn't got the picture. Gave me an injection, shoved a bottle in my hand.

I posed for another hour, unable to feel a thing except the blood that kept dripping into my left eye, which they loved because it made the image *darling*.

When they finally took me to hospital I had a fractured coccyx and a severed eyelid. My eyelashes were lost somewhere in the dirt and the sand. And when Diana saw the stills she went ballistic. Said the shoot was too gory, scrapped the lot.

I would never wink again thanks to one junked spread, one damn-fool idea too many.

And that was it for me. Like a soldier missing a leg, I was invalided out of service, never to work again. It all ended, with a snap of the fingers: just... like... that.

The Spaniards did a good job of pinning me back together. The insurance paid out. I decided to move back to London. It seemed like the only place to go. I didn't want to stay in Paris. I sold Frank's studio and bought my house, began the lengthy process of renovating it. I decorated each wall with paper; I wanted to recreate my travels – flamingos in the bedroom, monkeys in the bathroom, lizards in the kitchen – so whenever I unravelled I could concentrate on the walls.

And I kept going for quite some time before I fell apart. I tried, I really tried, to keep my spirits up. But what use is an aged, disabled model? I was one of countless redundant things. Even now, whenever I see a red telephone box, I feel a twinge and suppress a sob. For that's what I'm like. An iconic design, no longer needed. Utterly useless in every way.

And I spent the next five years staring at the walls.

I don't like to think of the time I wasted lying in bed. I couldn't stop thinking of my mother, and how I left her, not quite dead, not quite alive. How she lay, in great pain, all alone. And how I'd left her. How I'd betrayed her. And I thought of Frank, falling asleep by my side. Often I'd wake up in the morning and reach out my arm, searching for his body, finding nothing in his place.

I didn't sleep. I didn't eat. I couldn't read. I felt nothing, absolutely nothing. Nothing whatsoever at all. It was as if I had died, but no one had told my corpse.

Dr Traub said I had to get out of the house. That walking was the best cure. So I forced myself, and that's when my wandering started. First I walked in the garden, later the street, after a while the whole city, still lost to everything.

And then one autumn, on one of my interminable walks, I got lost on the wrong side of the Thames and I stumbled across my mannequin. She looked so beautiful in the window, in the dying October light. I just knew I had to have her. She was me – as I had once been – famous and fearless and free. She was me – as I never was – fresh and pure and whole.

I stood staring at her for the best part of an hour, thinking how she was deprived of all the insides that make a woman's life hell. She was only velvet skin and piercing eyes. No brain, so she never had to think. No womb, so she never felt the ache. No heart, so she never felt it bleed.

I was seized by the urge to buy her. To have her. Take her home. To treat her as I would wish to be treated myself, if found locked up in a window, abused and abandoned on some back street.

A week later I unpacked her, proudly, from a polystyrene crate. I tried her out in several different places. She liked the bedroom best. I felt her presence like a tonic. I began to recuperate. I started the lengthy process of unpacking all my things, all the dusty boxes in the attic, untouched since they had arrived from France.

One by one, I took my precious things out, to arrange beside her. Almost in spite of myself, I found I was enjoying it, sorting through all my make-up and brushes and perfumes, reminiscing with all my accessories and dresses and shoes.

And we started to play a game then, my mannequin and I. We would paint our faces very carefully, the way Frank liked. We'd laugh at how he used to scream if we had a hair out of place. I took my time, made us identical in every way, until our faces loomed like twin moons in a vacant sky.

And then we would dress up.

I took out Frank's equipment, established a small darkroom in the garage. I'd always had it in me to be a photographer. Even Frank admitted that I had imagination. I started to play around with light and colour. I'd take a picture, shake it out, pin the Polaroid to the board. Then another image with the camera on timer. I cleared the whole bedroom, created a sprawling smorgasbord on all four walls of me and my mannequin at peak glamour: the golden girls with platinum skin and silver eyes. I had a damask curtain fitted to hide the images away.

And over the years that I came alive again I started to talk to her and ask her advice. It was a pleasant process because she never imposed her views. She just listened, passively, tirelessly, sympathetically, enabled me to reach my own conclusions. Sometimes, if I were really desperate, I'd ask her, flat out, what to do. And, in such cases, she arrived at the most ingenious answers. So I became a little reliant on her. I had to have a little conversation with my best friend before I left the house.

There is a reservoir of calm within her. That is what I admire most. I felt sure that had she lived my life, she would have managed it much better. She would not have lost her dignity. She would not have allowed herself to be trampled underfoot. She leapt up, fully formed, when I was successful, so she hadn't acquired the tastes that took me apart. She was too great a lady to drink her weight in champagne or wrap her legs around a perfect stranger. She would not have been seized by that unbearable urge to dance.

She was happy in the corner, staring straight through people. Yes, I'm well aware: she'd make a better woman than I.

And she never liked you at all.

Right at the start, she warned me, you'd do me no good. 'A bastard, if ever I saw one,' that's what she said, and she never swears. After a few weeks, she poured out her wisdom. She told me she could see the way you were tending, that you'd worship my body and despise my mind. It was obvious, the way you behaved, so brash and self-regarding; you didn't care about me at all.

Why didn't I listen? In my gut, I knew it too. Just as I've always known when I lock eyes with a man of your sort.

Dr Traub told me to take a holiday. He said I needed warmth in my bones. He might have meant somewhere easy – the south coast or Spain or France. But I bought a ticket to Rio, my favourite place on earth, and then I lay on the beach for a month and felt so alone.

I picked *you* up on the flight back home. That is the saddest thing of all.

The airport had been fiendish. The bits of metal that hinge my spine set off every single alarm in the whole damned place. The plane was delayed. I sat in one spot, dying of thirst, desperate for water, but unwilling to move and create another security alert. By the time I got on the plane I was so dehydrated, I felt downright ill.

But the air hostess was caught up with your carping and whining about the flight delay. I wasn't having that, so I told you to shut up and leave her alone. Take it up with the airline – like a real man – that's what I said. So you directed your anger at me instead. But already your pupils had widened in homage to my face, your vituperation eased. We shared three bottles of champagne and, by the time the plane touched down, you were offering me a lift home in the Jag.

It was only when I got home, peeled off my shoes, massaged my feet, that I went over some of the things you'd said and remembered I didn't like you very much. The next day I could have slept you off, along with the hangover, if I'd been able to sleep. But starting at eight o'clock, and from then on hourly, the doorbell rang, relentlessly, as you bombarded me with flowers.

Lilies and hydrangeas, sweet peas and tuberose, wild roses, peonies, hothouse blooms. Forget-me-nots, love-in-the-mist, coxcombs and snapdragons. The whole house was alive with the intoxicating stench. It made me sneeze so violently I couldn't breathe. By the afternoon, it was no longer funny; it was just… quite appallingly flattering. I fixed myself a Bloody Mary and asked Marzena to take the arrangements outside. I stood and watched her arrange them, so beautifully, in the garden as I ran a bath and dialled the number scribbled on the cards.

But if you want to know the truth…

And do you, darling, or shall I lie…?

You know, you look like Frank, horrifically so. You can see it, he'll be there, among my photographs. You inflame me because he did. So I can't let you go…

You can see that, can't you? When you understand how he – you – are absolutely integral to my soul?

I should have been smarter. Should have held out longer. Played harder to get. But it had been such a long time. Sex, with you, was an assault. And I liked, afterwards, lying with you in the dark.

From the first, you were obsessed with my body. Absolutely engrossed. Even in my prime, I never experienced anything like it. If we were alone, you'd strip me naked within seconds. Tearing at my clothes with your fingers and your teeth. Slitting dresses off with scissors. And I'd be so panicked, watching you seize a knife when I was midway through cooking dinner, and ripping the seams of my dress. I can't say I enjoyed it. But seeming to be petrified only added to your excitement. You loved it if I lay there like a doll, unable to move.

You were a brute, an utter brute when your blood was up. You'd stare at me, with starving eyes. If we were at a friend's house for dinner, you'd drag me into the bathroom. We'd be in a restaurant, and you'd do the same, tipping the waiters while they laughed.

I was so taken aback I never quite worked out what to do. You'd bring me a bag from Selfridges every Friday evening with ever more depraved lingerie. You insisted on the most obscene contraptions. And if I didn't change into it at once, you'd bare a blade, a razor, annihilate another dress.

I put all my best outfits away to protect them, started wearing sweatpants and jumpers. That only encouraged you; there was a new present every day.

Lying down, trussed up, that was one thing. However little I contributed I could do no wrong. But standing up, fully clothed, I could do nothing right. You didn't agree with anything I said or approve of anything I did. You'd cause a row and then we'd make up. Cause a row, then make up. Row – make up.

And you were so enthusiastic in the making up, I did start to wonder if I'd truly done anything wrong. If I became tearful it made your need for me quite desperate. I never had any rest. I never had any time to myself. You dressed me up and rearranged me. Until occasionally I'd rebel. Thinking all the time, I am not a bloody Barbie doll. I am not...

When you went away for business, I'd start to relax, fall into old habits. I'd take a long bath, paint my nails, attempt to read a book. Once, you said you'd be away for a fortnight, so I decided to give myself a treat, and play dress-up with my mannequin again.

I'd stopped all that soon after you arrived. I didn't want to give you an excuse to get irritated. It was a foolish thing to do, for you came home unexpectedly right in the middle of it, when my mannequin and I were starting to enjoy ourselves again. You came home, but instead of interrupting us you hid behind the rhododendrons in the garden, watching. You'd seen it all, it was impossible to deny. But, to my surprise, it didn't annoy you; you didn't fly into a rage. Instead, you asked to join in.

First, you wanted to take the photographs. Then you wanted to direct the tableaux. Soon enough, you demanded to be in the photos too. You'd stand, proudly, in the middle, as we hung, identical, off both your arms. Later, you'd want something 'more interesting', so we'd be wrapped around you in just our stockings and suspenders. Before long, you wanted us naked and spread-eagled in the most humiliating ways.

I'm used to maltreatment. But my mannequin is too good for that. A strong urge to protect her welled up within me. One morning, when I was out shopping, I came home early to find you on your knees, struggling with straps and hooks, redressing her on your own.

I didn't mind, I never mind. I'm a very placid person these days. But she didn't like it. You dressed her up all wrong.

The aesthetic of an outfit is very important, as any designer will tell you. You must construct it around the body to flaunt its advantages and conceal its flaws. You must acquaint yourself with the colour and the fabric, the bias and the fit. You can break all the rules once you know them, but first you have to learn. I tried to explain, patiently and reasonably, where you were going wrong.

You flew into a violent rage, the like of which I'd never seen before. I fled to the bathroom, carrying her with me, and we stood there, putting all our weight against the door, as you battered at it, trying to get through. The neighbours must have called the police. I know you don't believe me, but I didn't make the call. All I did was plead with you to quieten down.

When the police released you – I wouldn't press charges –

you had no further interest in the game. Instead, you turned nasty, teased me about it in public, and made me seem absurd in front of everyone we knew. So I too gave it up and didn't dress her at all. I left her in the corner, naked as she was. But you didn't like that either, claimed that she was watching you as we made love. 'Don't be so ridiculous,' I said. I never heard anything so pathetic. But, eager to please, as ever, I took your part over hers.

Every night, I'd throw a shawl over her. Every morning, I'd rearrange it round her neck. She stood there, loyally, uncomplaining, watching me put up with it all. Until, one afternoon, you came home in a vile mood, and had me submit to various acts I don't want to recall, and then, when you could not reach a satisfactory conclusion, purple of face, you told me it was her fault. She'd been staring at you, putting you off with her vicious, watery eyes.

I never did say no to you. It's not a word I use with a man. I often wonder what my life would have been like if, early on, I'd ever learned that magic word. You wanted her taken up to the attic. So we hauled her up the ladder, then and there, in our dressing gowns. I made her as comfortable as I could, made sure that she would not be troubled by mice or dust or damp. I apologised to her, under my breath. For it was a cowardly act, on my part.

I didn't think it would help. But, in fact, the moment she was banished, you and I started to get along. We were planning to spend Christmas together. I got quite excited, buying the tree, putting up decorations, starting on a crate of champagne, singing carols. I was going to cook a goose. You bought tickets to the ballet.

And then what happened? One day you were there, and the next you were gone. Saturday I went to Mass, and we spent the evening together. Sunday morning, you left a poinsettia for me by the bed with a barely legible note, saying you didn't want to wake me, that I was so very beautiful – when unconscious.

But I didn't take the hint. I made dinner, expecting you to return that evening. And when you didn't, I became wild with worry. Couldn't calm down. Phoned all your phones, left all my messages. Drove round to your house, knocked frantically at the door. Your neighbour said you'd not been home in months. Pointed to the For Sale sign at the bottom of the garden, and, beneath it, a SOLD. I called your office. No one picked up. Phoned everyone I knew you knew. None of them had heard from you. Or that's what they said. I reported you missing – for Christ's sake – to the police.

On Boxing Day, I had a call from a withheld number. It was a woman who claimed to be your secretary, calling me on your behalf. She said you'd had to leave the country, told some ridiculous story, adding that you'd be certain to call me the minute all the trouble was resolved. It was all very complicated, she said, she couldn't quite grasp it herself. Well, what was there to do? There was nothing. I stared at myself in the mirror, took many deep breaths. I tried to remind myself – oh, I always remind myself – I've been through far worse.

And since there was nothing else I could do, at least, I thought, I'd make amends to my mannequin. I apologised profusely, reinstalled her downstairs. I cleaned her very attentively, made up her face, smothered her in Insolence. And then I got out her all-time favourite to give us both a treat. That stunning vermilion Galliano no one knows I've got.

I took a picture of her, alone, reclining on the banister. Swathes of sumptuous silk, gushing down the stairs like blood.

I hired a private detective to find out where you went.

It took him a week. When he was done, I paid up and retired to think.

Oh, it was the best Valentine's present of my life, now I come to think of it, almost running into you like that. For if I'd not had that chance, I'd never have known what a fool I was. Now I laugh to think of it. To be confronted, so unexpectedly, with the truth. Now I laugh. I laugh ceaselessly. At the end of all your lies.

Because they weren't lies. Not mere lies. Not mere *lies* – you see. They were a special breed. A new kind: they were super, absolutely super-sized...

Not so long ago, you swore you couldn't live without me, that my being was essential to your mortal soul. And if I died, you'd embalm me in order to keep me, to do with as you pleased. Such strange protestations, such sinister homage, it never occurred to me that you never meant a word. In so many years of searching, you said, you'd never found a woman with a body so sublime.

I'm impressed, I can't deny it, that an inveterate liar such as myself should have been so easily duped. But now I know. There are lies, damned lies, and the lies we tell. Not lies, not mere *lies*, my dear, super, super-lies.

It was such a cliché, so infinitely beneath you, to leave me, for a younger woman. So you tarted it up, made the circumstance special, by making a present to her of all my clothes. I understand, of course, you need to impress her; twenty-somethings can be hard to land. Hourly flower deliveries can't have done the trick. The best way to woo a woman is with incessant, spectacular gifts.

At least she has impeccable taste. But is that a compensation to me? My dear, not at all; it seems almost calculated to infuriate me, worse than anything else could. I can imagine her sitting there, delighted with all my possessions, holding the emerald salamander up to the light, watching as the jewels glint and flirt with her. Slipping into my Dior gown, twirling as it swishes, kicking her legs up to admire my Ferragamos, since she'll never be able to walk in them; they're meant for lying down.

Alas, the file my detective drew up contains nothing about her at all. Her name, her age, every fact eludes us. All we know is she's statuesque and she's young. You worship at her feet. You've won her, and she can have you, I don't care. But she needs to know that what you gave her is mine and I want it back. You – both of you – must surrender my mannequin, immediately. That is a provocation too far.

Whenever I need clarity, I go to the hairdresser. So I called Leonard, told him he had to slot me in. 'Darling,' he trilled, 'come straight over.' And he got down to work, fixed me, and now I feel brand new.

Afterwards, I walked across Covent Garden to correct the rest of me, face, neck, legs, nails. A seaweed wrap, a caviar facial. Gleaming and polished, gripped by a feverish enthusiasm I haven't felt in years, I hailed a taxi and went to Harrods. There I bought a black silk jumpsuit, sunglasses and a fedora.

Now I drive over every evening, and I sit here, pondering exactly what to do.

I can see her sitting in your armchair by the window. Perfectly poised. Perfectly still. Her head doesn't move. She's waiting so poignantly. I wonder if, inside, her nerves boil. Already, I feel, she's a better actress than I am. Even when you're out she barely stirs. She watches television for hours and hours, reclining there in the dark. Idly, she changes channels, the blue light flickering on the walls.

If I climb up the drainpipe, and onto the balcony, I might be able to see her through the blinds.

I know I can't complain about her, necessarily. Over the years, I wasn't fussy when it came to tearing a man in two.

Most often he belonged to another woman. And I didn't care. I devoured him all the same.

It is a large flat in one of those neat art deco estates. You tend to come home around eight, park your car under the moulting cherry tree, and hurry inside. You kiss her on the neck, and then you lift her dainty hand and kiss her on the wrist, then all the other places she's dabbed in perfume. Afterwards, you open a bottle of wine, bed down on her lap, and *talk*, I suppose. Or you change channels, catch up with the news.

I used to get so damned bored of watching you watch television. You never mind what's on, you just sit there and stare at it and claim to be relaxing. You're always so tired, you say. I'd be trapped there, on the sofa, with your head like a great paperweight, weighing me down.

I suppose she doesn't mind.

I've been watching her for days and she's a patient, passive creature.

She lets you wait on her hand and foot. You get her meals, feed her forkfuls, I can see it all through the binoculars. It's sickening, absolutely sickening. At a quarter to midnight, you emerge from your bath, wearing what I believe to be my strawberry-patterned kimono, you come out, untie it, let it fall to the floor, like you're seducing her in the manner of a geisha.

Then you hurry towards her all at once, kiss her smack on the lips. You pick her up in your arms, as if she weighs nothing, and sweep her off to the bedroom as she sprawls about like a gigantic, lolling baby. The rest I am spared, since it is impossible to see the bedroom from the street. She is such a slender supple thing. No doubt she cavorts in ways quite depraved.

After an hour, all the lights go out and, depending on my state of mind, I go home or try to sleep in the car.

After several nights, I started drinking. I keep a bottle of gin in the glove compartment and pass out on the back seat.

I have decided to go in and talk to her.

I need my things back and she's more likely to let me have them than you are. You'd call the police, who have already taken your side. Also, I want a proper look at her. And to let her know – for she deserves to be told – exactly what you are. How you love the chase and loathe the conquest. How she mustn't talk too much. Or drink too much. Or do anything that might possibly embarrass you.

So one morning, just after you left, I rang the bell downstairs. I rang and rang and rang and she wouldn't answer. A resident came out. I slipped in, went up three flights of stairs and started tapping at the door. No doubt you've told her not to let anyone in. I could sense her there, loitering behind the door. So I've decided that I'll have to climb up the outside, as stealthily as I can, and meet her that way. But then – this is my worry – what will I do if I climb up and she is lounging about up there, wearing my clothes?

I can imagine her, not even close to thirty years old, playing at being a woman, admiring her own violent beauty. Casually propping her head up in what she considers to be a sophisticated pose. Painting her eyes with smooth, dark flicks, a typical ingénue. Kicking her legs up, just to admire her thighs, reflecting on her delicious little toes. Splaying her painted fingers across her taut, flat belly. Resting her wrists on her angular hips. Oh, the exquisite narcissism of the young.

Well, now I'll get my revenge, once and for all.

The street is getting slightly dark. And she sits there just the same.

Do you keep her up all night – is that it? Do you exhaust her so, she sleeps all day?

I'll soon find out.

*

I'm not as agile as I once was but it's not a hard building to scale. Between the drainpipes and the ivy and the balconies there's plenty to grip. I take my heels off, lock the car, sling my bag across my shoulders, and start shimmying up the wall.

It's even easy to get to the first balcony. I need to stop panting. My heart is beating too fast. I get up to the second balcony. Only my hat falls to the ground.

Now the third balcony. *Et voilà!*

I'll test the door. And, yes, of course, it's locked.

The window is open on the casement, just slightly to one side. I can see her, now. Sitting in a draught, the little fool, wearing next to nothing. And so, I think, I'll call out to her. That will be the best thing. Maybe we can talk through the open window.

But the haughty little madam doesn't deign to turn. So I get my hand under the latch and the frame swings towards me. I get my foot up and the leg of my suit gets caught on the sill. I'm careful, I disentangle myself: I must not fall. My arms are trembling but I take a leap and swing the rest of my body inside.

So I'm in your flat now, which might as well be my flat, since it's obvious, straightaway, that it's crammed full of all my stuff.

I'm so furious with you, my thoughts have slowed; I'm not making any noise at all. So she doesn't hear, she doesn't hear a thing as I creep up behind her. She's reclining there, pretty much naked, with her head, so affectedly, resting in her hand. She has stockings and suspenders on and my apricot Jimmy Choos.

On the coffee table, three scented altar candles are burning to the wick. There are great piles of Polaroids and negatives strewn all over the top. And I start to think. What the hell have you done to her, to leave her like this? Drugged her, doped her, to keep her here against her will? I pull at her hair for some reason, I can't help myself. That great blonde backcombed mess that perches, like a nesting bird, on top of her head. And, to my horror, it comes off in my hand.

I start to scream. But there's no response from her. And I start to think: my God, you've killed her, and are keeping her up here, to do all these deranged things to her corpse. But then I realise. She's not cold. She's not dead. She's familiar. I've seen her before. Sitting there among my knick-knacks. My diamonds on her fingers. My varnish on her toes. I know her like I know myself.

And so, I see now, I realise now... she is me.

She's my goddamned mannequin.

I lose track. I'm so stunned. I just stand there, as if paralysed. I am... I must have been... on account of the shock.

How long did I stand still?

(Because I didn't hear you come upstairs. I didn't hear your key in the door.)

For some reason, you're on the scene; you're not supposed to be home for hours. Did I trip some alarm?

No, the first thing I know about it is your hands closing around my throat. And somehow, I must have taken my phone out to call. I have it in one hand, dialling 999, and my mannequin in the other, though you're throttling me, you're throttling me, until my hands go limp, and I drop them both. I scream out, scream out, at the top of my voice. Won't someone hear me? I yell out where we are, what you're doing, as I summon all my strength to wriggle one leg out from underneath you. And kick you in the testicles.

Your grip slips. I've got her back under one arm; I'm gripping the coffee table with the other. Every time I turn my head, I see more signs of your sick, sick mind. The flat is strewn with paraphernalia. And I can see exactly what you've done. My damned doll is absolutely covered with the fruit of your loin. Outside, a whinge of sirens. A fire has started, races over the floor. All my things, my pretty things. My life's work goes up in flames. But as you drag me back, into the smoke, I'm still not letting her go. I'm choking and I'm coughing, when all of a sudden you take your hands away. Because I can't breathe, I can't see, I roll around on the floor. I hug her to me, because you're not having her, you're not having her anymore. With a sudden surge of strength you lift us both. Hurl us both through the glass door.

And I only realise, when I wake up in the ambulance sick and sore, that all I'm clinging to is my mannequin's head. You and the rest of her lie on the pavement below. Smoke streams out of the window. The whole flat has gone up in flames.

And while you may prove hard to scrape up and reassemble, landing, as you did, head first, looking, as you do, all covered in jam, my mannequin is made of sterner stuff. She's come clean apart but I'll put her back together. Reconstruct her, limb by limb.

For the thing about my mannequin is she can't be beaten, she won't surrender, she will never, never give up. She trusts to her unconquerable soul.

For, after all… she is my perfect replica.

Acknowledgements

First, to you – specifically you – who shall remain nameless, and Alexandra Townshend (to whom this book is dedicated...). Then, to Sarah MacKinlay (first and faithful reader who always said we'd get here in the end).

To Felix Lloyd (for all her fierce advice), Polly Dunbar (who kept coming to see me when everyone else had flown), Ariane Sherine (plus husband), Marzena Lubaszka (angel) and Oli Foster (comrade).

To Mary Wakefield (heroine – who let me do a bad impersonation of her for a year) and Sam Leith (who mounted manuscript rescue by shoving me towards Cathryn Summerhayes, fearless agent).

To *all* my family but most particularly my brother, Alex (for the sports metaphors – yes we skinned them in extra time) and my aunt, Lisa (who went in to bat for me when I couldn't hold a pencil).

To everyone at Unbound but most especially Katy Guest, Imogen Denny and Anna Simpson. (You know what you did.) And Justine Taylor and Miranda Ward, for their kindness in the edit.

To each and every one of you who pledged, I mutter your names with eternal gratitude.

And most of all to you, dearest, who reached the end of the book, conscious that 'Reader, I didn't marry him' is a triumphant ending too.

Supporters

Unbound is a new kind of publishing house. Our books are funded directly by readers. This was a very popular idea during the late eighteenth and early nineteenth centuries. Now we have revived it for the internet age. It allows authors to write the books they really want to write and readers to support the books they would most like to see published.

The names listed below are of readers who have pledged their support and made this book happen. If you'd like to join them, visit www.unbound.com.

Super friend
Klaas Jan Runia

Supporters
Kia Abdullah
David Allen
Kate Andrews
Susan Angoy
John Auckland
Juliet Baillie
Katy Balls
Houman Barekat
James Bartholomew
Aloysius Basingstoke
Gary Bell
Matthew Bell
Asa Bennett
Robyn Benson

Lauren Bensted
Alex Black
Eleanor Black
Jill Black
Terence Blacker
David Blacow
Jean Blacow
Kara Blacow
Matthew Blakstad
Annie Blinkhorn
Margaret Blinkhorn
Josie Bloom
Catherine Blyth
Joe Bond
Tristan Bradley
Flora Bradley-Watson
Kate Bulpitt
Miranda Bunting

Christine Burns

David Butterfield

Zack Cahill

Eleni Calligas

Sam Cane

Tracey Carey

David Catley

Elaine Chambers

Kate Chell

Teresa Clarke

Julian Clyne

Stevyn Colgan

Harry Come

Dominic Connolly

Samantha Conway

Roger Cosson

Silvia Crompton

Sarah Crouch

Dolan Cummings

Alka Sehgal Cuthbert

Fraser Daisley

Stewart Dakers

Iain Dale

Dan Dalton

Danny

Gill Darling

Andrew Davies

Melissa Davies

Sue Davis

Kim de Ruiter

Debbie Deeley

Jess Deeley

Lester Deeley

James Delingpole

Alastair Donald

John Donaldson

William Donaldson

Kirsty Doole

Eleanor Doughty

Kathy Draxlbauer

Edward Druce

Oly Duff

Polly Dunbar

Ben Elton

Simon English

ER Queen of Scotland

Catherine Evans

David Ewart

Claire Faragher

Jamie Fewery

James Fisher

Molly Flatt

John Fleming

Chloe Fogg

James Forsyth

Oli Foster

Piers Foster

Ceri Fowler

Claire Fox

Adam Fox-Rumley

Trilby Fox-Rumley

Julie Foxall

Spenser Frearson

Justin Freeman

Laura Freeman

Laura Fulcher

Laurie Garrison

Rebecca Geller

Dashiel Gettings

Luke Gittos

Katie Glass
Tom Goldsmith
Sophie Goldsworthy
Tom Goodenough
Priscilla Goslett
Sarah-Jane Grace
Ysenda Maxtone Graham
Grampsie and Granma
Anna Gray
Rachel Green
Charlie Griffs
Katy Guest
Helene Guldberg
Douglas Haddow
Liam Halligan
Dan Hancox
Andrea Harman
Rob Harris
Melinda Haunton
Patrick Hayes
Carole Hayman
James Heartfield
Will Heaven
Bríd Hehir
Tom Higgins
Alexander Hill
Anne Hill
Brent Hill
Nick Hilton
Johanna Hogan
Chris Holbrook
Mary Honeyball
Krista Horn
Holly Howells
Christina Hughes-Onslow

Flora Hughes-Onslow
George Hull
Julia Hull
Thirzie Hull
Mick Hume
Stephen Hussey
John Iris
Biliby Iwai
Christopher Jackson
Zoe Jardiniere
Alice-Azania Jarvis
jayoaks.bandcamp.com
Misti & Henry Jeffreys
Tiffany Jenkins
Angella Johnson
Anne Jolis
Alison Jones
Caitlin Jones
Emma Jones
Claudia Joseph
Adam Juniper
Kamal
Lesley Katon
Elena Kaufman
Felix Kaufmann
Sarah-Jane Keeble
Sophie Kelly
Emma Kendrew
Imran Khan
Dan Kieran
Patrick Kincaid
Pierre L'Allier
Cosmo Landesman
Victoria Lane
Laura & Antoine

Jonathan Le Page
Jimmy Leach
Sam Leith
Lisa
Liz B
Felicity Lloyd
Joy Lo Dico
Chris Locke
Wendy Lord
Will Lord
Suzanne Lowry
Jadwiga Lubaszka
Marzena Lubaszka
Robert Lyons
Deborah Maby
John R. MacArthur
Stef Macbeth
Cait MacPhee
Mali
Robert Jesus Marney
Lavender Marsh
Jessica Martin
Helena Mathes
Michael May
Tessa Mayes
Siobhan McBride
Paul McCallum
Siobhan McFadyen
Sarah McLaughlin
Catherine McNamara
Kat Metcalf
Luisa Metcalfe
Erinna Mettler
Munira Mirza
John Mitchinson

Amanda Moffat
Natalie Moorse
Charlotte Morton
Emily Mules
Jenny Munro-Hunt
Carlo Navato
Joshua Neicho
Fraser Nelson
Alison Newton
Jeremy Norman
Graham Nunn
Gary O'Donoghue
Brendan O'Neill
John O'Neill
Gregory Olver
Charles Orton-Jones
Richard Owen
Kelly Palmer-George
Rosalind Parkes
Christina Patterson
Benedicte Paviot
Poppy Peacock
Alex Peake-Tomkinson
Hugo Perks
Helen Perry
Harry Phibbs
Rice Pile
Justin Pollard
Laura Powell
Nina Powell
Lara Prendergast
David Prew
Marleen Raaijmakers
Yuan Ren
Zelda Rhiando

Emily Rhodes
Lisa Richards
Jane Richardson
Andrew Ritchie
Claire Riviere
Will Roberts
Frances Robinson
Emma Rowley
Lydia Ruffles
Barbara Rumley
Tom Rumley
Jez Rushworth
Josephine Russell
Nigel Ryan
Chris Ryland
Elizabeth Sanderson
Sandra and Ron
Danny Scheinmann
Hannah Riviere Scott
Cesca Service
Ariane Sherine
Sonia Sodha
Alice Squires
Louise Stephens
Mark Stephenson
Joanna Sterling
Jane Stewart
Tabatha Stirling
Jennie Stolpe
Brendan Strong
Camilla Swift
Alicja Syska
Elsie Temple
Jane Temple
Sally Temple
Victoria-Anne Tessa

Martin Thomas
Julie Throup
Ayo Tijani
Igor Toronyi-Lalic
Alex Townshend
Tiffany Trenner-Lyle
Trouble Club
Wendy Tuxworth
Cara Usher
Rebecca Veals
Lucy Vickery
Oliver Wadeson
Charlotte Wagstaffe
Kate Wagstaffe
Mary Wakefield
Jonathan Walpole
Emma Webster-Green
Jo Webster-Green
Barbara Weilgony
Peter Weilgony
Louise Welch
Lucinda Weston
Sam Weston
Francis Wheen
Chris Whitaker
Paul Wight
Fiona Williams
Jim Williams
Joanna Williams
Jane Withers
Ruben Wood
Alison Woodhouse
Tim Youd
Cathy Young
Toby Young